Arabella's Assistant

by

Judy Lynn Ichkhanian

Raised All Wrong, Book 1

Arabella's Assistant

Cover Art by *Debbie Taylor*

The Wild Rose Press, Inc.
PO Box 708
Adams Basin, NY 14410-0708
Visit us at www.thewildrosepress.com

Publishing History
First Edition, 2022
Trade Paperback ISBN 978-1-5092-4233-7
Digital ISBN 978-1-5092-4234-4

Raised All Wrong, Book 1
Published in the United States of America

Gabriel pivoted, expecting to see Arabella, but the space was a wash of lonely trees. He took a step forward just as nausea and dizziness speared through him. Though it felt like moving through molten sand, he stumbled on as an odd heaviness began dragging him downward. Another step, and the stinging in his torso flamed.

A glint of white, gold, and pink, almost covered from sight by a hillock of decaying leaves and green sprouts, caught his attention. Forcing his legs to advance, he staggered toward it, his feet unusually clumsy over the litter of foliage and roots.

He shouted, or thought he did, but Arabella did not move. As he flung himself to the ground beside her, he reached out to cup her cheek, willing those beautiful amethyst eyes to open.

A terrible bright stain of red painted the side of her gentle head crimson.

The world flipped again as the silk of her golden hair slipped through his numb fingers. The damp earth, loamy and dark, reached up to drag him down beside her. He closed his eyes and sighed.

Arabella was his epic love.

How stupid of him not to have realized it while there was still time.

Dedication

To Claude and Theo,
thank you for the incredible life you've given me.
I wouldn't want to go through this world
without either of you.

Chapter 1

Mayfair, London, 1859

The capture of a wealthy lord was a blood-sport. Support was required.

As a result, it took Gabriel Darkwood, Baron Brynley, exactly eighteen minutes to cross the ballroom once the niceties with his host and hostess had been performed. Nubile young women, out for blood, "accidentally" tossed handkerchiefs, fans, an odd assortment of clips, pins, and, in one case, a punch glass, directly into his path with unerring accuracy. Convention required him to bend, pick up, and return these items with a smile and a few gritted-teeth pleasantries. In three instances, doting mamas helped pitch belongings when their daughters' aim lacked precision.

He didn't take it personally.

Though normally quite adept at eluding such hazards, he found himself tripping and bending like someone new to the game because all he could think about was throwing his cousin through the tall windows to the lawn below.

He had just managed to spy his prey when, unfortunately, his prey spied him. He knew it by the way Justin Thauley, Viscount Manning, paled to the color of three-day-old fish, if such a fish could be counted upon to wear finely tailored garments of fabric luxurious enough to render a king envious. When the unscrupulous lout turned tail and hastened through the crowd, probably hoping to become lost among the wallflowers, Gabriel followed.

"Come out from behind Lady Numeraughton," Gabriel demanded as Justin circled the stout-girthed woman for the second time. "I see you, Manning. It would be hard to miss your copper-colored head, even in this sea of bright plumage. Coward."

Peeping from behind the blue-frilled matron, Justin made his excuses to the lady and stepped forward, his expression grim. "Ah, um, Darkie, I, um, didn't see you there. Fancy us both being here tonight. You aren't usually much for going out in Society."

"And I'm still not," Gabriel snapped, tamping down the urge to shake the man by his collars. "I had to hunt you down, you louse—"

"Sshh!" Justin swiveled to see who was watching.

Everyone was watching.

Gabriel didn't much care, except someone was bound to interrupt them soon, so he acted quickly. Throwing his arm about his cousin's shoulder, he leaned in and whispered, "Walk with me to less intrusive environs. Otherwise, I shall make a scene so enormous it will be discussed long after you've turned to dust."

It was a source of some small contentment when Justin paled further. Though the iniquitous rat ruffled his shoulders with discontent, he allowed himself to be prodded in the right direction. When they had adequately skirted the crowds and found themselves in a study doing duty as a cloakroom, Gabriel took a moment to growl some threats at the servants, scattering them, before turning his ire upon his cousin.

Shoving Justin into the edge of a movable wardrobe filled with cloaks, coats, and wraps, Gabriel demanded, "Tell me. Exactly what unscrupulous action have you planned? Don't bother to deny you are up to no good. My challenge to the title is meritorious, which means any defenses you and my cockroach-heeled uncle are in the process of mounting must be scurrilous."

Belaying the red-stained fluster that painted his cheeks, Justin calmly removed Gabriel's hand from where it twisted into his fine white shirt and black evening jacket. He smoothed the wrinkles from his clothing without haste. Though he breathed hard, he replied evenly enough, "Let's just leave the matter to the Court of Assizes to determine legitimacy, shall we?"

"Why? Do you think I cannot bribe them as well as you do?" Gabriel stepped back and clenched his fists, afraid he might strangle the rogue.

Given the number of witnesses at the party, someone was sure to mention his murderous demeanor to the investigators afterward. Even Queen Victoria would hesitate to save him should she learn he had dispatched his cousin during a Society event. She was a bit of a stickler about such things.

"I think," Justin drawled, looking up from his examination of his front, "that you don't have the grit or resolve to do what is necessary. Perhaps…not the imagination, either," he added, cocking his head.

"Try me. Know this, cousin; I am watching you. You and your father will not continue to hold that which rightfully belongs to *my* branch of the family tree."

"Your branch deserves nothing. Why don't you go bury yourself in some book and leave us alone? You're the one trying to rip the estates from us. You're the interloper, Darkie," he practically spat. He drew in a long breath and said in a more measured tone, "We will soon have irrefutable means of keeping our titles. You may be too weak to do the necessary, but I most assuredly am not."

Gabriel took another careful step back to save himself from prison, transport, or worse.

Justin shot his cuffs and *harrumph*ed. "Now, I am returning to the ball. There is a certain American heiress who possesses a fortune vast enough even for me. I am considering taking it off her hands once the court has ruled in our favor. Then, I shall happily repay you for the misery you have brought upon us."

"Perhaps the American's father should be warned."

"Perhaps he should, but you will not offer him your slander. If the justices were to hear of your slurs, they would look unfavorably upon your appeal."

"It is only slander if it isn't true," Gabriel pointed out.

However, in this matter his cousin was unfortunately correct. While he could probably prove Justin was in massive debt to numerous creditors, so too were many nobility. The viscount still held a prestigious title, which was in many ways equal to, or better than, a fortune. A daughter's luck in becoming a viscountess was all most grappling fathers would see.

His cousin studied him in a way Gabriel couldn't quite interpret before turning his back and stalking out of the room. The reverberations of the slamming door danced across the floor and under his leather soles.

It was as he feared. His uncle and cousin were plotting; curse them.

Considering the documents Gabriel had attached to

his suit for the earldom of Kildare and all its lesser titles, Justin and his father should be packing their bags and getting ready to steal whatever had not already been pawned, sold, or lost during the present earl's reign. Justin should not be met at balls, courting wealthy American women for their gold. His confidence was almost unnerving.

"Your cousin truly is a vile piece of handiwork," Peter Bartholomew muttered as he stepped from the shadows that blanketed the corner of the room.

Gabriel startled before he realized who it was. "He hasn't changed much these past thirty-odd years, has he?"

"He's still the same donkey's buttocks who pushed me down the well," Peter replied.

In the soft-lit chamber, his golden angel curls refracted the light like a halo. He crossed the room and sat down before the desk where Gabriel leaned.

"Once I saw you pounce upon Justin in the ballroom, I guessed this was where you would end up. We need to talk."

"Words I'm certain you've repeated to far too many women, leaving all of them broken-hearted." Gabriel smirked as he rolled his shoulders, trying to ease the tension knotting them.

"You will remember Lady de Veer?"

Gabriel raised a tired eyebrow.

"Aside from the fact she made a rather intrepid bed partner for a small while, she is rumored now to be sleeping with your uncle. That means she likely knows what those toads are up to. Realizing that, I took it upon myself to visit her before coming here. Well, never let it be said I can't pry open a loose woman's legs, even when she has them wrapped tightly around a rather portly earl."

Peter shuddered delicately. "I can't imagine how she stomachs that stomach."

"You are, as ever, a poet with the spoken word," Gabriel remarked dryly.

"A poet sheathed in lamb's intestine. I took the necessary precautions, not wishing to travel the same road behind the earl, lest that swine carry the pox. At any rate, my efforts upon your behalf have yielded fruit. You're welcome."

"Happy to hear it…and, thank you. Is there a point?"

"A very sharp one and I'm sure you'll see why." Peter rose and glided toward a bookshelf. He picked up a statuette of a hunting dog and examined it. "It seems your uncle has been making inquiries about one Lady Arabella Warwick, daughter of the late Earl of Winslow." He replaced the object and faced Gabriel. "For his son. Justin," Peter added pointedly. "Lady Arabella is rumored to be a penniless, well-shelved bluestocking, and Justin is a persnickety snoot who thinks himself too fine even for royalty, so the only explanation for any such interest must be tied to your suit for their titles."

"Yet he is searching for an heiress, as he just admitted."

"*Penniless* bluestocking. If those curs are interested in Lady Arabella, then she must be an interesting clue worth pursuing."

"Then pursue her."

Peter slowly smiled. "Unfortunately, this time it is you who must fight the front. She is presumably an innocent of high station. Your milieu, *my lord.*"

Gabriel snorted and shot his friend a pointed look. He stalked toward the window as he considered the matter. Outside, the lights that banked the front staircase blazed.

Through the leaded glass, figures arriving and departing were little but a blur of vaguely colored shadows against the night.

By the time he turned from the window, Peter was already at the door.

"Lady Arabella is having a belated sortie into society this Friday evening," he remarked lightly, hand on the knob. "I have procured an invitation for you as the escort of Lady Aimsbridge."

"Dear Heaven!" Gabriel sputtered, stepping back until the windowsill hit him in mid-thigh. "That violet-haired, decrepit harridan?"

"The same. If you want to gain those titles, you will have to do as Justin suggests and scrabble around a bit in the mud. The best way to gauge Lady Arabella's appeal to your cousin is to, er, *gauge her appeal* if you take my meaning?" He smiled mischievously.

"I couldn't mistake it were I illiterate."

As Peter escaped through the doorway, Gabriel turned to look back out the window into the gas-lit ink, already longing to be safely home. His library and his studies of the Gilgamesh Epic, the place he always longed to be and the thing he always longed to be doing, would have to wait. Justin and his misdeeds could not.

Lady Arabella had better be a clue worth unraveling.

Chapter 2

Lady Arabella Warwick tasted blood and winced. Once again, she had abraded her tongue in her efforts to ignore the feather and sugar-plum assault lobbed by her helpful mother. If matters continued apace, she might soon have no tongue left at all.

Her fingers tightened around the water glass as she took three deep, calming breaths. She would not respond. She would not argue. She would remain as calm and composed as the crystal she held so tightly she feared snapping the delicate stem.

Her small and extremely late debut into Society was going well, except that the main guest, upon whose favor they all waited expectantly, had yet to appear. Because of their necessary frugality, Lord Manning's absence was easy to remark. The guest list was extremely limited.

"Lady de Veer tells me he is quite well-endowed," Glenda Warwick, Dowager Countess of Winslow, whispered excitedly into her daughter's ear. Then, she quickly leaned away, blushed, and looked down at the Champagne flute she held.

The bubbly brew had cost them almost their last crown, but even so, it had needed to be sugared to be drinkable.

"Er, financially, that is," she amended after a pause. She shot her daughter an enigmatic look.

Arabella nodded. "I'm certain the viscount will arrive

shortly," she replied, before adding in a whisper, "the hunchbacked toad."

"I am reminded once again I have given you far too much leeway all these years since your father's death that you could be so uncharitable now about the man who will save our lives."

Well, there was that. Arabella sipped from her glass as she looked around the ballroom.

Their efforts had transformed the decrepitating room nicely. Burning candles, borrowed chairs, and hand-picked nobility altered the space into an impermanent wonderland. In reality, the room was hung with only threads of genteel splendor. Wallpaper that must have looked outdated when it was installed showed signs of yellow age where paste had separated from wallboard. The hunting scene, a bloody affair with stags' heads lying all about, was mercifully fading a little more each year. There was a reasonable expectation one day it would fade into oblivion completely. A single Chippendale side table remained, only because any value it once held had been destroyed by her father in his youth. Remnants of his childhood scribbling peeped from beneath the painted, flower-adorned façade.

Across the way, the only remaining portrait of Earl John Winslow, whom Arabella resembled down to her pale blond hair and pansy-colored eyes, mocked her efforts at gilding the pig. Genteel poverty was only a pinky's breath from destitution, after all, and it still showed at the seams.

As Arabella peered at Lady Winslow beneath her eyelashes, she couldn't help but notice the heightened spots of rose that dotted her mother's pale cheeks or the wheeze that ended each intake of the older woman's breaths. Had a reminder been required of why they needed Lord Manning's rumored interest to be true, her mother, whom she loved in a completely unfashionable but true and deep way, provided it. The doctors had unanimously agreed Lady Winslow's breathing problems would soon kill her if she didn't relocate to the cleaner air of the South of France.

Without the viscount's purse, however, there were simply no funds. It was that uncomplicated. For gently bred women living in Queen Victoria's England, the only way to obtain money was through marriage.

"Why, Lady Aimsbridge, how lovely you could join us for this most special evening," Lady Winslow gushed.

Looking up, Arabella was all but struck dumb at the sight of the heavily-wrinkled face gazing down at her, surrounded as it was by pounds of glittering jewels and mounds of purple hair. Somewhere behind the behemoth's shoulder, she caught a glimpse of an escort, but whoever the man might be, Lady Aimsbridge's over-weighted person rendered him invisible.

Pasting a polite smile upon her lips and studiously ignoring her instincts to stare, Arabella muttered a greeting, then did her best to blur her vision.

When the couple moved along into the ballroom, Arabella and Lady Winslow greeted their next guests until finally, the receiving line ended.

"Still no viscount," her mother warbled.

Arabella sighed. She was certain the lack of a viscount was a good thing, though it boded ill for the future.

"Mother, perhaps you should be a bit more realistic where this gentleman is concerned." She tried to choose her words with care since they seemed set to fall from her lips no matter how abraded her tongue. "Lady de Veer's assurances notwithstanding, surely so extraordinary a man as you have described is unlikely to hold an interest in someone like me, someone whom he has never even met?"

"Nonsense, darling. The Winslows have held high office in this land since William came over from that heathen country. You are a catch. At any rate, I know why you have caught the viscount's attention."

A small smile played upon Lady Winslow's lips.

"And that is?"

The arrival of Lord Percy and his wife, Lady Percy interrupted them. Once they had all exchanged pleasantries, the couple moved on to the interior, taking entirely too long to do so.

"Mother?"

"The viscount is also rumored to harbor a passing interest in Jellyfish."

"You never said!" If true, the information might change everything. She shut her gaping mouth before her mother could lecture her on proper comportment. "And it's Gilgamesh, not Jellyfish."

"It's one and the same." Lady Winslow's gaze darted toward the door. "Gillymeed. Jellyfish. It is true. I have it from Annette. The viscount is a scholar obsessed with Assyriology." She shot her daughter a pointed look. "I do hope, however, you are able to refrain from boring the poor man with your endless inquiries about this demented personage. Not everyone will be equally besotted. His lordship will likely hold other interests as well, and your job must be to entice him into telling all of them. Oh, dear. Now what?"

Arabella followed her mother's gaze to lock upon

Lady Annette de Veer, who frantically bobbed her chin toward the far end of the ballroom. Frowning, Lady Winslow set off to calm whatever storm brewed.

"Gilgamesh was not demented," Arabella muttered, aware her words were not, strictly speaking, true.

The tiny parts she had managed to translate of the Sumerian king's tale demanded a few questions about his mental faculties. A bit of a braggart and impossibly impulsive, he seemed to hie hither and yon without a care at all for the kingdom he had been given to manage.

Still, if she didn't defend him, who would?

When Lady Winslow returned, she grabbed Arabella's arm just above her long white gloves and whispered, "Darling, you simply must do something about your cat. Kismet has already knocked over a tray of Champagne, as well as ruined three coiffures, including that of Lady Riffinger, who, as you know, wears a wig to cover her baldness." She nodded toward the area in which the guests were visibly skirting away. "She is quite upset. Didn't I tell you to lock that nasty creature in your bedchamber? Whatever will Lord Manning think if he should arrive now and witness this debacle?"

"That he should run as if the hounds of Hades pursued him?" As her mother's lips twisted in response, no doubt to issue yet another long lecture on the subjects of gratitude and necessity, Arabella touched her elbow. "Be calm, Mother. I shall take care of it immediately."

Lady Winslow waved her fan with fury, the rasp of her breath loud even over the babble of cacophonous good cheer. Arabella patted her glove, set down her glass upon the side table, and made haste toward the disruption. When she arrived, she buried her smile behind her fingers. Their borrowed butler, James, wrestled her squirming cat, one hand gripping the ruff of its neck. Judging by the loud shrieks piercing the air, a battle had been waged.

James shrieked, not the cat. The feline had the benefit of very long and razor-sharp claws, and he seemed to be enjoying himself immensely, to judge by the lopsided grin he sported. James, whose dignity was in almost as many tatters as the sleeve of his jacket, threw Kismet into Arabella's waiting arms, where he settled down nicely and began to purr.

How had the cat escaped her room? She was certain she had locked the door behind her to keep out unwelcome guests. Having once been startled awake to find one of her mother's guests climbing into her bed, she had been assiduous ever since in locking her door, whether she was within or without. A large and heavy volume of Egyptian hieroglyphs wielded like a club had saved her virtue then, but the *Epic of Gilgamesh* was much lighter and couldn't be counted as an adequate deterrent.

"You've been imbibing, haven't you, naughty boy," Arabella whispered to the purring, grinning gray fluff in her arms as she sought the back staircase.

He must have imbibed the Champagne while tumbling the tray. He loved wine. Even as a kitten, he had been known to knock over a glass or two to take a sip. She planted a kiss on top of his head.

"You must think of these as punishing kisses, you villain, although I suspect you were just uncertain without me there to protect you. Were you lonely without my company, my darling? Were you frightened?" she asked as she reached the second floor.

Perhaps the only cat with such a phobia, Kismet was

terrified of the dark. It was her fault he had sought escape to the brighter lights of the ballroom, as she hadn't wanted to leave an untended flame burning in a locked room.

She had secured the door, hadn't she?

"I would far prefer to stay with you, my heart," she assured the cat, "but, alas, I must see to the guests. Duty before pleasure." She snuggled her face into his sonorous vibrations to borrow some of his contentment. Then, she sighed and turned the knob.

****

Baron Brynley had wasted little time escaping Lady Aimsbridge's clutches and heading above-stairs. If there was a connection to be found between Lady Arabella and his dastardly relatives' opposition to his title suit, he had been determined to find it. That determination had flagged, however, as he had closed the door to Lady Arabella's room, the only chamber he had come across that had still held any furnishings. All the other portals had revealed spaces long since emptied of goods, the only remainder being a wash of dust upon the floor, like sand within a desert tent.

The rumors had been accurate. The ladies were obviously in financial straits.

Unlike the other doors he had tried, Lady Arabella's had been locked, but a few swipes with his favorite picks had opened it right up. Something gray and fast had streaked by his feet as he pushed open the entry, but he had paid it little heed as guilt had dogged his heels.

Tossing dresses and knickers, powder, and a few pieces of paper he had reluctantly skimmed, as it was not in his nature to abuse the privacy of innocents, if that was indeed what Lady Arabella was, he had finally and happily admitted defeat. The papers held only a list of necessities for the party below. It would have taken suspicion beyond his abilities to find conspiracy in the words, "rose bowl filled with garden flowers," and "exotic rice and raisin dish."

Now, closing the door softly, the heinous chore behind him, he became aware of soft footsteps climbing the back staircase and a female voice uttering sweet words in dulcet tones.

A lover's words.

Quickly, he dashed to one of the empty rooms across the hall and secreted himself within. Leaning his head against the jamb, heart pounding with adrenaline, he found himself strangely disappointed to realize the voice had to belong to Lady Arabella herself. There weren't many young women present, the party consisting mainly of friends of Lady Winslow, of like age and demeanor, but this voice definitely possessed the timbre of a younger woman.

The rustle of the woman's skirts grew louder. A knob turned. Lady Arabella gasped.

"I am certain I locked the door. Quick, let's get you inside before you make any further trouble."

She took no care to soften the volume of her words, the brazen thing. The door shut. More words followed, too low-voiced for him to hear though he pressed his ear to the wood until it throbbed.

She laughed, a delightful tinkling sound, and the volume increased as she exclaimed, "Just look at that tipsy grin you are sporting! This calls for severe punishment, and I know just how to go about it. First, a few quick kisses to your belly."

He gritted his teeth, his initial impression of Lady

Arabella spoiling in his stomach like rotting meat. While he had walked the receiving line, all but invisible in Lady Aimsbridge's shadow, he had studied this paragon his cousin was rumored to desire. Despite his initial prejudices, he had thought her rather lovely. He had even much admired her noticeable efforts to hide her shock at his partner's purple beehive, a coloration almost matched by the shade of Lady Arabella's own wilted-pansy eyes. It would be difficult not to admire the kindness of character such restraint indicated, though she had missed greeting him.

He hadn't minded. His invisibility had been a blessing, allowing him ample opportunity to slip past all the guests unnoticed. It would appear, however, Lady Arabella was now rudely interrupting his illicit search with her own illicit tryst, and with the same man who had sent him here on this furtive mission in the first place. It was galling.

The girl murmured sweet nothings into his cousin's ear. Strange, he wouldn't have thought her loose. At first blush, she had appeared staid. To drag a man up to her bedroom in the middle of her party seemed a bit excessive for even the lightest of skirts, no matter how much she might wish to net a fellow.

Her ivory lace had seemed made of heavier stuff. Perhaps it was the wanness of too many dim rooms reflected in her face that had formed his opinion. Peter was forever telling him the same color lightened his complexion. Musty gray, his all-but-brother called the look. Not that he was right, of course, since Gabriel knew his skin was rather too bronzed ever to be termed gray. Still, there was a certain indoor pallor to the girl he recognized. It bespoke libraries. Or boudoirs. Just because a band across the ridge of her nose indicated spectacles didn't mean her eyesight had deteriorated from reading educational treatises. Perhaps she had merely been born with insufficient vision.

When Peter had mentioned in his biographical compilation of rumors and surmise that the lady was an ardent Assyriologist, Gabriel's heart had quickened. However, Peter hadn't mentioned that the girl was happier lying upon her back than sitting upon her haunches. All that pale hair and those limpid violet eyes. Of course, she was too lovely to actually be intelligent and interesting as well. To her further discredit, it appeared she preferred the company of boors.

Abruptly deciding he should return downstairs rather than attempt to wait the lovers out, he opened his door just as the one opposite was flung open. Gabriel stood, startled eye to startled eye, with the woman he had just been considering.

"Ah!"

In the next instant, Arabella slipped back inside her room, no doubt intending to lock him out.

He didn't hesitate.

Chapter 3

Just as her door closed, Gabriel pushed it open with his right arm. In his left hand he held, like a knife, the picks he had originally used to jimmy the lock.

Once through, he shut the portal behind him in a single motion. Lady Arabella, violet eyes wide with shock, slid backward until her legs braced the bedframe.

"What are you doing?" she demanded. "Who are you?"

As he stared at her, catalogued her, incredibly, the world stilled.

Locks of curling golden hair, some so light it looked almost white in the clear glow of moonlight shining through the open draperies, escaped into tendrils that framed her face and brushed her almost naked shoulders. The slope of skin led his examination downward to the surprisingly ripe bosom encased by the aged-lace gown. For a moment, he feasted on the sumptuous display more hinted at than revealed. He did so enjoy using his imagination. A slim waist gave way to what appeared to be more ample hips. Hers was a figure that invited a man's hands. His gaze darted back up and rested again upon her bosom.

How had he missed these facets of her before? It must have been Lady Aimsbridge's girth and the fact he had been trying to see around her beehive of purple hair. As he had fought the lavender-hued monster and a socially inappropriate sneeze, he had been unable to take in the full magnificence of the bluestocking.

Finally, Gabriel managed to lift his gaze to meet Arabella's. She looked as stunned as he felt. Did she feel the earth tremble beneath her feet as he did? Was her belly also constricted with air she could not expel? Proving him wrong, Lady Arabella inhaled sharply, and he remembered.

Her lover.

Striding forward and capturing her arm, he pushed her behind him as he prepared against an attack from the bed. However, that piece of furniture was empty save for a long-haired gray cat watching him rather expectantly, rather like one might regard a comedic actor in an amusing play.

"I am not here for your amusement," he muttered, spinning around again and taking the lady with him.

He ignored her sounds of distress as he searched the largely empty space. He couldn't spot a single nefarious cousin, let alone any other sort of human.

The wardrobe. Unheeding of the protesting form he dragged behind him, he rushed the cabinet, threw the doors wide, and then stepped into the best fighting stance he could achieve. Lady Arabella twisted and thrashed about, but she did so, thankfully, without making a sound.

"Come out, you cad," he ordered.

When the few billowy dresses stopped moving from the rush of air, he noticed a decided absence of human beings within the closet.

"Where is he?" Gabriel demanded. "Where is your lover?"

Her gaze darted toward the bed again.

"Aha!" he exclaimed. "Under the bed. Of course.

Stay here, and don't move a muscle."

He released her and stormed the enormous furniture. The hangings gathered neatly around the poles, framing the smirking cat. Flinging himself to the ground, he pulled the dust ruffle up and out of the way.

And sneezed violently.

"Gads, have your servants ever cleaned under here? There are enough dust bunnies to knit sweaters for everyone in this kingdom."

His eyes watered as he flung himself up to a standing position again. It was clear no one was hiding under the bed. Anyone attempting such an act would have been suffocated in short order.

The metallic scrape of the lock alerted him as he rubbed away the dust, and just as the door opened, he flung himself against it, trapping the lady's warm, lithe body against the portal that slammed shut.

"Oh, no. You'll not escape me yet," he growled, reaching to turn her around so she rested frontal against his chest.

Her breasts pressed to his body, and her hair feathered his chin. She was soft, golden, and warm. He removed one hand from her hip and pushed the picks he still held into his pocket. It would not do to mar her perfect skin accidentally.

"Let me go, or I'll scream," she rasped, pushing at him ineffectually.

"Like some penny-dreadful heroine?" he asked, as his gaze raked her features.

Perfect. She was just perfect. Her face was an exact oval, the details small and centered but for the wide amethyst eyes. A faint smell of some sweet flower, maybe gardenia, wafted from her hair. There was something about her that seemed almost familiar, something that put him immediately at ease and made him want to joke and jostle her. Other things about her, such as the perfect weight of her body pressed to his, made him want to do different things. Bedroom things.

"Are you insulting me?" Lady Arabella demanded. "A penny-dreadful heroine? Truly? Well then, I suppose your assessment must make you the villain of the piece, barging into my bedroom, manhandling me, threatening me with those sharp, pointy, metal, pokey things. You do know what happens to the villains in those books, don't you? Or, I'm sorry, perhaps you cannot read?" Her tone was withering.

He shook his head and backed off a few inches, but only a few. She was more formidable than he had supposed, but her body was also a lodestone, pulling him in.

"I meant only a sensible woman would forbear screaming in this particular situation, as she would realize that, while I am harmless, the risk to her reputation, should someone come running, is great. She…you… would be ruined."

Her shoulders, held in tense readiness for sparring, lowered. "Threatening my ruin doesn't commend you, you know," Arabella muttered.

It didn't. Clearing his throat, he tried again. "Speaking of ruin, where is the cad who accompanied you?"

"You're the only one here of that description." She pushed against him again, but he refused to notice.

"Perhaps. How did he leave? Is there a secret passage?"

She bit at her lip and cocked her head, and then,

suddenly, all traces of ire melted from her face. Slowly, her lips slid into a captivating smile. "Are you mad?" she whispered as if his insanity might be delightful.

The question stalled him, not because he was insulted, but because the mental state would explain a lot of the mixed emotions he was currently experiencing.

"Perhaps," he finally answered, inching her closer again.

Chapter 4

"Mad or not, I'm afraid you must unhand me," she said in a reasonable tone.

"Or you'll scream?"

"As you not-so-gallantly mentioned, I cannot afford the scandal." She frowned. "My mother would collapse and never recover. Why is it, do you suppose, innocence is such a tricky thing for a woman? It is a much-vaunted virtue, endlessly coveted, and yet easily lost without so much as a by-your-leave. It just doesn't seem quite fair, does it?"

"Life often isn't."

Unfairness brought to mind his cousin and his machinations, which in turn reminded him he was in his present situation for reasons having nothing to do with flirtation. Instead of moving back or releasing Lady Arabella, Gabriel pulled her with him to the bed, ignoring her protests.

"Enough," he finally muttered, placing her gently onto the soft coverlet.

Before she could spring up and away, he flung himself beside her, wincing as his hip jarred the edge of a book. He took it up, about to read the cover, when she distracted him.

"It is enough, isn't it? While I enjoy reading about mad escapades, I'm discovering it is entirely different to live one. You must leave at once. I warn you," she continued, skittering away as far as her skirts would allow, which wasn't very far since his leg held down one corner, "I will scream if I must. I may lose social standing, but you will be placed behind bars for the rest of your days. You'll be hanged, boiled in oil…eradicated completely."

"Boiled and eradicated, before or after they hang me?" he asked, curious.

She was funny, this female, and intrepid too. This bluestocking with her iron-melting body was far more than merely a pretty pair of eyes. She had some lip on her as well. Her fearlessness was intriguing. So far, she hadn't raised her voice, which was quite something given he had pulled and pushed her all about the room. There wasn't another female he could name who would not have screamed down the house by now.

"I will defend my honor, even if it should mean my ruin."

Gabriel frowned. "Lady Arabella, I promise you, I would never force a female in that manner, not ever. You have my word." He paused. "I find, however, I might not be averse to any liberties you might wish to take with my person."

A blush suffused her cheeks and went as high as her hairline, dissipating her indoor pallor. With her hair loosening from her carefully constructed coiffure, the temper in her eyes, and the lush sweetness of her figure, she was temptation on a plate.

Without thinking further, he leaned over, intending to press his lips to her rosy, parted ones. Halfway there, sharp pain needled the back of his neck.

Snapping back quickly, he turned his head just enough to see the fuzzy, grinning, gray cat stretched to imbed tiny sharp claws into Gabriel's skin just above the collar line. Letting go of the lady's wrist and the book, he used two hands to remove each sharp nail, one by one. When he drew his fingers back, he was dismayed to discover blood.

"Gad, but this will ruin my shirt," he grumbled, wiping his fingers upon his dark pants. "Stay right there," he added, reaching for the woman who was fast moving away.

She was as slippery as an eel. With little effort, he dragged her back beside him.

"Please," she pleaded softly, "please, let me go back to my party. You have no idea how important it is. I don't know what you want, who you're looking for, but there's no one here and nothing of value, believe me. If there were anything valuable, it would have been sold long ago. In fact, that's why I must return below. Immediately. I'm the next Winslow possession on auction."

Her lip caught in her teeth, drawing Gabriel's gaze again to her mouth. He found his desire to taste her had not diminished in the least.

"Where is your lover?" he asked, struggling to keep his mind where it ought to be stuck.

"I don't have a lover, not that it's any of your business. I don't even know you."

"Funny. We were formally introduced not an hour since. I'm not sure you noticed." At her quizzical look, his voice hardened. "Perhaps you do not recall the moment because you were occupied with dreaming of how you would sneak away from your party to press soft kisses upon your lover's belly."

"There is no lover. Furthermore, had we been introduced, I would certainly have remembered you, sir, I assure you. With your dimpled chin, ebony hair, and those forest-green eyes, you are quite memorable. You do not look very English at all, and…oh!"

Gabriel found himself inordinately pleased she found him memorable, even if she did not remember him. Deliberately, he pushed the ridiculous notion away.

"Did you accompany Lady Aimsbridge?" she demanded, squinting at him. "With the purple hair?" She gestured high above her head and waved her hand.

"Guilty as charged, but yes. I even attempted a fleeting kiss above your glove before I was stampeded into the ballroom. You never even blinked."

She blinked now. Several times. "Why, then, you must be a guest."

"Always that quick, are you?" He laughed as a flush of red suffused her cheeks again. "No, tame that temper I see brewing. I jest. I have already remarked to myself upon the amazing quality of invisibility one attains next to dear Lady Aimsbridge. The government should employ her for all those tricky missions that require furtive maneuvers."

"Droll sense of humor you have for a thief and a lecher."

"Lecher?"

"Absolutely. Don't think I missed your perusal of my person or that you were about to, er, um…"

"Kiss you?" he finished softly. "Is that what you would like me to do?"

"No, of course not," she whispered, averting her gaze.

"Liar." He smiled.

His words goose-bumped her skin between sleeve and glove, he noted with pleasure. That was certainly a good sign.

"Tell me," he continued, before he could do something stupid, like kiss her against her will, "if you haven't a lover, then to whom were you speaking in the hallway? Don't deny it. I heard you quite clearly."

Her confusion did not appear feigned. Odd.

"You kissed his belly," he urged, "and—oh." He tossed a glance at the now slumbering cat whistling through its nose.

A terrible realization swept over him.

Lady Arabella burst out laughing. "You thought I'd taken a cat for my lover? Fie, sir, I think my virtue safe with Kismet."

Gabriel scowled as he accepted his monumental gaffe.

"Yes, an apology is in order, Mister…?"

"Lord, actually. Gabriel Darkwood, Baron Brynley, at your service." He inclined his head.

Arabella stopped laughing. "And because you thought I had taken a lover, me, someone you do not even know, such belief gave you the right to haul me about, threaten me, and put me in fear of my life?"

"*Pff*!" he exclaimed, before he could consider his words, "I see very little fear. In fact, you seem rather the intrepid sort."

She nodded, accepting the compliment as if it matched her own self-assessment. She really was extraordinary.

"I am a scholar. Of course, I am intrepid. One cannot read without developing an understanding of the need for courage. Broadening the mind is not a task for the anemic."

He quite agreed, but he had never thought to hear a

woman utter such sentiments. It was almost shocking.

Gabriel cleared his throat. "And what is it you are studying?" he asked, reaching for the book lying next to him to hide his confusion.

It wasn't every day he attacked incomparable women, accused them of having lovers, and been mauled by a cat for his troubles. His stomach wobbled as he looked down at the book. "*The Epic of Gilgamesh?*"

It couldn't be, but the cuneiform inscriptions embossed upon the front leather were unmistakable to those who could understand them.

"You recognize the title?" Her mouth rounded until she snapped her lips shut.

"You are reading this?"

"How?" they demanded in unison.

"As much as I am able," she allowed, breaking the silence. "There are a great many symbols, of course, that have not yet been translated. I am trying, in a small way, to remedy that lack." She scooted an inch or so closer to him.

The rumors had, unaccountably, been true. Something flip-flopped within his chest.

"Have you read much of the tale? You are obviously able to translate the title." She laughed, an abrupt sound, and reached toward the nightstand for her glasses. Slipping them onto her nose, she held out her hand for the book, which he gave her. Without bothering to smooth the fabric, she crossed her legs under her wide skirts, party slippers and all. "I'm only a beginning student, I'm afraid. Have you read Rawlinson?"

"Rawlinson?" he repeated, flummoxed by her posture. For the life of him, he couldn't remember when a woman had crossed her legs in front of him, probably because it had never happened. "Oh. Yes. Henry," he answered, trying to recapture his wits. "We are members of many of the same clubs."

"He's amazing," she gushed.

Gabriel's smile faltered. "Well, I too intend to make discoveries of my own. Soon. It is my dream to read the messages left to us by those who lived thousands of years ago."

She frowned suddenly, her eyes narrowing behind the façade of her spectacles. "Are you mocking me?"

Surprised, he shook his head.

"Because it is my dream as well," she continued sheepishly. "To see Sumer for myself. My mother calls it all sand and noise, but what must it be like, to touch the stone hewn by a hand so far in the distant past as to be mythological in nature?"

No one could fake that intensity. He knew the passion well, for he had been ridiculed for it his entire life. He had it still, though lately it had been dimmed by duty, business, and court battles for titles that should already be his. For a moment he could only stare at the lady, at the gentle beauty that could easily make up for lack of fortune in anyone of honest intent.

Perhaps his cousin's interest was not so hard to understand after all. One look from those crushed violet eyes would drive any man to the edge of the altar.

Finally, he murmured, "You are an original."

He leaned forward and brushed a curl back from her forehead. Gently. Provocatively. Then, remembering his cousin, he pulled back from the cocoon Lady Arabella wove around him. Justin wanted less learning in his women than in his saddle. Crushed violet eyes would not hold the cur. Justin sought riches, fame, and his own brand of secret infamy. He was cruel and delighted only in the misfortune of others. So then, why was he interested in this delightful female?

Shaking his head, Gabriel cleared his throat again for good measure.

Tapping the book she held, he asked, "How did you come by this copy of the Epic tablets? The British Museum is still translating them and has been ever since they were discovered at Nineveh by Sir Austen Henry Layard. I wasn't aware copies had been printed for the public."

"Oh, they haven't, at least, not to my knowledge. This is one of the special editions Sir Austen had made for himself. The symbols are drawn by hand, and the back holds a few colored plates and partial translations. I am very lucky to possess such a treasure. Sir Austen is a great friend of my mother's, you see, and she begged this for me."

"Ah." He sat up straighter and held out his palm. "Since you are interested in such things, please allow me to read one of the most fascinating aspects of the story. I've managed to decode a tiny part over the course of some rather long and sleepless nights." When her head tilted, he explained, "Large donations to the museum have given me the access I need to work."

As an explanation, it was good enough, although not completely correct.

She tossed him a glance he could only read as a mix of understanding and complicity. It confused him and sent some odd rush of fire through his blood. He wanted to shrug out of his tailored black evening jacket and rip the constricting knot from around his neck. His fingers sought his collar, but then she handed him the book.

Their pinkies brushed and his chest contracted tighter than his cravat. It wasn't a pleasant feeling, not exactly.

Clearing his throat again, he flipped through the pages. "Utnapishtim, the Noah figure who survives the deluge, was given immortality for his great deeds in serving the gods and surviving the flood, or, one supposes, for his general piety. But here," he added, locating the section and roughly translating as he went, "it reads to the general that, having been granted such a boon, he and his wife are to live at the source, or base, of the two rivers. Gilgamesh, the hero, is journeying there to meet Utnapishtim, or so I believe."

"Remarkable."

"Indeed. The most intriguing part for me is how real the direction to the location appears to be. It makes me wonder whether I might be able to locate this exact spot at the mouth of two rivers. That is to be my life's work after I am done with my responsibilities here."

"In Genesis, too, there is a description of the Garden of Eden much like a map," she agreed in an excited voice. "Four rivers are precisely described."

"Like Dilmun from the *Epic*."

"Yes," she whispered.

A strange fluttering caught in his chest and rose to his throat. It rippled along his veins. It was the oddest sensation, yet she seemed similarly beset, as if she too would like nothing better than to fly about the room.

There was nothing he could do. She was already leaning forward. He reached to meet her, his hand gently coming around to cup her head from behind and draw her lips closer. As if every second slowed like melting molasses, he counted the light splattering of bleached freckles upon her cheekbones, noticed the way her upper lip plumped at the edges, found himself amazed by the creamy expanse of seemingly poreless porcelain skin.

Then, his eyes closed as he saw hers gently dropping. His lips parted, less than a finger's breadth away, when a sudden banging reverberated through the room, sending them both crashing back and away.

In the next instant, the room was far too crowded. Skirts swirled, but it was a silver blade laid against his throat that caught his attention.

"Well, well, what have we here?" the too-familiar voice asked softly.

Chapter 5

The knife edge dug deeper, almost certainly drawing blood. Gabriel winced. No doubt about it; the shirt was definitely ruined. He groaned and briefly shut his eyes as the enormity of his mistake crashed in upon him.

"Mother, I can explain," Lady Arabella said firmly.

Peter had been wrong to have trusted him with this mission. Lady Arabella was not a clue to be unraveled at all.

She was a clue that had unraveled him.

The serene space with its lavender wallpaper and pristine white linens had become chaotic. Lady Winslow, perched precariously on the edge of weeping, wailed as she leaned upon Lady de Veer, who was nearly bent double with laughter. Justin, standing beside him, bent over and snarled a continuous line of threats into Gabriel's ear. Next to his hip, the cat began to snore sonorously, as if too used to such carryings-on to bother to lift an eyelid.

Meanwhile, Lady Arabella's smallest gloved finger crept out and touched the tip of his pinky where it lay upon the spread next to the feline. Prevented from fully turning his head to look at her by Justin's blade, he allowed the small touch to calm his initial panic. She really was quite remarkable. Worse fates could befall a man.

Breathing in a long, deep breath, he prepared to do

what duty expected of him. He would, once the others settled. He counted to ten and then ten again, but the uproar only increased exponentially.

"Enough," he finally snapped. Unaccountably, the others fell silent, one after the other, excepting the cat, who continued to blister the air. "Now, if you would be so good, Justin, I prefer to keep my head attached to my shoulders." He grabbed Justin's wrist and tried to force the blade away.

"I should see your neck severed instead," Justin growled, resisting, leaning in, so his face nearly touched Gabriel's.

"You're always welcome to try."

His cousin's face screwed tight as if he would force his point, but it seemed the muffled cry from Lady Winslow reminded him in time that murder might have consequences, even in the present situation. Swearing softly, he stood straight and removed the blade. Once the knife was sheathed and pocketed, Gabriel stood as well, deliberately bumping him. At Justin's muttered oath, Gabriel's lips twitched, but he took care to hide his humor as he brushed the creases from his jacket. All attention was upon him, waiting.

Well, they would stare. His was the only power to undo the damage, unfortunately.

He opened his mouth, but before he could utter a sound, Lady Winslow wailed into the waiting silence.

"Oh, Arabella, how could you have done such a thing?"

"Really, Glenda, give the girl some credit," Annette de Veer purred, her voice chocolate-smooth as her glittering gaze raked over Gabriel. "What girl wouldn't give her eye teeth for a few moments alone with Lord

Brynley? In my opinion, it's the first sign of good sense Arabella has exhibited to date."

"Your opinion is not wanted," Lady Winslow snapped. "Oh, everything is ruined!"

"Mother, calm yourself," Arabella ordered, voice stern but concern etched her beautiful face.

Gabriel sighed. He ran his hand through his hair. What a mess. The Darkwoods were infamous for slithering out of tight situations, but he had just been caught sitting upon an unwed lady's bed about to kiss her. There was only one remedy for that sort of thing, one he would have preferred not to provide despite how undeniably attractive Lady Arabella was. Still, his preferences were not the issue, and many men had married for less. He squared his shoulders.

"Despite the circumstances, there was no impropriety," Lady Arabella objected.

Her voice was steady, and for a moment Gabriel was distracted by her unaccountable bravery. Not many women could comport themselves so well in this ruinous situation. There probably weren't any.

She truly was incomparable.

Lady Arabella still sat cross-legged, calmly holding the book from which they had been reading. The spectacles on her face were only slightly askew, and if she looked like the most passionate bluestocking ever to grace the planet, the good news was she indeed appeared interested only in bookish pursuits. Her aspect might help wash her reputation, which would suffer even after they wed.

He tried to ignore the guilt that crept up his spine with scabby fingers. There was no way around the knowledge: the entire situation was his fault.

"What interests me about Lord Brynley is not his, er, physical properties, as Lady de Veer suggests," Lady Arabella continued evenly, "but rather his mental ones. Did you know he has translated part of the *Epic*? It is so exciting I can hardly credit it."

The rabid disinterest this startling news had upon most of those present was almost comical. Lady Winslow's expression glazed as her lip continued to tremble. Lady de Veer groaned loudly and rolled her eyes. Justin, however, glared at Gabriel before turning his attention upon Lady Arabella, eyes narrowed.

That was concerning. A focused Justin was a dangerous Justin.

"Enough about Gilded-dish, Arabella, you promised to behave," Lady Winslow wailed. "You were supposed to entertain your guests in the ballroom! Oh, Lord Manning, what must you be thinking?"

Glenda Winslow leaned resolutely upon her friend's shoulder. They might have toppled to the floor if Annette de Veer had been of less sturdy build.

"No doubt about it. Arabella has captured the viscount's attention," Lady de Veer murmured, her voice thick with amusement. She clicked her tongue and tilted her brazenly orange head. "Toothsome though the baron is," she added, sending him a wicked smile, to which he returned his most withering frown, "I yet think Manning has a chance with her. What say you, my lord?" She raised an eyebrow.

Gabriel focused once more upon his cousin. Justin was indeed a handsome devil if one liked that too-perfect, almost doll-like figure and face. His russet locks curled just enough. His Champagne eyes were cat-like. He cut a fine figure in his evening wear, and if one didn't look deeper into his eyes, one might indeed miss the malice that sat there like a fat worm.

This would be tricky. His newly favorite bluestocking was a stalwart figure, and he admired her calm more than he could say, but she was unequipped to handle Justin's machinations…if she were as innocent as she seemed.

"*Gilgamesh*, Mother, not Gilded-dish." Lady Arabella frowned and adjusted her slipping spectacles. "Please be calm before you inspire another breathing attack."

She turned her attention toward Justin and unpretzeled her legs. As she scooted toward the edge of the bed, her movements tousled her wide skirts, revealing a length of leg that was pleasing to behold until Justin began beholding it with every appearance of pleasure. Quickly, Gabriel reached over and tugged the fabric into place, jostling Lady Arabella in the process.

Sending Gabriel a forbidding frown, she turned back to his cousin and extended her hand. "Please excuse the drama, my lord," she chirped, re-plastering a polite smile upon her lips. "You must be Lord Manning. I had so wished to greet you below, but Kismet, my naughty cat, managed to imbibe a bit too much Champagne." She slanted the cat a fond look. "I was forced to return him to my room, but then," she shot a sideways look at Gabriel from the corner of her eyes, "I encountered Lord Brynley. We began discussing the *Epic*, and…" She shrugged. "I understand you also harbor a passion for Assyriology, so perhaps you might comprehend how distracting the subject can become."

"Do not mistake this dandified buffoon for a scholar," Gabriel objected.

Justin ignored him and bowed over Arabella's hand, kissing her glove as he lingered overlong. He left behind a wet patch upon the delicate kid when he stepped back. Lady Arabella's eyes briefly narrowed, but if disgust had ever been etched into her features, it was there and gone before Gabriel could be certain. His fists clenched, but there were more important matters before him. Again, he opened his mouth to do the right thing, but his cousin interrupted him.

"Lady Arabella, I have long wished to meet you. Well, I've made no pretense of my interest, have I? Rumors of your enchanting occupation immediately caught my notice. Now, seeing you, I am overjoyed to discover…well, no. It would not do to comment upon your beauty, though I might say I am enormously pleased by it."

Gabriel didn't like the weasel-like, leering look his cousin wore.

"Lord Manning, I must assure you this-this lapse is completely out of character for my daughter." Lady Winslow breathed heavily. "I have no idea why this-this person is above stairs, and what could you be thinking, Brynley?" she demanded, rounding upon him. Maternal wrath incised her every syllable.

"I assure you, Lady Winslow, I wasn't considering causing a debacle," Gabriel murmured, keeping his gaze upon his unctuous cousin, who looked at Lady Arabella's bustline with too much intensity. "I apologize for any part I have played in causing my cousin to lose interest in your daughter." He took a moment to smirk at Justin, who frowned. "There is no cause for alarm, however. A simple remedy for this sort of thing is well-known, and I am ready to—"

"On the contrary, dear cousin. I fully realize, knowing you as I do, that you are incapable of true impropriety." Justin turned to face Lady Winslow. "Given the large book lodged between Lady Arabella and Brynley, I am absolutely certain they had only lost languages on their minds. Quite forgivable. And forgettable." He approached Gabriel and whispered, "The entire Assyriology interest is, of course, the approach I intend to use myself."

"Unbelievable," Gabriel snapped.

Turning back to face the ladies, Justin added in a louder voice, "Allow me to assure you all that, far from losing interest, I have instead become even further enamored of Lady Arabella. It is obvious the tales of her enterprising interest in Assyriology were not created simply to catch my attention, as I had all but feared. Indeed, though our introduction is, admittedly, unfortunate," he said pompously, slanting a glance at Gabriel out of the corner of his eye, "this moment has simply served to justify my initial interest."

Conceited, diabolical, crusty-panted buffoon. He waited for someone to put those words into the air, but no one did.

"Lady Arabella," Justin continued, a too-wide smile stretching his otherwise handsome features, "I am delighted by your intellectual fervor. I hope we might share some mutually gratifying moments poring over old texts together. Nothing would give me greater pleasure than hearing your views on ancient matters. Soon."

"Lovely," Lady de Veer cooed before his cousin had even finished his sentence. She obviously recognized a rescue line thrown her friend's daughter's way. "Well, that's all sorted then. It is such a relief when logical minds prevail in unfortunate circumstances. What a marvelous example of tolerance you portray, Lord Manning. You are to be congratulated upon your aplomb."

"Oh, yes," Lady Winslow choked out as Lady de Veer elbowed her in the ribs. "You are indeed… possessed of…superior reason, my lord."

"Er, yes. Quite," Arabella agreed slowly.

But her expression had suddenly hardened. She stared at her mother, whose skin had turned the color of old cod and whose lips were bluing at the edges. Gabriel swiftly stepped toward her as the woman tried and failed to inhale deeply.

"Lady Winslow, will you sit?"

If he had thought she would be grateful for the support, he was mistaken. Instantly, her back sprang rigid as she threw off his touch and shied away.

Arabella was there immediately, covering her mother's movements. "Come, Mother, let us go below."

"Excellent idea," Justin crowed, pushing Gabriel out of the way. "Lady Arabella, might I interest you in a turn about the dance floor?"

"In a moment." Having arrested the group again, Gabriel scrambled for something further to say. The *Epic*. That would do.

"Lady Winslow, while it was not my intention to cause an incident, I wondered if Lady Arabella would do me the great honor of allowing me to assist with her studies of the *Epic*? I believe we might make wonderful progress in uncovering the words of the ancients."

Arabella instantly cooed with delight and clapped her hands together, but the collective objections of the others quickly drowned the sound. None of their opinions mattered, however, because Arabella was beaming.

"Yes! I would be delighted! Honored. I accept. Isn't this the most wonderful news?" she asked her mother.

Although the volume of protestations increased and Justin's nostrils flared to murderous widths, Gabriel didn't care. He met and held Arabella's purple pansy gaze. Her countenance, lit from within, was an unanticipated reward. Her expression suggested he had just managed something heroic.

Who knew breathing could be so difficult?

Before this moment, Gabriel had possessed no notion of acting as a scholarly assistant to anyone. Something told him, however, it would prove the very greatest occupation he had ever attempted. Not only would he ferret out his cousin's reasons for wooing the remarkable Lady Arabella, he could spend time with the lady herself.

Perhaps, he had not failed Peter's faith in him after all.

Chapter 6

Several blocks away and long hours later, Justin Thauley, Viscount Manning, paced his father's library. Back and forth, from wall to wall, he stalked. His father, Robert, the Earl of Kildare, sat comfortably ensconced in an overstuffed library chair of bronzed leather, his ascot undone, his jacket unbuttoned, and the long greasy hairs usually combed over his prominent bald spot pushed back in the wrong direction.

Justin ran his hand over his eyes, trying to ignore the fear and rage that filled him, feelings not calmed by his father's incessant chewing. No matter how many times he reviewed the evening, he came to the same conclusions.

"It is no use, Father. To keep our titles and what few assets remain, we must obtain the Kildare seal ring, but to obtain it, I am required to play nice with Lady Arabella." He paused. "I don't think she desires to play nice with *me*."

"Please. You worry over trivialities," the earl grumbled, waving the free hand that wasn't knuckle-deep in a bowl of candied ginger. "As I said, Annie told me—under the covers, so it must be true—Glenda Winslow is desperate. Between us, we've laid a foundation so sturdy a deluge couldn't wash it away. Lady Arabella would have you even if you were covered in spots. Besides, you did say the gel was fixed to you for the remainder of the evening, did you not?"

Reluctantly, Justin nodded, but he continued to pace. "I suppose she was. I sensed, however, a certain disinterest, as if she would rather have remained in her room with Darkie."

His lip curled as he reviewed the scene into which he had stepped earlier that very evening. If he hadn't been aware of just how urgently they needed Lady Arabella's ring, he would have spun on his heels and decamped, affronted to have witnessed such a revolting display.

His father made a clicking noise. "What matters her thoughts? The mother is for you, as is Annie, who is like a favored aunt to the gel. Besides, I am happy to twist my nephew's nose."

"How so?" Justin paced toward the other chair adjacent to the fire and flopped himself into it.

"You saved him from offering for her, that's true—"

"Which still vexes me greatly. I would have loved to have seen him forced to swing from a marriage knot to an impoverished bluestocking, except…." His voice trailed off, as he didn't want to admit he had found Lady Arabella strangely sweet, especially given her age, lack of fortune, and unmarried state. Most women of their class wrapped themselves in pretension, but she hadn't bothered to seem better than she was. In a different situation, her attitude might have even seemed admirable.

"But did he want saving?" the earl continued pointedly. "Say what you will about Darkie; he has never been one to place himself in compromising situations. He is far too conscientious. No, if he entered Lady Arabella's bedroom and had the temerity to sit upon her bed and kiss her—"

"*Almost* kiss her."

"Then he knew what he was doing, at least on some

level. He understood the risks, and he took them anyway. That speaks of emotion." The earl tapped the side of the nut bowl, the hollow tinging noise of plated-silver grating down Justin's spine. "We might use that sensibility against him."

Justin glared at his father. Dishes and bowls of nuts and dried fruit vied for his attention. Beside his elbow, a cup of tea heavily laced with cloves, cinnamon, and honey sweetened the air. Despite their current financial woes, the man would not give up his expensive, imported sweets.

Justin snorted.

His father leaned forward, no mean feat considering his ever-expanding girth. "Listen, boy, and listen well. You will put your quavering aside because we need that ring to complete the will, and the ring is in Arabella Warwick's possession. Without the will, our claims upon the Kildare and Manning titles are imperiled. With it, Darkie is sure to lose. Therefore, you will court the chit, and you will keep her happy until the bloody piece of jewelry is ours. You will also marry the lady to get us an heir with impeccable bloodlines. Do you understand?"

Reluctantly, Justin nodded.

With a *harrumph*, the earl sat back again. "Good. That is settled then."

Once again, Justin sprang from his chair and paced to the other end of the library. Settled it might be, but that didn't mean *he* was happy about the course of events.

"I've always remarked that your fine sensibilities were an impediment." His father tossed the words over his shoulder as he picked at a plate of apricots. "Just remember, as all three of my wives kindly demonstrated, women make a habit of dying during childbirth. No one important will inquire too closely if your first wife pops out a boy and then rapidly stumbles into a grave. It is a sequence greatly preferred."

"Death does remedy many an entanglement," Justin agreed equably as he paced back to the fire.

The earl beamed. "Indeed, and it is so easily arranged. When Lady Arabella passes on, heiresses will be lining up to commiserate with you, my son. A bereaved viscount is a heady draw, especially to those American fillies long on *lucre* and short on standing. One of them will fill our coffers nicely, not to mention Darkie has no heir, nor even the hope of obtaining one before this affair is settled. If we time events correctly, we might inherit the Brynley estate as well. Won't it be lovely to have a full chest?"

Justin nodded absently as he adjusted his cuffs before leaning against the chair. He focused upon a small portrait over the hearth that portrayed his grandfather as a young boy, playing in green grass with a small dog. Looking at the aristocratic features of the child, it was difficult to imagine he would grow into such a short-sighted man. Russell Thauley, future Earl of Kildare, had made an absolute mess of what should have been a simple line of succession by secretly wedding Darkie's grandmother, Bertha Darkwood.

A commoner.

Oh, it had been no secret Darkie's father, Oliver, had been Russell's first-born son. It had come as something of a shock when Darkie discovered the certificate proving Russell had married Bertha in a secret ceremony some nine months before Oliver's birth, thus legitimizing Oliver and his line. Unfortunately, that piece of paper made Russell's subsequent marriage to Lady Mary

Reichtin bigamous and Robert Thauley, their son, nothing but a bastard through and through.

And what did that make him, Robert's son, other than a spendthrift commoner? Justin shuddered. It was a life-station too terrible to be borne.

Still, all was not lost. His inspiration had been forging a will to explain away Russell's marriage to Bertha Darkwood. He had employed the best and most nefarious artisans he could find to do so. The will was perfect, but it lacked only the seal. No one would believe Russell's claims written there, that he had lured Bertha into his bed by playacting a marriage, unless his testament specifically laid out such an admission in his hand, affixed with his insignia. His hand had been easy to copy. They had found documents sufficient enough to recreate his writing. Aged paper and ink had been easier to find than clean water. However, they hadn't managed to find a legible copy of the emblem.

"I could forge the seal," Justin said, repeating a previous argument.

His father sighed.

"I cannot forge the seal," Justin agreed, tapping the chair.

If Darkie had a clean copy in his possession, and the court eyed too closely the forgery, which they would do, then all their plans would unravel when the lines did not perfectly match.

The problem was, the seal was on a ring, and that ring, once given to Darkie's dissolute father, Oliver, had been lost by him in a card game to Lady Arabella Warwick's dissolute father, Lord John Winslow.

Justin studied Robert, who was currently knuckle-deep in a dish of honeyed figs. Dissolute fathers seemed to be a common problem among his generation.

He punched the chair lightly before flinging himself around it and back into the seat. He propped his feet on an ottoman upholstered in dark royal reds intersected with strands of gold, specifically chosen to pick up the golds in his auburn highlights and reflect his much-commented-upon, astounding, Champagne-colored eyes. He always insisted, where possible, upon matching his environment to his person. After all, what was the sense of being born with such devastating features if one was only going to exhibit them in an unflattering light?

"I swear to you, I will be the next Earl of Kildare when you are dead," Justin muttered, staring at his grandfather's portrait.

"With all your siblings gone to the grave, you are next in line, providing Darkie loses his suit." His father shelled a pistachio. He threw the empty casings into the fire where they popped. "They were a useless lot, weren't they? None of them had your fire, boy, or your brains." The earl's fingers stilled. "Justin?"

Justin turned his head and caught his father's gaze.

"I'm very proud of you, son," the earl added gruffly before turning his attention back to his nut.

Heat rushed through Justin's body, a warmth that had nothing to do with the flames at his feet. He had never heard those words before.

He vowed to hear them again soon.

Chapter 7

Bang, bang, bang!

Arabella was startled awake as something heavy hammered at her door. Squinting toward the offending portal, she raised her head a few inches off the pillow, swallowed a yawn, and then mumbled something even she couldn't decipher. Then she turned over.

Bang! Bang!

"Lady Arabella?"

A deeply masculine voice tried to rouse her with a whisper so loud it might have been heard in any theater's back row, even one with poor acoustics. The birds twittering outside the window momentarily stilled, proving the man had the lung capacity of the greatest of thespians.

"Open the door," the voice insisted and hammered some more.

Foggy-brained with sleep, she might be, but Arabella was suddenly alert enough to realize, if the birds outside could hear the voice, then so could her mother, asleep down the hall.

Quickly slipping from the bed, she crossed the room. Her white eyelet nightgown swirled around her ankles, threatening to upend her. When she managed to turn the key in the lock, she was unprepared for the door's force swinging inward.

Tripping backward, it was a moment before she could

focus fully upon the person barging inward. When she did, she gasped.

"Please don't scream," the incredibly beautiful stranger instructed quickly, holding up his hands. "I mean you no harm."

It was an angel. It had to be an angel. His features were simply too perfect to belong to mortal man. Possessed of wavy, white-gold hair and pale blue eyes the color of soft aquamarines, the features of his angled face looked hewn of strongest marble. Though not quite as tall and muscled as, say, Lord Brynley, who had immediately become the standard against which she feared she would forever measure a male, the angel's chiseled body, encased in dark blue and tan, was certainly what Lady de Veer might characterize as "toothsome."

"Lady Arabella?" he demanded, closing the door quietly behind him.

"Shh!" she whispered quickly, holding her finger to her lips. She squinted. "I should find my spectacles."

"And, perhaps, a robe?" he pointedly stage-whispered. His voice was no softer than it had been on the other side of the door.

Arabella looked down and gulped. Her face heated. "Excuse me."

She turned back toward the end of her bed and hurriedly shimmied into a covering. After fitting her spectacles upon her nose, she found herself truly gaping. The angel was even more beautiful when sharply edged.

"I understand better now why a certain gentleman rushed me from my sleep this morning," he whispered, proving he could indeed lower his voice. "The sights in this part of London are unassailably superb. In any event, kindly allow me to introduce myself, Lady Arabella, while I beg forgiveness for this unacceptable intrusion. My name is Peter Bartholomew. You may call me by my given name, as I am a confirmed egalitarian." He bowed slightly at the waist, his eyes sparkling with mischief. "Lord Brynley has asked me to direct you—"

"Gabriel?" she demanded, her feet surging toward him.

His brows rose in surprise before he hastily got them under control.

"Er...Lord Brynley, I mean?" she promptly corrected.

He hesitated. "Er, yes." He tilted his head appraisingly. "*Gabriel*," he added, stressing the name, "has charged me with escorting you to your first tutoring session. He didn't think it wise to come to your chambers himself, given the events of last evening. I am to direct you to make haste. Lessons are to begin within the quarter-hour, downstairs in your library."

"Lessons? Here? Now?"

"Yes. Lessons. Gabriel. Library. Now...ish. I think the man might keep his patience another ten minutes, but surely not longer. May I rely upon you to find your own way and quickly?"

Arabella nodded because it seemed she had lost her voice. She swallowed. Lord Brynley, he of the wide shoulders, sparkling green eyes, dimpled chin, growly voice, and command of cuneiform, was in her library.

"Wonderful. Then I see no reason why I shouldn't further neglect my escort duties to facilitate my search for a cup of very strong coffee. You will thank me for it, as *Gabriel* isn't tolerable until he has downed several cups. I understand you haven't a cook? No?" He sighed. "I will find my way to the kitchen and root around, shall I?

Perhaps I'll just whip up an egg or two while I'm there? You must have eggs. Everyone has eggs, which is rather a wonderful fact as I find myself a bit peckish at the moment."

He nodded, and then was out the door before she could recover speech sufficient to inform him there were coffee beans in the cupboard. Baron Brynley. Downstairs in *her* library. Baron Brynley, with his long legs, sharp-hewn cheekbones, strong grasp, and sweeping dark brows, waited to speak with *her* about cuneiform inscriptions.

A little corner of her chest felt as if a light had been lit within. It was a very peculiar feeling.

The door opened again, and the angel peeked around the corner. "Just a thought, but you will change into something decent, yes? That's a relief. Something high-necked and sack-like, if you have it? His lordship and I are fairly evenly-matched at swords, you see, but I am a bit better, and though it would be an honor to shed blood in your defense, I'd prefer not to have to do so until after I have breakfasted."

"Oh. Yes, of course," she replied.

But he was already gone.

Without time to ponder the matter further, she sped through her ablutions, pulled out the necessary undergarments, and began shoving herself into them.

She stalled when she viewed the steel-boned corset lying upon her trunk. There was simply no way to lace it up on her own. Without it, she could not wear either of the two dresses she normally wore for visits, which was a shame as they were both icy colors that accentuated her skin tone.

With no other option, she slipped into her blue at-home gown with its front buttons and tiny embroidered flowers along the hem. She would look thicker in the waist, which was unexpectedly upsetting, though she had never cared about such useless facts before. The good news was breathing was far easier to accomplish without the boning. Perhaps she could use oxygen to her advantage? She surveilled herself in the mirror and frowned.

Snatching up the brush, she pinned her hair back into a neat bow. Then, for good measure, she pinched her cheeks, hard, to add some color, before grabbing the spectacles from her nose and slipping them into a pocket. A moment later, she was ready. After giving Kismet one last kiss on the top of his fuzzy head, she slipped out the door and turned the key, pocketing it as well. Only as she neared the bottom of the stairs did she realize she had forgotten to put on shoes. For a moment she paused, and then decided footwear was the least of her concerns.

Unaccountably, there was an angel in her kitchen and a devil in her library, both of whom must remain hidden from her mother. She would tackle the devil first.

Arabella took a deep and steadying breath at the library, flung wide one side of the double pocket doors, and then stalled. The room was vacant.

Vast empty shelves, their precious volumes long since sold, edged the space. Only a few books remained, those used for her translations she refused to part with. Threadbare Aubusson rugs, with their gentle blues and soft reds, added a touch of color to the otherwise dark-wood shelving. A small and weathered blue couch lay between equally weathered upholstered chairs, flanking a small tea table. A larger library table still rested to the side, but one of the legs had been broken, so the table was now propped up level by two heavy volumes on farming practices no one with any sense would want to read. However, two hardback chairs that should have sided that table were pulled before the fire, which had already been lit. Flames danced merrily against the dim room.

"Hello?" Arabella stepped into the room.

Behind her, the door slid shut. She jumped and found herself nose to chest with Lord Brynley. The scent of fir, lime, vanilla, and something else, masculine and elusive, enveloped her.

"Oh!" She stepped back.

Lord Brynley grinned and advanced. Instinctively, she retreated another step, but somehow he moved her around so her back pressed to the wall adjacent to the door. He placed a hand next to her ear, effectively trapping her.

"Lady Arabella, you are a cheerful sight on this rainy day," he murmured.

He leaned over and inhaled deeply, the full breadth of him crowding her senses. Attired in a forest-green jacket with a matching vest and a simple white shirt, he was devastatingly masculine. Little trills of awareness danced upon her skin as she studied him. His ebony hair was swept back, caressed by the merest hint of silver at the sides, foils that heightened the startling color of his green irises.

Her knees buckled. He tugged her against the stone-hard length of his torso. He leaned toward her lips; his breath gently fanned her skin.

"I believe you were about to kiss me last night, before we were so rudely interrupted."

She gasped, helpless in anticipation.

"Tell me you want me to kiss you," he demanded

gently, so gently.

His lips brushed against hers, but only like the wind moving past a flower. She leaned forward, closing her eyes, wanting to deepen the connection, but he pulled back a terrible inch.

"Tell me," he repeated.

"Please." Her arms reached up to snake around his neck of their own volition.

What was taking him so long to cross such a short distance? Her fingers pulled at his head.

His responding smile was feral and self-satisfied, but she didn't care, not when he began to comply. He leaned in again, his mouth touched hers, almost a ghost of a touch, not quite real yet. Her lips parted as she gasped in anticipation.

And then the doors beside them opened wide.

Chapter 8

Gabriel growled, pushing Arabella behind him as he pivoted to face the doors.

The angel in the entry didn't seem the least bit shocked. "Am I interrupting?" he asked mildly, eyes sparkling. "Well, never mind, there's always time for *studies* later. I have come equipped with a rolling cart that quite refuses to roll, but which I have managed, through Herculean efforts, to fill with tea and coffee, rolls, and eggs. Gabriel, if you would lend a hand?" he asked, dragging a cart into the library backward.

Arabella jumped out of the way just as the rickety wicker contraption trundled by. Its wooden wheels didn't quite rotate anymore.

With no more than the smallest of disgruntled sighs, Gabriel lifted one end of the cart and helped maneuver it over the carpet to set it down before the snapping flames. As the men passed her, Arabella pressed her fingertips into the wood paneling, her other hand flattened to her heart that beat too fast, whether from the surprise of Peter's entry or the near kiss, she could not say.

From across the room, Peter darted a searching look toward her before clapping the baron on the shoulder. "Patience."

"Exigency trumps patience," Gabriel retorted in a quiet voice, although Arabella had no trouble hearing him from where she stood.

The acoustics in the library had always been tricky.

"You ache," Peter replied sympathetically.

"I do," the baron admitted. "Isn't that odd?"

"Not at all. I find it refreshingly wonderful." Peter glanced down at the cart and then back to her. "Lady Arabella, you may cease clutching the doorjamb. I've quite rescued you from milord's dastardly clutches. He'll behave now, or will, at least, once he's broken his fast."

Gabriel rolled his eyes, and Arabella found herself smiling despite her startlement.

"Friends are often a trial," Gabriel groused, his deep, rich voice reaching easily across the space. "But come, Lady Arabella. Please, sit." He gestured to one of the rickety chairs. "Ignore for the moment, if you would be so kind, that we have usurped your home. It is only we have much to discuss."

Arabella rushed to comply. Once in the chair, however, she found it necessary to take a few deep, steadying breaths to still her racing pulse. The effort proved impossible. His very proximity energized her blood. She looked at his bowed lips, and the tip of her tongue absently tested her own.

"You've met Peter, of course," Gabriel added, in a voice as steady as a well-cobbled street.

He was not as overwhelmed by her presence as she was by his.

Peter bobbed his head.

"I thought you were an angel at my door," Arabella said, still staring at the baron's mouth.

No sooner had the words passed her lips than she wished them back. What was wrong with her, commenting upon a gentleman's appearance? She fluffed her skirts to hide her shaking fingers and cover her stocking-clad feet.

Peter sputtered, and Gabriel burst out laughing.

"He's a rogue with the face of an angel, Lady Arabella." The baron seated himself next to her. He reached for the teapot and poured a cup, which he placed into her hands.

"Yes, but now you are forewarned." Peter crossed to look out the window. He turned back. "Gabriel hopes to ensure this face will not sway you."

"The threat has been neutralized."

"There was no need, I think."

"Despite the fact he is often a rogue, Peter is eminently trustworthy, Arabella. May I call you Arabella? I realize it is an impertinence even to ask, but given our peculiar association thus far and the fact we will be studying closely…"

When she nodded, he relaxed his shoulders. "And you must call me Gabriel."

"Already done," Peter murmured. "Thoroughly perplexing, but probably not the most perplexing part of all this."

They ignored him as they stared hard at each other while time skipped, paused, and then started again. After many moments, Gabriel cleared his throat, breaking the spell as he glanced away. Arabella dropped her gaze to her lap, where her trembling fingers clenched around the teacup. Thankfully, he had only filled it halfway, or her skirts would be a mess by now.

"So, it is to be that way," Peter remarked blandly. "I cannot see how the cause of Assyriology will be advanced if the both of you are tongue-tied. Languages require tongues, I'm told, as do other pleasurable things. Speaking of which—" He shifted back to the cart. "I have whipped up a credible brew of beans to tickle those organs."

He poured a cup of dark liquid. Its acrid smell bit at her nostrils.

"Do you take milk, Lady Arabella?" he asked, hand upon the ceramic pitcher.

Arabella nodded and then shook her head. "I would, er, normally," she stammered, "if-if, well, if I didn't already have tea, which I prefer black." She gestured with the drink she still held.

"Ah. So you do. Would you prefer coffee?"

When she shook her head, Peter shoved the cup into Gabriel's hands instead. The liquid sloshed and just narrowly missed bubbling over to burn the baron's long fingers.

"Have some eggs, then."

Peter proffered a plate heaped with more food than she might eat in three meals, along with a fork and napkin. She set her cup down upon the side table to take them.

"Thank you." She placed the plate next to her tea.

"Did you add soured cream, as Reggie does?" Gabriel inquired, taking the dish Peter handed him before poking at the rapidly cooling mountain of eggs with his fork. Then, he paused. Long moments ticked by.

Some sort of struggle crossed his face before he slanted his eyes toward her.

"Reggie is ostensibly my butler," he explained, marking out each word. "My parents died when I was quite young, so the current Earl of Kildare, my father's half-brother, Lord Manning's father, became my guardian. Kildare was not pleased about raising his bastard half-brother's offspring, so, to demonstrate his displeasure, he picked a village drunkard much damaged by war to watch over me. We were installed in an outbuilding on the estate and largely forgotten." The baron smiled softly, his features briefly relaxing. "Reggie was my saving, and not just mine." He nodded his chin toward the angelic-faced man. "When Peter's mother, an unmarried village lass, died, Peter joined us, and he became my brother in all but name. Reggie saved Peter as well."

"Should you be so bold as to put words into my mouth?" Peter grumbled. He eyed Arabella and then smiled. "Nevertheless, Gabriel is correct."

"I see," Arabella murmured.

"Of course, my scandalous upbringing is not common knowledge," Gabriel continued seriously. "Many would shun me because of it. My uncle and cousin don't mention it, of course, as it reflects just as badly upon them."

"Is that why you are telling me this?" she asked quietly. "Because it reflects poorly upon the viscount?"

For a moment, Gabriel's expression fell, but then he shook his head. "No. Yes. Perhaps." He rotated his hand. "I'm not certain. It is true Justin and I do not harbor much affection for each other, as you must have guessed. However, with Reggie mentioned, I suppose I took advantage of the moment to express the oddity of my past, perhaps so you might better excuse the unnatural liberties I've taken with you. I do respect you, Arabella. Please, believe that."

At their societal station, her name upon his lips was equally as intimate as a public kiss. It thrilled her down to her stocking-clad feet and curled her toes.

"There is also the matter that, if we are to be…

friends, I would have you understand. Peter and Reggie are my family, as dear to me as if we were connected by blood."

Friends? He thought they might become friends? She thought back quickly over her twenty-seven years. Acquaintances, she had had, and a family, yes, but a friend?

"How enviable you have managed such a close camaraderie," she replied, wistful.

Peter and Gabriel exchanged a look.

"I told you she was incomparable," Gabriel murmured to Peter, who continued to stare at her as if she had sprouted another head.

Heat rose to her cheeks, and a full flock of butterflies seemed to beat inside her chest at the baron's compliment, though it may only have been guilt as such approbation was undeserved. She swallowed hard.

"I was also unusually raised," she ventured. "It has always been just my mother and me. And Lady de Veer, I suppose. She and my mother have been best friends since they were young girls, so they're more like sisters than mere friends." Arabella paused and looked between the two men. "I am rather envious of those able to forge such close friendships they become like blood. I…I wonder if I am not too cold for such a thing."

It was a galling admission, and she had no idea why she had just made it. Heat rising to the roots of her hairline, she glanced away before forcing her gaze back again.

"I thought as much, given your intrepid nature." Gabriel bobbed his chin, appearing satisfied, but then he added quickly, "Not that you are cold, no, not at all. Why, I feel warmed just having you near."

"That's likely the hearth," she quipped.

He laughed, a large staccato burst of sound that caused her to smile in return.

"I assure you, the fire plays only a minor part. In any event, what I meant to say before my tongue tripped over itself, is that it takes having been incorrectly raised to foray outside the conventions of one's station. I have always been most grateful for my unusual cultivation. I am doubly grateful for yours; else, you would have screamed down the house last evening. Had you not been raised all wrong, as it were, neither of us would be here now." He stared at her a moment longer, then turned his attention to his plate.

"Where would we be?" she asked softly.

He threw her a glance that said a thousand words, but what he meant by them was still unclear.

Something unfurled within her, a white and gentle excitement as if her insides understood his unspoken communication. Perhaps they were building a friendship? Or was it more? How would she know, never having been in love, never before having had a close friend? The Sumerian Gilgamesh, and the gods of Egyptian myth before that, had always been her only true companions.

"There wasn't any soured cream and not even a hint of Devonshire cream," Peter said into the void before forking eggs into his mouth. He chewed, then swallowed. "Not terrible, but Reggie's are better."

Arabella tapped her heels as the two men turned their scrutiny toward their plates. For something to do, as she couldn't swallow food, she sipped tea, then practiced hiding her grimace as the tannin assaulted her teeth. She danced her heels some more. When it looked as if their immediate hunger had been assuaged, she could stand it no longer.

"Unusual upbringing notwithstanding, I'm still curious, my lord. How is it you are here, within my home, and why? Were our doors unlocked? Were you in need of a good meal?"

The two men exchanged another look. Peter raised his eyebrow.

"This was your idea, my friend," he said, sauntering off with his cup and another serving of eggs to the window seat. "Never mind me. Just us draperies sitting idly about the window, waiting for the play to begin."

Carefully, Gabriel placed his fork upon the edge of his plate before lowering the objects to the bottom of the cart. He searched for something he could not seem to find, which she guessed must have been a napkin. He ended up dabbing at his mouth and wiping his fingers with his handkerchief before replacing the folded square into his pocket. Then he stood and extended his hand toward her.

Without hesitation, she allowed him to pull her up and walk her over to the library table where the *Epic* lay. She waited as he fetched their two chairs and dragged them over so they might sit.

"I'm…we're here for a higher cause." Gabriel tapped his fingers upon the leather-bound collection of cuneiform etchings. "You did agree I might offer assistance in your translation of this work. Fortunately for me, and unfortunately for your security, your locks are insufficient to stop a five-year-old child from gaining entry. As to the 'why,' I thought it would be best to study secretly, given your mother's obvious disapproval of me. If we meet early in the day, I believe we might advance our scholarship without the interruptions your mother and my cousin will surely do their best to provide."

Secret meetings with the handsome baron, studying her favorite subject? The difficulty would be in restraining her body from flying about the room.

"They have already declared their intentions to attend our sessions in the afternoon," she acknowledged, but then her stomach wobbled, as it usually did when she thought about her mother.

"While it would be a lie of omission to hide our mornings from Lady Winslow, it seems the wiser course to forbear speaking of them." Gabriel shuffled in his chair. "Arabella, my impropriety where you are concerned has thus far been a horrendous breach of etiquette. A whole series of horrendous breaches. I am aware that even calling you by name is inexcusable. Nevertheless, I must beg you to overlook such egregious failings. I am…consumed, you see."

Consumed. Her toes curled again.

"I am a scholar," he continued softly as if that was all the explanation she would need.

And, strangely, it was. As her toes uncurled again, she found the knowledge already inside herself. It had formed as a hard kernel she had unknowingly avoided biting into, fashioned the moment she had recognized his need last evening, when his eyes had widened and glowed as first he had read the title upon the book he stroked now with his fingertips.

"You wish access to the *Epic*."

He blinked. "Access," he repeated, and paused. "Er… well, that does seem the best explanation."

He must be embarrassed. In many ways, he should be. He was flouting convention in a ruinous manner that should have seen them both excommunicated from

Society. His actions in dragging her with him into his passion were morally bankrupt, completely unacceptable, save for one thing: his motive was knowledge. To acquire the wisdom of the ancient world, almost any deed short of murder could be excused. The scholarly milieu was cutthroat. Would she have behaved any differently if access to the *Epic* were otherwise denied to *her*?

She might have behaved even more brazenly. After all, at least the baron was wearing shoes. She, in her eagerness to "study," had forgotten hers. Her cheeks heated once more.

"I am twenty-seven years old, my lord," she said slowly. "It would be difficult for my mother to forbid me anything, although her wishes are naturally an important consideration. However, I do see your point, and I agree. We shall study secretly in the mornings if that is what you wish."

He released his breath in an audible rush. "It is." His face cracked into a beaming smile. "Thank you, Arabella. You will not regret allowing me to assist you with the translations."

Of course, the handsome, intelligent, and fascinating man was not interested in her romantically. Whyever had she even imagined it possible?

Except, there were those almost-kisses last evening and this morning. That touch of the butterfly wings as his lips had brushed hers. The sensation made it difficult to remember what she had always known to be true: she was not the type to engage the enthusiasm of a man like him.

But why should it even matter if Gabriel was not interested in her romantically? He had suggested they could be friends, and she had never had a friend. They certainly had much in common. She admired him enormously. He seemed to hold her in a certain regard as well. Perhaps that could be enough?

Except, he had almost kissed her. Twice. Kissing indicated romantic feelings. It certainly indicated romantic feelings inside her, but then, she was a woman. Perhaps a man could kiss and still feel only friendship? How was it she had attained such a ripe old age without having the least notion of such things? How had she never considered their importance?

"There is also the matter of my cousin, which I would like to discuss."

"Lord Manning?"

Gabriel's expression hardened. "Excuse my presumption, but I believe he has expressed an interest in courting you, one which you might not be averse to receiving." His fingers drilled upon the book. "You are, as I mentioned last evening, a woman of unparalleled sense, clearly, but on this score, I feel I must warn you. Justin Thauley is no scholar. Assyriology holds little fascination for him. Indeed, although I cannot, at this time, give you any particulars, I feel I must advise you to be wary of his attentions."

Wary? She was desperate for his considerations, or supposed to be.

It was true the viscount's pretense of scholarly leanings had already proved thin. Last evening, during dinner and between dances, he had glued himself to her side, and not once had he mentioned Gilgamesh. Instead, he spent the span of hours pointing out the flaws in the attire of the other guests and gossiping about people she had never met. Still, he had been kind enough and certainly earnest in his wooing. It hadn't been his fault she had already been turned by a dark-haired stranger with a starched personality and a comedic, somehow farcical, turn to his humor that matched her own.

"Yes, well, the viscount proved exceptionally honorable last evening," Arabella murmured, her voice tight as she was forced to defend the man in his absence.

From his seat on the window, Peter cleared his throat then muttered something incomprehensible. Arabella startled, having forgotten his presence. The two men, who noticed her jump, exchanged another impenetrable look.

Gabriel's fingers drummed more rapidly, until finally, he sat back in his seat with a long sigh. Running a hand through his hair, he shook his head.

"If I have offended, I apologize. Moreover, I do apologize again for hauling you about your room last night. My actions were, in retrospect, unforgivable."

"Were they?"

He shrugged. "Like most of my sex, upon occasion, I tend toward action first. Well, without thoughtless movements by men, the *Epic* would be abysmally thin. 'I, Gilgamesh, ruler of Uruk, etc., sat home and considered my intended pursuits, and only then realized I was about to make a complete hash of myself, while simultaneously endangering the lives of countless thousands of others, so I decided to go down to dinner instead. I passed a lovely evening before the fire, a very good book about ziggurat construction in my lap. The pudding was also pleasant.' "

Arabella startled herself by laughing, the sound earning a broad smile from the baron. When he was pleased, a little light flared in the area just surrounding the pupil, a spot of gold in an otherwise forest-green sea.

Strange. She had never noticed someone's irises before.

"I am sorry for tarnishing your reputation with my

cousin last evening, although I still must warn you to be wary," he murmured, though a smile still lifted his lips.

She nodded as her laughter died. She wasn't sorry at all.

She should be, her conscience quickly reminded her. Her life was already set. Marry the viscount, send her mother to France, and push out some babies before it was too late. There was no place in her circumstances or her thoughts for a handsome lord who obviously wasn't interested in wooing, at least, not as interested as he was in deciphering an ancient tongue. If he had wanted her at all, he would have said so last evening, when convention dictated he remedy his wrong.

She could respect his decision, but that didn't mean it wasn't an unpleasant realization.

"Excellent." He opened the book and flipped through the pages. "Now, let's see. This part has been translated, as you know, although there are a few symbols that are still unclear. Look, here." He pointed to the text.

For the first time Arabella could ever remember, her mind wandered as cuneiform failed to hold her interest. Gabriel's gravel tones pulled her into something like a trance, his words washing over her like sweet, warm honey.

She had never been less interested in Assyriology.

Chapter 9

"How wonderfully kind of you, my lord. I'll just run and place these in water before they wilt." Lady Winslow buried her nose within the bouquet of violets Lord Manning had just presented. "Arabella, please pour our guest a cup. I shall return momentarily."

"How lovely you have joined us, my lord," Arabella murmured, bowing her head.

She remained seated at the tea-table installed years ago in the tiny windowed room that had once functioned as an additional conservatory for her orchid-mad grandfather. When the viscount approached, she held out her hand, allowing him to place a kiss upon its back. Because she was at home, she wore no gloves.

The absence of a saliva trail gladdened her. That was progress of a kind.

At her request, the viscount withdrew the chair next to hers. As Lady de Veer had not yet sent her grooms to repossess the lent furniture, they had seats aplenty for the moment. The chairs surrounded the small, scarred table purloined from the kitchen once the last of the servants had been let go. Covered in blue linen, an accent to the periwinkle-painted walls, and white paneling, the table overflowed with plates, napkins, cups, and food.

A cleared spot in the center just large enough to hold a nosegay of flowers glaringly revealed Lady Winslow's hope the viscount might surprise them.

When his regard settled upon the empty spot, his expression lightened.

"There is an excellent vanilla cake from yesterday evening I've only just discovered. Do let me serve you a slice?"

"I'm certain it's delicious, but I am not one for sweets." His gaze raked her face. "I will avail myself of a cup of tea if you don't mind," he said, slipping into the seat.

Careful to use porcelain that wasn't badly chipped, she poured him a cup. "Sugar? Cream?"

"Black," he replied absently, still surveilling her intently.

She placed the tea before him. "I'm sorry, but do I have dirt upon my face?"

He raised his brows. "Pardon? Oh, no." He smiled. "Forgive me. It is just I am finding it difficult to reconcile how lovely you are with your…um…availability. I cannot imagine my good fortune." He leaned over so that he invaded her space.

Arabella moved back in her chair as subtly as she was able. Their class followed many rules that narrowed their lives in unforgivable ways. However, the positive aspect of those strictures was they saved unmarried women from the difficulty of rejecting blatant pursuit. Indirect and unwanted interest was normally easily avoided.

Not that the viscount's interest was unwanted, she quickly reminded herself, trying to ignore the unpleasant feeling in her middle as she surreptitiously scooted another half inch away.

"I'm pleased you are pleased."

"Your face. It really is a perfect oval, isn't it?"

She had no idea how to respond to that statement.

What was keeping her mother? It wasn't even proper to have left her alone in Manning's company, especially not this early in their relationship, if a relationship was even to form. Last evening, they had spoken for many hours, it was true, and she hadn't found his presence completely odious, but there had been movement then, and other people. Today, without any distractions and in the space of five minutes, she was already lost for conversation.

For something to do, she reached over to the cake and cut herself a hefty slice. While she transferred it to her plate, he cleared his throat. The gruff sound resonated. Darting a glance his way, she had no trouble interpreting his admonishing look. For a moment, she paused, the slice of cake held tenuously upon the server in mid-air before she reluctantly placed the sweet back upon its original platter. Then she folded her hands in her lap.

He beamed with approval.

The silence deepened. Had her mother gone to Saint-Martin-in-the-Fields to recover an adequate vase?

"Where do you make your home?" she finally inquired, to be polite.

"My father's townhouse is here in Belgravia," he murmured. "The Kildare seat is in Ireland, as I'm sure you've discovered. There's an adjoining parcel there of a hundred acres and a comfortable country house to which the viscountcy lays claim."

Arabella nodded, then looked at her hands. She tried to find an interesting thought that might hold the man in conversation. "And, er, do you have a separate residence in London?"

To that sterling bit of spoken eloquence, he frowned

and drew his back even straighter. "Would that matter? My father and I are quite close, and there is plenty of space at the Belgravia residence, I assure you."

She had insulted him somehow.

As she tried to find the words to apologize for what she did not know, he added, "There is property in Hertfordshire I rarely attend, and there used to be land and a hunting box in Sussex. I'm told that the Sussex property was quite fine, but it slipped through the entail and was sold off two generations ago. My forebears failed me, you see, just as your father did you."

"I'm sorry?"

"Every family has its black sheep, those we wish had been born sensible." He tilted his head in a condescending manner.

Arabella wanted to slap him. Although she regularly insulted her wastrel father, it rankled when someone else did. "That was slightly more information than I sought, my lord, but thank you for it all the same," she replied carefully.

"I trust nothing I've said repels you." The viscount's fingers reached out to where hers had retreated to lie next to her plate.

She started but then resisted the urge and allowed him to take her hand. She had to start making an effort, even when it seemed herculean to do so.

He nodded. "We need not prevaricate when it is just the two of us. I believe you mentioned that for those who study Assyriology, the normal rules of Society are to be easily transcended?" He looked at her pointedly over lowered brows.

He was goading her.

"I don't believe I used those exact words. Still, you

are not entirely wrong."

She looked toward the doorway, impressed her mother must have traveled all the way to America to find adequate crockery. The flowers must be very lovely, indeed.

"I'm certain you will happily grant me the same trespasses you granted my cousin."

She cleared her throat. "Yes, well, as to that, I believe we are all grateful you chose to handle that misunderstanding last evening with such...diplomacy." Lifting her long-tepid cup of tea, she took a large sip, not because she was thirsty but to forestall that unwelcome line of conversation.

He stroked his fingertips upon the blue linen as if testing the quality of the weave. That he was unimpressed was evidenced by the way his nose wrinkled.

Arabella took another hefty swig of tea and almost choked.

"I enjoyed dancing with you," he said suddenly. "You have a lovely figure. Quite lush."

Which was taking openness just a little too far. Proving she had not traveled across the sea after all, Lady Winslow returned at just that moment. It was almost as if she had lurked in the adjoining doorway, waiting to time her arrival to the viscount's leave of his senses.

Dramatically, her mother placed the vase of violets at the table center, then shot her daughter a triumphant look.

For the next fifteen minutes, Lady Winslow engaged their guest in convivial conversation about people and things in which Arabella had little interest.

All she needed to do was smile and nod her head when anyone glanced her way, which wasn't so terribly hard to do.

Still, it was a very long fifteen minutes.

****

The bell chimed. Arabella jumped from her chair and practically ran to the front door without waiting for her mother to offer. Given their lack of servants, they usually shared the butler duties. As few people visited, it wasn't a terrible burden most of the time. Just now, it offered escape, not to mention she knew who would be on the other side of the portal.

Something in her chest lifted as Gabriel stepped through the doorway, his large form crowding her in a way that rushed blood through her veins. Her stomach flipped as he leaned past her to drop his hat and walking stick upon the hall tree.

He smiled at her conspiratorially. "We're to be a foursome?" he inquired softly.

"I'm afraid so."

"Adequately chaperoned then," he murmured in his growly voice. His eyes sparkled. "How delightful."

Arabella nodded, then led Gabriel to the small conservatory. No sooner did they step through the door than both her mother and the viscount rose and whisked everyone to the library. Arabella couldn't help but notice Gabriel had not been offered tea. The lapse was telling. Even a murderer could count upon an offer of a good cup. It was also quite puzzling.

But then she put the thought from her as seats were sorted and the *Epic* opened.

A half hour later, Arabella recognized Gabriel's prescience in arranging for their morning studies alone. Lord Manning and Lady Winslow had done little but impede progress. Her mother, ostensibly embroidering a pillowcase for charity, had shot thunderous looks at the baron while encouraging the viscount's every smallest thought with a lovely, tinkling laugh.

They might have ignored her, if not for the viscount himself. He must have been sporting crab pants, for he squirmed as if a thousand crustaceans pinched him in inappropriate places. Having seated himself at the long library table, the better to torment the true scholars, he had done little with the marks Gabriel had written out for him—three carefully penned lines of cuneiform in need of translation—other than crumple the paper and blatantly ignore it. Instead, he had loudly engaged Lady Winslow in conversation concerning the Esterhazys' new salon.

It had been a relief when, finally, alleging an aching back due to an inauspicious saddle just purchased for his horse, the viscount had moved to the couch to converse with Arabella's mother. His three lines of cuneiform had fluttered to the floor and lain there like an unwanted orphan. Now, with their time nearly spent, Arabella was uncertain whether she should be provoked or amused by the viscount's inattention. The baron, however, seemed clear on which way he leaned, if his thunderous eyebrows could be interpreted correctly.

"Empty-headed, prattling fool," he muttered.

"I beg your pardon?" Lady Winslow demanded from her seat quite a few feet away. As always, her hearing proved impeccable at the worst possible moments.

"Gilgamesh," Arabella said quickly. "He's doing something silly again, Mother."

"Like going on a quest for immortality without packing a nightshirt." There was a twinkle in Gabriel's eyes that made Arabella smile complicity. She dropped her gaze back to the paper on which she wrote.

The two of them worked in companionable silence as

the viscount and Lady Winslow discovered the even more interesting topic of the queen's recent squabble with her husband over how many dogs they should acquire. However, when the viscount asked whether Arabella preferred horses to dogs, she finally snapped.

"I like them both better than most people," she retorted, only to be cut by guilt as her mother gasped at the impolite response. "Present company excluded, of course."

"Easy," Gabriel whispered as they turned back to their pages.

He slid his hand along the table until his pinky surreptitiously touched her own. She had done the same for him last evening when chaos had claimed her bedroom.

So, this is what friendship was. She had never been so readily understood before.

It was exhilarating.

Chapter 10

As he lay beside Annette de Veer, Robert Thauley, Earl of Kildare, couldn't decide if he was bored or intrigued. Annie had always had that effect upon him, even when they had been affianced in a very casual and completely deniable way.

On the one hand, while he was certainly delighted to accept her well-practiced, lascivious attentions, on the other, he was loathe to return her favors. Deep diving in skunked waters was unpleasant, no matter the potential reward for his efforts. Not only that, age had diminished the firmness of her bosom and the once-taut expanse of her stomach. Voluptuousness was admirable, but only when it was on the right side of lumpy.

He grabbed at a roll of fat around her midriff and squeezed it in a manner he intended to pass off as playful. If she weren't careful, she would exceed his own magnificent girth. Rollyness on a man was one thing. It spoke of a certain libertine lifestyle. Fat on a woman was another thing entirely.

"Ooh!" she squealed.

Pain flashed in her eyes, exciting him.

"There's so very much of you to hold tight. Come, you've brought me to fine form again, you daring wench. Just see how the years have failed to cool my ardor."

He maneuvered Annette to a position over him where he wouldn't have to exert himself, then climaxed yet again while he envisioned the new full-lipped kitchen maid riding him to perdition. By his count, that made four successful couplings in the space of an hour, all of them fueled by the power of his imagination and the skill Annette had amassed over the years. Only now he found himself quite depleted and in need of a good breakfast.

However, when he turned his head to mention eggs and kippers, he couldn't help but wince. She lay sprawled in the manner of a flophouse whore, legs angled and wide. Less than gently, he pushed at her limb in the vain hope she would close the pair of them.

"It was just like old times, wasn't it?" Annette cooed, running a finger down his naked chest and completely ignoring his efforts to force her into a more attractive pose. "You were my first love, Robbie. You taught me all about passion, and I've never quite recovered."

"Minx," he growled and pushed at her leg again.

This time, success was realized. However, a moment later, her fingers wrapped around his exhausted worm.

"My little Robbie," she warbled.

He winced again and pushed her fingers away. They found their way back immediately.

"Shh. I often felt intimidated, desperate, and confused when you were younger. Now I've brought the devil to heel, haven't I?" Her fingers stilled. "Though, I confess I'm still uncertain how you have come to be with me of late, especially seeing as how we've passed each other at social events for years with barely a nod between us. You did always seem keen to keep your distance."

An anxious expression alighted in her eyes as her lips pouted. He strove to hide his impatience.

"Annie, we've been over this road many times now. You know our parting was difficult for me," he lied. "I had to heed my parents' wishes and marry elsewhere, as did you. It took some years to realize I might act upon my wishes." He paused and reached out to stroke the pudgy part of her thigh. "That is why it is so important my Justin attains his one true love in marriage. I want for him what I was denied. What *we* were denied, Annie."

As he had known she would, Annette wrapped herself under his arm and trilled, "Oh, Robbie! You know I will do anything to ensure your happiness. Arabella has always been a strange girl, but if that is who your son wants, then that is who he will have."

"If only I could be certain," he murmured, looking woefully up to the ceiling of the rented room of the Pig and Thistle Inn. He slid his glance sideways to see if he was over-acting, but no, she seemed all melted and soft-eyed.

"Put this worry from you, darling. I will make certain Arabella stays the course."

"If only I could be absolutely sure. It has been a week, and Justin worries about the lady's tepid response to his address. What is a loving father to feel but concern for his child's every happiness?"

As she sat up, her pendulous breasts fell over the rolls of her stomach in a bit of welcome concealment. "You can rest easy, Robbie. I have a perfect plan. Glenda has allowed Arabella too much head over the years. Without a father's guidance, she has become woefully independent. She has forgotten she is a woman, with a woman's needs. What is required is a gentle push, just enough to make her realize how wonderful it can be to have strong, male arms wrapped around her."

"Compromise her?" Robert pretended to be shocked.

She held up two fingers, a small space apart. "Just the

tiniest bit. A kiss, no more. I warrant she will fall nicely for your son once she has felt the force of his lips pressed to hers."

"How Machiavellian of you," he purred.

"Needs must. Besides, Glenda is growing more prone to attacks of late. Without putting too fine a point upon it, Arabella needs to marry Justin quickly. It would be best for everyone were she to be desirous of the only positive outcome available to her."

When Annette leaned over and used her clever tongue against his nipple, Robert forced himself not to push her away. He closed his eyes and sighed.

The things he did to keep his title were really quite debasing.

****

A few hours and two meals later, the earl found himself on horseback, skulking in the bushes that bordered his Hertfordshire country home, the only property left to the Thauleys if Gabriel Darkwood succeeded in winning the Kildare title.

Ripemoor had been handed down through his mother. It might even have proved sufficient had it held some sort of title. As it stood, the twenty-room cottage and its meager fifty acres had not been worth the trouble of upkeep. The estate was blighted and completely unsuitable for their future needs, should they lose the suit. Besides, farming was for other people.

He turned up his nose at the whiff of manure stinging his nostrils. Everything in this place smelled of waste.

Next to him, Justin's horse skidded and tossed its head. Though likely more accustomed to the estate's odiferous charms, the beast was as bored as they were.

As his horse skidded in response, the saddle chafed

parts of him that had already seen a good excoriation that morning. Robert's mood grew fouler and fouler. He had better things to do than stalk a poacher, but Justin had been insistent they capture whoever had been using the back entrance of the cottage to clean and gut his kills. His son wasn't wrong. Order must be kept, especially as they might have need of this dilapidated parcel of land should matters proceed in an unfortunate direction.

"I agree a man might easily store a lass here without anyone being the wiser," he said quietly so as not to spook their game. "However, Darkie knows of this property."

"Which is to our advantage as the corridors were positively made to murder intruders, especially unruly cousins. If Darkie didn't know of the place, how could I hope he would appear for his summary execution?"

Robert snickered. He quite liked the idea of a kebabbed nephew.

"Should Lady Arabella continue to treat me so shabbily, I see no recourse but kidnapping. I have searched everywhere below stairs for that blasted ring these past days without any success." He paused and then sighed. "I'm not even certain she'll agree to marriage."

Silence descended as the men waited, their horses more jittery with each passing moment. The equines pulled at the reins, fighting to reach the sweet grass below.

"Enough, you stupid nag!" Robert whispered and pulled with such force his horse backed up three steps.

When he managed to get the animal under control, he said, "Annie faults the books the gel reads. You'll have to keep her away from such unhealthy pursuits."

"I plan to. Shh!" Justin held a finger up to his lips.

Robert was about to snap a retort when he heard what his son's better ears must have picked up. From somewhere in the forest, getting closer, the base and classless sound of whistling reached out to him.

"Five minutes, I think," Justin mouthed.

They waited. Sooner than anticipated, movement sounded to their left, where the darkest part of the forest stretched. Justin hunkered down lower over his steed and edged his way around the brush toward the far side of the small patch of clearing.

The poacher was just behind the large oak now, not fifteen feet away. Abruptly, the man's whistles cut off before he began to whine and plead.

Smiling, Robert directed his recalcitrant nag around the trees, only to find the poacher's temple attached to the business end of Justin's shotgun. Two dead pheasants ringed the man's feet.

"Look what I've caught, Father," Justin snarled, his Champagne eyes sparkling with malice even in the dim light.

His horse shook its matching auburn head as if mirroring his rider's mood and kicked at the birds, spraying last autumn's leaves.

"Well done, my boy," Robert responded gleefully, poking the edge of his rifle toward the poacher's face. "The law hangs thieves," he added conversationally.

The man swayed and spasmodically reached for his temples, his hands arrested by the realization they could do nothing to stop a bullet. The rheumy, colorless gaze lifted beseechingly, but quickly dropped. "My lord," he whispered in recognition. His bladder loosened.

The scent of the long flush of acrid liquid grated in Robert's nose, and he laughed. "That, my son, is the smell of victory."

Justin smiled back, and Robert beamed. It was nice to share these father and son bonding moments. So few of their class did.

Suddenly, Justin's hand swung down and connected with the man's nose. The shifting of cartilage cracked through the silent clearing. Toppling to the ground, the poacher recovered with surprising dexterity and scrabbled into the underbrush. From there, he gained his feet and sprang back into the forest.

"The hunt is on," Robert whispered, excitement bubbling through his blood.

For the next half hour, they chased the man throughout the wood, certain they were on him at any moment, only to find he knew the woods better than they. Reluctantly, they admitted defeat.

"I wanted blood, Father," Justin growled, scowling at the trees around him. "I *want* blood."

Robert wiped at his sweating brow with a silk handkerchief. "Then blood you shall have. Soon. Let's off to the village church for a license. If Lady Arabella doesn't respond as she should to the little surprise you will spring at tea tomorrow, then take her by force at the first opportune moment. There is no blood finer for slaking a man's thirst than a virgin's smear upon his sheets."

Justin looked almost weepy. "You really are the best father in the world."

Robert glowed.

It was so nice to be appreciated by one's son.

Chapter 11

Arabella sighed and pushed her glasses further up her nose. Why had she ever considered herself a scholar? Compared to Gabriel, she was a bumbling novice, unfit even to lay a finger upon the *Epic*, let alone attempt to translate it.

Before the baron had appeared in her life, she had worked tirelessly comparing symbols to texts and thought her progress rather remarkable. The most remarkable part of their work together was that he didn't scream with boredom and snap her nose in the book.

She peeped at him sideways, but no, he still hadn't stalked out the door, vowing never to waste another moment with such a hopeless cause. His determination in the face of her obtuseness had to be admired.

"Perhaps we'll put this symbol aside for later," he murmured as he wrote out another line of cuneiform and handed it to her. He shot her a patient smile. "Don't despair. We will arrive, eventually, I am certain of it."

"I think I am done with Gilgamesh forever," she exclaimed.

Lady Winslow looked up abruptly from her perch on the sofa, where she was pretending to read. She met Arabella's gaze with a hopeful look of her own, and then harrumphed softly and returned to her book. Even from the room's distance, Arabella saw her mother held it upside down.

For once, the viscount was absent for their afternoon study session. Arabella had expected to see him for tea, which they had taken in Lady de Veer's front parlor, but he had sent a note explaining he would be tied up all afternoon at his country estate. With his absence, she and Gabriel might have made some real headway with their translations, but instead, Arabella found her mind strangely unfocused.

"I wonder if the tablet was too damaged here to make sense of this symbol?" she said, proving her earlier exclamation a lie as she forced her attention to the paper.

Gabriel shrugged, his concentration square again upon the page in front of him. He seemed relaxed, despite Lady Winslow's presence and her less-than-completely-veiled dislike of him. There was some reason for his ease. The library was cozy, after all, despite the rickety chairs. The *Epic* was spread between them. A fire burned in the hearth, one Gabriel himself regularly laid each day after tea. He never complained about the servant's work he performed. The ash was starting to overtake the kindling, however, as there was no one to clean the grate between lightings. The hired girl came only twice a week, but with two study sessions a day in ever-damp London, they needed to see more of her.

Of course, Sally demanded a wage for her efforts. They would likely be seeing her even less unless Arabella could marry Justin quickly.

Arabella glanced toward her mother again. Lady Winslow's spine was rigid. Her gaze flicked back and forth between the upside-down book of poetry and the baron, where it would stall. Her lips frowned, and her brows furrowed as if she worried Gabriel might suddenly draw a knife from his pockets and attack them both. How was it that the viscount's presence was deemed beneficial when the baron's was about as fulsome as poison? No matter how many times she asked Lady Winslow that very question, she received no truthful answer.

"Are you memorizing a particular passage, Mother?" Arabella demanded as Lady Winslow's lips drew back into what could only be characterized as a snarl.

Lady Winslow jolted. Her rabid expression disappeared. "Er…yes, I am."

"Really? Well, we would love to hear it, wouldn't we, Lord Brynley?"

Arabella wasn't certain why she goaded her mother. It wasn't well done, especially considering the woman looked so tired and disheartened. Uncomfortable guilt rose within her. She truly was an ungrateful daughter.

A worried daughter too, she suddenly remembered. Passing the time with Gabriel had a way of distracting her from her obligations.

He looked up from his notes, his expression vague. "Indeed," he finally mumbled, although Arabella suspected he had little idea to what he responded.

"Oh!" Lady Winslow dropped the book and bent to pick it up again. "Never mind. I don't quite have it just yet."

Arabella nodded and turned her attention back to Gabriel, who was reading the *Epic* from an angle she never could have managed.

"We know this symbol represents the god, Enki, and this one, Ziusudra." He pointed, frowning in concentration. "With all these animals mentioned, and rain, I believe it might be a warning of the coming flood, much like the biblical story of Noah. And these…might these be the instructions for the ship's building? If so, we could undertake the construction of a scale model and try to sail the result up the Thames." His lips turned upward, and his green eyes sparkled, catching her again with his infallible good humor.

As she leaned in toward him, he subtly moved back in his chair, the sparkle vanishing.

It was the third time he had inched away from her. She suspected he simply didn't wish to hint at any impropriety, especially in front of Lady Winslow. He was correct, of course, for both their sakes. He had neatly escaped once, thanks to the viscount's extraordinary reaction to finding them together on her bed. There was no compelling reason for him to test his luck again, especially if he no longer found her to be kissable.

A week of study sessions, during which he had not made a single attempt, suggested he did not.

The thought clawed like nails against the inside of her stomach, although she shouldn't have been thinking of him at all.

"We should consider how we might build a similar large ship today. Find comparable words for tools and materials in the text, even in the broken fields." He pointed to an open glossary of terms they were compiling. "For instance, if 'isu' is wood, and we think to look for it, and we have an 'i'…"

Gabriel shrugged. When he glanced up again, their gazes locked.

Arabella swallowed. "That's quite perceptive, actually."

"I do manage to be less shallow than a plate from time to time." He laughed. It transformed him. The dark part of his eyes lit with fire.

He was devastating. Arabella melted across the table,

her fingers splayed flat, snaking toward his like stems seeking water.

He cleared his throat abruptly. His expression hardened, and he looked away.

Embarrassed, she retracted her fingers and moved the *Epic* a hairsbreadth, as if that had been her intention all along.

"Let's look at that last section again, the one that began with 'everything.' And here's the symbol for 'strength.' " He translated the cuneiform in his growly tiger voice. The timbre of it sent goosebumps down her arms.

"Yes. It is." She swallowed.

"Is he bragging that his goods are the strongest? I confess I'm finding this passage most difficult. What about here?" He frowned again and pointed.

She squinted through her lenses. "Silver?"

Gabriel did not look up. "Yes. Silver, whatever that might mean in context." His head swiveled toward the window as if he thought the strange land and the extravagant ship might have popped up in her garden. Then, carefully, he closed the *Epic*. "I think that's enough for this afternoon. We've done exceedingly well, for once."

He stretched his shoulders, a gesture that brought the coat of his fine burgundy jacket almost in line with his ears. The tight collar of his shirt slipped upon his elegant neck. A mad urge to press her lips to the ticking pulse just above his jaw possessed her. Of themselves, her hands knotted in her lap, ink stains from her fingers transferring to the rose of her gown. She reached up and pushed her spectacles further up her nose.

His gaze tracked her movement, like a hound on a

fox, before slipping just off to the side again. Her goosebumps grew goosebumps.

"Do you ever do anything else but study cuneiform?" she asked suddenly before she could consider her words. "I mean, in your spare time?"

The warm, slow, upward turn of his lips lit a ready ember in her belly. The glow spread through her veins. Once more, his eyes sparkled with refracted light that drew her toward him. "You mean, am I just this obsessed with cuneiform symbols, or am I sometimes aroused by other subjects? Tell me, Lady Arabella, do you think that possible?"

If there was a suggestion in his low-voiced growl, and she hoped there was, it skipped along her pulse. A heated flush rose from her throat to her cheeks, so she turned away, pretending a great interest in the needlepoint-upholstered arm of her chair to which time had not been kind. Threads were splayed every which way, and one could barely tell the subject had once been pastoral. Reaching out to trace the lines of a tree, she noted the ink upon her fingers and quickly pulled them back.

"I think you are capable of a great many things, my lord," she finally whispered back.

She hazarded a peek from beneath her lashes to see what he thought of her statement but then was immediately sorry when her stomach turned over yet again with the strange molten desire he unwittingly inspired.

"What I wondered," she said, despite the array of butterflies racing up to play in her windpipe, "is if you only study or if you have other business interests? Or perhaps you ride, or like to sail boats, or-or hang about the court wearing pink velvet jackets?"

His burst of laughter probably furthered the heat in her cheeks, but she was so busy being arrested by the play of emotions across the angular planes of his cheeks, she barely cared. Laughter gave him his own roses, and softened his hard edges until he looked far younger than what she now knew, through careful pestering, was his thirty-six years.

"Oh, wouldn't Reggie and Peter just love to see me gander about in pink velvet?" he asked. Chuckling, he stood and circled the table to lean against the window sash.

Lady Winslow closed the book in her lap, her pretense over as she tracked the man like he was a wild creature. Gabriel, no fool, inclined his head toward her, acknowledging her regard, before turning to contemplate the garden.

"I have a reputation as being a man of business, and I confess it is business that occupies me most of my hours." He enunciated each word, but Arabella wasn't certain whether for her benefit or Lady Winslow's. "I have had little time to play of late. However, though gossip might label me as no more than codfish aristocracy because of my commercial success, the Brynley title is quite old. It passed to my father through a quirk in the entailment. I have been fortunate to do well by it, enough so, at any rate, my heirs need never work. Although," he added, revolving to face her again, "I do hope these mythical beings enjoy laboring at interesting pursuits. I've no wish to father a bunch of simpletons concerned only with dress and gossip."

Arabella's mouth dropped open. It was clear talk, in an age when no one spoke clearly.

"I shouldn't trouble myself with that, my lord," she managed to reply after a moment's hesitation. "I cannot imagine you creating a simpleton."

It was his turn to flush, even as he pointedly stared at her across the room.

Part of his meaning was obvious, at least to her. He was warning her Justin's children might very well be the scourge he was describing since his cousin's interests ran to little more than said gossip and clothing.

But why did he elaborate on his circumstances? Could she hope Gabriel might be excited by more than the *Epic*, even if he didn't seem to want to kiss her? When Lord Manning had informed her of his present and future estates, she had understood immediately. He had already made known his intentions. With Gabriel, however, there was no reason to discuss, even vaguely, his worth unless—

Lady Winslow suddenly stood, interrupting Arabella's train of thoughts. "My lord, it grows late, and we wouldn't wish to hold you, lest the rains return."

"I dare say I won't melt, Lady Winslow, but you are correct," he agreed, pivoting toward the elder woman and nodding his head. "It is time for me to take my leave. I thank you for your gracious hospitality. Studying the *Epic* this closely, in such comfortable quarters, is indeed a scholar's dream."

Arabella looked around the room, the room that might not be truly comfortable on most days but which had been made so simply by his presence.

When she spent time with Lord Manning, it was as if she perched upon a cushion of pins, desperate to avoid being stuck by some barb. When she was with Gabriel, she lost sight of the perception of others and simply did as she liked. That was comfort, to be herself, even when with so desirable a man.

It was not lost upon her how different she felt about the two cousins. She simply did not know how to resolve the difference, given the man she wished to know better worked to evade her, and the one she didn't wish to know at all was anxious to further their intimacy.

It really was a conundrum.

Chapter 12

If only he knew Arabella better. Gabriel paced the length of his stable the next morning, miserable with indecision. How to proceed? Back and forth, he stalked the aisle, but the motion didn't help him determine what to do next. Up and turn, down and revolve, back up again. He chased the empty corridor between the rows of stalls, his once-pristine black boots covered with dust, hay, and horse-fouling.

As he evaded a bench, his foot tapped the edge of a mucking rake. The stick flew into his cheek, and he pushed it away. When it bounced back, he picked it up and threw it to the ground with more force than was necessary. He closed his eyes and shook his head.

It was no good. He could no longer study with Arabella.

He couldn't bear not to.

Pacing again, he cursed his own impatience. No matter how calming the horses normally were, today their warm, musky scent and softly voiced ruffles of air did nothing to ease the headache behind his eyes. He flopped down on the bench and threw the saddle over his lap. After grabbing a cloth, he bent to forcefully polish the leather into a pristine shine.

This morning's secret study session had been torture. The one hour in Arabella's presence had dragged on for days while simultaneously winging by on feathered feet.

Such was the usual course of their afternoon meetings when he was forced to navigate the morass created by his cousin's essential uselessness and Lady Winslow's avid dislike.

When he and Arabella were alone, a kind of rhythm existed, a sort of peace that made the minutes fall away gently. This morning had been different. Sharp desire to pull her close and kiss to distraction those gorgeous, tempting, rosebud lips had needled him, perhaps because she had looked so particularly bedraggled, sleepy, and warm. Her hair had floated about her head like a mass of dandelion fluff. Two deep crevices beneath her eyes had spoken of lost sleep. He couldn't help but hope thoughts of him were keeping her awake.

He hoped they were not.

Though he had ignored his most ignoble impulses and behaved like a gentleman ought, it was becoming more and more difficult to stay the course. Reminders Justin was up to his usual nefarious deeds and Arabella might be involved up to her golden eyebrows were no longer affecting his mind as they should.

Instead, every single time the lady translated a cuneiform symbol and lit up like a flame on a cold, remote, starry night, his resistance faded a little more. Her smile of delight, the way it reflected in her crushed-pansy eyes, pulled him to her like iron to a lodestone so he simply forgot her potential malfeasance.

It was a few moments before he realized a shadow stretched from the doorway, over the saddle, and down past his feet. Reggie appraised him from the open doorway

"Boyo, I've been lookin' all o'er fer ye'," Reggie said.

A breeze blew in past the little man, bringing with it the smells of hay, cut grass, and livestock. Reggie followed the scents on his bowed legs, his thick shock of gray hair standing on end, as usual, and his merry green eyes twinkling even in the dull stable light.

"I'm just polishing Shu's saddle," Gabriel replied.

"Aye. And thinkin'."

Gabriel nodded. "And thinking."

"About yer cousin, the weasel?"

He paused as the old man drew up a stool and sank heavily onto it, keeping his right leg extended. Shu immediately leaned over the stall window to ruffle the old man's hair, which she could just about reach. Reggie waved the horse off, though his face cracked into a weather-beaten smile.

"Get off me, ya ole' nag, else I make glue from yer hide," Reggie said when the horse again pulled at a few of the tufts upon his skull.

Shu whickered, but it seemed as if the horse smiled. That was the thing about horses, though. One could generally surmise what they were thinking but never be absolutely sure. They were like women that way.

"I was dwelling on matters concerning Lady Arabella." Gabriel sighed. "I'm afraid I'm no closer to discovering Justin's interest in her, nor whether she is involved in whatever scheme he might be hatching."

"Must be hatchin', or he ain't yer cousin." Then, discarding the brogue he used only when he was in the mood, Reggie added, "Peter told me Lady Arabella is a fine-looking lass. Smart, too, and interested in the same ancient writing you are. An earl's daughter, no less." He shrugged. "You could do worse."

Gabriel bent to polishing again. "She's all that,

Reggie, but she may be more."

The old man tipped his stool and leaned his upper back against the wall between the stalls, removing himself from the horse's reach. Shu whickered again but withdrew her head back into her cubby.

"Peter says he hasn't found a single bit of evidence to prove the lady's in league with that devil. You find the lass interesting. Perhaps Justin does as well."

It was true. Peter had investigated every angle he could, and Gabriel had done a little investigation as well. All his many business contacts had been mined. The multitude of their street sources had been shaken, but all they could find was that Lady Arabella was exactly what she seemed: a penniless bluestocking, an ardent Assyriologist, an innocent kept sheltered and out of Society by her widowed mother, and a woman in urgent need of funds to take that mother to a place possessed of breathable air. London, he had learned, was rather infamous for its smog and pollution. All of them would be better off afar.

"Even if Arabella is as perfect as she seems, and I can't know that yet, can I? But even if, I'm not in the market for a wife." Gabriel pulled the words from his heart. "There is the court case to determine first, and perhaps I am selfish, but I did wish to travel more before settling down to the procreative duties of the title. How long have I dreamt of seeing Sumer?" The cloth stilled upon the saddle.

Reggie leaned forward and cupped Gabriel's knee with his hand. "Forever, and that's the truth."

"Of course, Arabella has had the benefit of an unconventional family situation as well. It is not impossible she means what she says and that she, too, would like to visit Sumer."

"An unconventional family brings out a person's greatest resourcefulness."

"On the other hand, I have been happy, genuinely happy, without any attachments save for you and Peter. I've had my books, my studies, my business interests. Isn't that enough?" Gabriel demanded.

Reggie smiled. "Ah, lad. That's the thing about falling in love."

"I didn't say I was in love."

"One day, you're going on your way, perfectly fine, and the next day, you meet her, and your life is never the same again. Happiness is never the same again." He patted Gabriel's shoulder, put the stool back on three legs, and fought his way to a standing position, keeping his bad leg out in front of him. "Just let me know when the wedding is so I can iron out the creases in my good suit," Reggie mumbled, limping to the door. He whistled softly under his breath.

It was a happy tune.

Suddenly, with nothing actually decided, Gabriel felt a whole lot better.

Chapter 13

That afternoon, Arabella nodded sleepily over her cup of black tea, the flow of conversation around her like the calming waves of an ocean lapping against a beach. Interspersing the somnolent noise were the myriad sharp lectures about all manner of wrongs it seemed she had committed. According to her mother and Lady de Veer, chief among those breaches was her inability to net Lord Manning before he lost interest and swam away.

If ever there was a fish patiently waiting for capture, it was the viscount. Perhaps that was the problem. He had the personality of one of Mr. Darwin's barnacles and didn't seem to see a need to avoid the snare. All that was actually required of her was she not drop the mesh that held him.

The same was not true of the baron. Gabriel was an advanced species and one that refused to be hooked. He was a marvelous assistant but slippery for all that. His extensive knowledge of Assyriology fulfilled her mind when she could manage to concentrate in his presence. His compliments, the way he treated her as if her brain were a match to his own, energized her.

It was heady, being treated as an equal partner.

Unfortunately, despite their compatibility, his apparent disinterest in her romantically was quite remarkable in its steadiness. He had not made a single attempt to kiss her since that first morning, not even this morning when she had used every opportunity to stumble into him or accidentally touch the strong bone of his wrist where it peeked from his starched cuff.

She took another sip of tepid tea and sighed.

"Do not yawn at the table, Arabella," her mother complained. "Men abhor sleepy women."

"It is true, dear," Lady de Veer confirmed but then reached out and patted Arabella's hand. "The viscount's tardiness today is enervating, what with him having begged off tea yesterday."

"Should we be concerned, do you think?" Lady Winslow worried her lip with her teeth.

The two women conversed with telling looks. Arabella was exhausted enough to speak plainly.

"Has no one considered Baron Brynley might possess an equal interest in courting me? Is there a reason I shouldn't try to net him instead of the viscount?"

The way the two women turned to ghosts was interesting enough to pull Arabella from her languor.

Swallowing hard, flushing, after having turned so pale, Lady Winslow demanded, "Has Brynley mentioned an interest?"

"No," Arabella replied truthfully but was surprised all the same by the ladies' mutual, voluble sighs of relief.

"That's fine then," Lady de Veer said. "We had hoped that Brynley would take himself off once he found you suitably chaperoned at your so-called 'lessons,' so we forbore telling tales. Yet, he did not quit."

"Vile, deceitful, villainous, ruinous..." Lady Winslow muttered.

Lady de Veer leaned over and poked Lady Winslow's wrist with her fork. Then, she speared Arabella with her stare. "The baron is unacceptable for many reasons, none of which should ever be relevant to you. Focus upon the lord at hand with the grander title and the willingness to accept a woman too far from marriageable age, Arabella. All your attention must be focused upon keeping Lord Manning happy if you are to keep your mother alive."

"Brynley will ruin you if you aren't careful," Lady Winslow warned.

Arabella burst into laughter. She couldn't help it. She had been trying to maneuver Gabriel into kissing her for the better part of the past week and had nothing to show for her efforts. If he was a cad, he must be the most inept one in history.

"Brynley may be interested in this Gillywood person, or he may simply be trying to derail his cousin's pursuit out of spite. It is not beyond the man," Lady de Veer continued. "I know Kildare is simply plagued by Brynley's evil cunning in matters concerning the title."

"What matters?"

"Again, it is none of our affair," Lady de Veer replied firmly. "I declare, you are reaching for defeat with both hands, my dear, with all this interest in such an unsuitable person. We must be thankful indeed the viscount is wise enough to attend your dreary study sessions to keep his cousin in check."

"Marking his territory," Lady Winslow said. "It is very reassuring." She exchanged another look with her friend, then exhaled. "It is almost time for Brynley's arrival. I vow, it is difficult to be pleasant, despite his fortune, knowing what he truly is."

"Is there a fortune?" Arabella asked, curious about this substantiation of Gabriel's own words.

After a pause, Lady de Veer conceded. "Terrible

though he is, his business acumen is almost to be admired."

The ringing of the bell interrupted their conversation.

"Arabella, do run and get the door; there's a darling," her mother ordered, relief written upon her face. "This early, it must be Manning."

Her mother's fish-eyed stare was enough to move Arabella from her seat.

When she opened the door, the viscount whipped a bouquet of violets from behind his back like some deranged magician. Reluctantly, she reached forward to take the flowers. Twice before she had suggested she quite preferred roses, but he had only shuddered as if repulsed by the proletarian notion.

He was, as she remarked to herself daily, a very odd man.

"Violets to match your eyes," he said, smile too wide as he placed his hat upon the hall mantel. "There is simply no other flower that should ever be held in your hand. I could teach you much about the symmetry of color."

He looked expectant, so she smiled back. This afternoon, his coat and pants were colored a burnished bronze with matching accents of golden yellow at the cravat, the colors doing exquisite things for his pallid complexion and unique Champagne-colored eyes. At least his choices were always interesting. Perhaps they were also fashionable. She wouldn't know. She didn't care.

"Thank you, my lord," she replied. "I look forward to hearing once again your theories. My mother and Lady de Veer are in the parlor. You know the way by now, yes? I'll just be a moment, placing these lovely blooms in water."

"Ah, but I would prefer to keep your company."

He grabbed her free hand and placed it around his arm. His lips were wet as if he had just licked them, and he had the grip of a crab upon a piece of chicken bait. She tried to pull loose, but he ignored her gentle tugs.

"Violets are the most delicate of blooms. They are innocent of unseemly robustness," the viscount continued, refusing to let go. Indeed, he looked positively feverish. There was a sheen to his skin, and his eyes sparkled wildly. "But come, I will walk with you to the kitchen to tweak our little buds here into shape. I confess I have never even seen a kitchen. It will be something of an oddity to visit such a room, much like an expedition to an unknown land. You do lead me on a wild ride, Lady Arabella." He simpered suggestively as they proceeded down the long hallway toward the back of the house.

Though she sensed from his hungry expression she missed some double meaning, Arabella resolutely ignored it as she fought, once again, to want to keep his interest, especially as every instinct urged her to push him into the umbrella stand.

"You missed a rather startling discovery in yesterday's study, my lord," she said, just to fill the uncomfortable silence. "Your cousin considered we might back into a meaning by looking at…"

"Fascinating."

As they swung through the kitchen doorway, he grabbed the violets and threw them onto the counter.

"The point is, Arabella," he said, suddenly serious as he leaned forward and backed her against the chopping block, "I never manage time with you alone."

Then, he leaned over and sniffed her, a long inhalation that was very unsettling.

"I think, my lord, it would hardly be proper to do so." Arabella attempted to put as much space between their bodies as possible. She was already leaning so far back her spine was stretched to its limit. "Indeed, I have not given you leave to use my name. We are not married or even engaged, after all."

Instantly, she regretted her comment. His gaze traveled down the front of her dress, stripping her as if the layers of clothing she wore were invisible. She shivered. It felt as if worms crawled over her entire body.

"No, we are not married. Nor are we likely to be at this rate. Perhaps you are wondering why I have not offered for your hand as yet, given my stated and obvious interest?" he murmured. "It is not that I am conflicted, you understand, but I am a man. I need something more of you than babble about ancient civilizations. I need a sign you are also well-predisposed toward me."

"Well-predisposed toward you? Of course. I must be." She was torn between pushing him from her in disgust and the need to keep him close. "I-I wonder if you might step back, as you are quite crowding me?"

If only she weren't so tired, she might better be able to deal with this sudden bout of inappropriateness. With the way things stood, she worried she posed upon a single toe at the far edge of a precipice.

His leg pressed between her knees.

"My lord!"

"I find I no longer wish to be bound by etiquette, Arabella. And what of it? I have already left off proper, as you will recall."

"You-you have?" She gasped, trying to close her knees against him.

"I was the one who discovered you in your room,

upon your bed, with my cousin. I very inappropriately failed to challenge him to a duel. Or ruin you," he added pointedly. "I might have and then had you for a mistress, you know. Well, perhaps you don't. Perhaps that is why you do not look at me with the full accord you should feel?"

"I assure you, my lord, you acted quite properly in that situation." She tried to slide to the side. There was no room. "I am not insensible to that fact. Circumstances were not at all what they seemed, as we all agreed." She tried to squirm in the other direction without success.

"That the situation did not become what it seemed was only because of our timely interruption. Gads, enough talk. I cannot wait to have you in my bed," he growled.

Before she could think what to respond, he pressed his lips to hers.

Her mouth opened to vehemently protest the two saliva-slackened slugs thrust against hers. It was a mistake. He filled her mouth with his tongue, a large intrusion that choked her and made her eyes water.

Had this been what she had been yearning for with Gabriel? Arabella used all her force to try to push the viscount as far from her as possible.

She must have been out of her mind.

Her struggles to slip away were futile. He held her so far over the butcher block with her arms trapped between his that she was hardly able to wiggle. He reached down one hand between them. She could feel a bulge in the front of his pants. Then he quickly grasped her arm and pinned it to her side again before she could think to use it.

Just as suddenly as he had caught her, he broke away, gasping hard as if he had just run all the way from his family's estates in Ireland to her door. Sweat beaded at his temples, his auburn hair damp at the roots.

"Just a taste of what awaits you, my sweet." A satisfied smile stretched his face. "Something to persuade you to look at me with a little more interest. Hmm? My God, you are ripe for the bedding, aren't you?"

She didn't think she was meant to hear the last sentence as he muttered it to himself, but she had inherited her mother's keen hearing. She didn't want to think about what the first part of his words meant. A lifetime of these kisses? Arabella rubbed her mouth with the back of her hand. Even for her mother's very life, could she stand it?

She turned at a sudden noise by the door and gasped. Framed in the lintel, his jaw tight, his eyes burning, stood the baron. He was rigid, his expression feral. Briefly, his gaze met hers. Then his excoriating stare dismissed her and focused upon his cousin instead.

"Justin," he growled.

The viscount grabbed Arabella's hand and held it tight in his fist, though she tried to pull away. He smiled. "Darkie. How appropriate you should find us here."

He pressed Arabella against his body, the whipcord lean strength of him surprising her again. She wanted to jam her elbows into his stomach and order him to unhand her, but Gabriel's expression was so empty and cold she froze and found herself incapable of movement.

"Please," she begged, not even certain which man she addressed.

A tiny sob escaped her lips. She pressed her free hand against her mouth, but tears flooded her eyes. Roughly, she tried to wipe them away but then sobbed again. The floor beneath her feet swayed as she tried to find her balance in a world suddenly grown slippery.

"Unhand her, Justin, or I promise you shall soon miss your hands."

For a moment, as Justin's grip tightened around her, Arabella thought he might kiss her again. Yet, with a mocking smile and a gloating tilt of his chin, he released her, just as Lady Winslow appeared behind Gabriel in the doorway. Giving the baron an unladylike shove, her mother charged into the room.

Lady de Veer smirked around the baron's shoulder. She waved at Arabella.

"Why are you crying?" Lady Winslow demanded.

Arabella collapsed, sobbing into her mother's neck.

"What did you do?"

"What did *I* do?" Gabriel glared at his cousin.

The viscount cleared his throat. "Lady Winslow, I must confess. The fault is entirely my own. A stolen kiss. I am rightfully ashamed."

If that were true, one couldn't tell by looking at him. He looked set to dance a jig.

"Still, there is no need for distress." He turned to Arabella and lifted her chin from her mother's shoulder. She tried to shrug away, but he was persistent and, as she had already noted, stronger than he appeared. "These tears of shame must cease, my dear. I will marry you, Arabella. There is no need to fear for your reputation."

Lady de Veer cooed. Lady Winslow stuttered.

"Justin, don't do this," Gabriel growled, stepping into the room.

"I have quite irrevocably ruined your daughter, Lady Winslow," the viscount continued. His voice was triumphant as if announcing a win at a boxing match. "Though Arabella is overcome, a tribute to her innocence, all is not lost, but instead, gained."

Arabella pulled her chin from his fingers and stared directly at Gabriel, whose face had become expressionless. She tried to speak, but her throat had closed. She swallowed and tried again to find her voice.

"No." Gabriel took another step forward. "I forbid it."

"I claim responsibility," Justin crowed, "and my duty is my pleasure. Please, Lady Winslow, cease your frowning. Your daughter welcomed my advances completely. More than welcomed, though my humility forbids me from mentioning it."

"You just mentioned it, and you're wrong," Arabella cried.

He chuckled. "We shall be happy in all things, my lady, I assure you. So, come, let us plan our wedding. Dare I add, we should make haste, given the fires that burn between us?"

The smile on his face was victorious, but the glance he threw at Gabriel, who stood with hands clenched, was vicious.

"No, Mother, please," Arabella croaked as her options narrowed. She swallowed again.

Gabriel's hands clenched into fists. She wished she could lift one of them and punch Justin in the face with it. The baron, however, looked so stonelike, he would probably crack if she tried to move him.

A hysterical laugh bubbled out of her. "I never *welcomed* you," Arabella cried.

****

Gabriel wanted to believe her. He wanted to believe anything that might make him feel better because right now he felt as if someone had set him on fire, stabbed him with a hundred knives, weighted him down with boulders, drowned him like a kitten, and flayed his skin from his body. He was in agony.

"I couldn't stop him. I couldn't get away." Arabella's words and her fear tore through him like bullets.

"My lord, is this true? Did you force my daughter?" Lady Winslow asked in a horrified voice.

"Of course not. I take exception to the very idea." Justin drew himself up fully, every inch the besmirched gentleman. "The very idea that I would abuse her is repugnant. Arabella wanted my kiss, I assure you. If she is embarrassed for her actions now, there is still no reason to blacken my good name."

"It was black to start with," Gabriel snarled.

He pushed himself further into the room until he stood in front of his bluestocking. Gently, he drew her away from her mother.

"Unhand her, Darkie," Justin ordered. 'That is my bride."

Gabriel ignored him and rubbed his hands gently up and down Arabella's arms as if to warm her. "Lady Arabella," he said, using the softest voice he could manage, "I am well aware of the lengths to which my cousin will go."

"You believe me?" she asked, her voice edged with desperation.

Her violet eyes were purple bruises, but the flow of tears made them shiny as jewels. How could anything on earth be so beautiful? How could such beauty enrage and calm him at the same moment?

"Of course." With his thumbs, he swept the bones of her cheeks and wiped at the trail of tears. "Calm yourself. I will not let him harm you."

107

"Darkie!"

"There is only one question." Gabriel took a deep breath, hating to even ask, and afraid of what her answer might be. In a voice that cracked, despite his best efforts, he said, "Do you wish to marry Justin? The choice is entirely yours."

It was as if his words gave her a new spine. He nodded at the realization in her widening eyes. Her lips tremulously twitched as she tried to smile.

Justin moved to where Gabriel could see him. He touched his trouser leg and inched up his pants. An object bulged at the base of his right leg.

"Get your hands off my bride, Darkie, or I promise you will regret your actions."

Gabriel cursed under his breath. Trust his cousin to bring a gun to tea.

Whirling Arabella behind him, he stilled, his mind flipping through the best responses to this ridiculous situation. Before he could find a good one, Lady Winslow slid between the men to confront him rather than his onerous cousin.

"You have no right, Brynley. Unhand my… daughter…at…once," she wheezed and collapsed heavily onto the cutting board beside her.

Arabella sprang into action. She grabbed a stool and eased her mother onto it, before dropping to her knees. Although tears still marred her beautiful face, she looked stronger, and much more focused. She took Lady Winslow's hand and slowly stroked it.

"Remember what the doctors said, Mother? You must concentrate on breathing. Nice and easy. Everything is peaceful. Everything is fine. There is all the air in the world here, all the air you will ever need. Your lungs are pumping, nice and slow, filling completely. They are becoming marvelously full as they easily allow fresh air in and out. Gently, now," Arabella cooed, in a voice one might use to convince a toddler to eat her peas.

Justin let his pant leg fall.

Gabriel released his breath.

It seemed like Arabella murmured forever until Lady Winslow's breathing slowed and steadied, though the shallow rasping that sounded under the intake and exhalation of air remained audible.

"My lords," Arabella finally said, "My mother requires complete calm and rest. I must ask you both to leave now so I may put her to bed."

"Of course," Justin agreed quickly. "Lady Winslow, please do not worry. I will set these matters right. I shall marry Arabella as I've promised, despite her accusations. Naturally, she was unnerved; that is all. It is a testament to her innocence I find most pleasing."

Before Gabriel could object, Arabella surprised him.

"There is no need for explanation, Lord Manning, or action." She rose to her feet. "I thank you for your offer. However, I don't believe we cosmopolitan fellows think such a draconian response to a mere kiss is warranted. We live in a modern age, after all." She slanted a glance at her mother. "I am not saying I would not welcome your proposal in the near future. Later, when we have both had a chance to know each other better, I have every hope we might revisit your...selfless offer. Perhaps soon. I-I just need time to consider."

Arabella lifted her gaze toward Gabriel. He thought he understood her diplomacy but wasn't certain. Perhaps he also needed time.

For a moment, it seemed like Justin might argue or

insist. Then he bobbed his head.

Though his cousin's teeth were gritted and he was obviously displeased, still it was acquiescence. Relief flooded through Gabriel, leaving him lightheaded.

"Well then, Justin and I will take our leave. Please rest assured, Lady Winslow, I will not spread gossip. Do not distress yourself on my account. Justin? There are some family matters I wish to discuss."

Though his face hardened and his shoulders ruffled, Justin nodded. "I will wait for you outside." Bowing to the women, he took his leave.

Gabriel followed him but then paused at the doorway.

"Come, Mother, let us get you upstairs under some nice fluffy blankets," Arabella said.

Down the hall, his cousin closed the front door.

Lady Winslow drew in a ragged breath. She hesitated. "You did willingly kiss Manning?" she asked.

Gabriel faced the room and stilled, waiting for the answer. Arabella didn't instantly respond. Over her mother's shoulder, she tossed him a helpless, wide-eyed appeal.

Then, reluctantly, it seemed, she muttered, "Of course, Mother. Nothing is wrong that a good cup of tea won't fix."

Lady Winslow patted her daughter's hand. "You're such a good girl, Arabella," she managed between wheezes. "Trust me; he will make an excellent husband."

Arabella's gaze searched him as she led her mother from the room, past Gabriel, and up the stairs, leaving Lady de Veer to follow. On the landing, she paused.

Gabriel had to strain to hear her words, but he thought he heard her ask, "What if…what if I did not care for his kiss?"

Lady Winslow rasped, "Perhaps that is for the best."
He turned away, his emotions in turmoil.

Chapter 14

The two men stalked the sidewalk, the rage between them palpable. It connected them, so others on the street unwittingly gave them a wide berth. When they approached an alley, Gabriel pushed his cousin into the narrow slit and up against the wall. Hard.

"You bastard," he hissed in Justin's face. "How dare you touch her?"

His cousin smiled, a cat full of canary innards. "Careful, cuz, lest you wrinkle my bow." He simpered and tilted his chin. "Have I struck a nerve? Do you, perhaps, hold tender feelings for my bride?"

"She's not your bride yet, or ever, if I have anything to do about it. Besides, she obviously doesn't want you."

Justin shrugged. "She is a bit missish, that's true, but it does her credit. I, for one, look forward to that very naiveté. Our wedding night will be scrumptious," he added as he narrowed his eyes. "All that wonderful pale skin and hair, spread out upon my burgundy silk sheets? Ooh. Perhaps I'll have her painted thus, all despoiled innocence lying within a pool of blood? Metaphorically, of course."

Gabriel's hands tightened upon Justin's shoulders. "You forced her."

"As my wife, she will receive more than my kisses, and she will welcome every single caress, I assure you. Now, if you are done meddling in my business?"

"I am not," Gabriel growled, releasing the villainous rat, then slamming him into the wall again. "Listen carefully, cousin. If you touch her again without her leave, I will call you out, even if I hang for it."

"What is it to you?"

That was a question Gabriel preferred not to answer. He pushed Justin again.

"Think of me as the man who will hunt you to the ground if you play wolf."

Justin shrugged, seemingly indifferent to the threat of violence. "If you care about her enough to hang for murder, then why not offer for her yourself? Oh, yes. You have plans that do not include marriage, not to mention Lady Winslow has the good sense to despise you. I find I quite like her for possessing such an enlightened view. Certainly, I intend to make use of it." His stare intensified. "Is that really all that is holding you back? Why, for example, didn't you come up to snuff when I discovered you in her bedroom?"

"You had the advantage of surprise," Gabriel muttered, "and I did not yet know the young lady well enough."

"You knew her well enough to have irrevocably compromised her, had I made a fuss." Justin smiled. "No, I think you hold back because you are weak at the core. You need time to weigh all the odds, the risks, before you are capable of acting, but I am giving you no time, am I?" He laughed. "Oh, I do so love it when your foibles bring you down, Darkie." He paused, then snarled, "I have decided to marry Lady Arabella, and that is what I shall do. Prepare yourself. It will not be long now."

He shoved Gabriel back, and Gabriel let himself be moved. Fixing his collar, Justin nodded and then strode back to the opening of the alley.

"Why?" Gabriel called, just as his cousin was about to slip into the main street. "Why her? She is poor."

Justin turned. His face was expressionless. "Because she is your undoing." He disappeared around the corner.

Gabriel ignored the hit and focused instead upon the fact Justin's words had been the confirmation he had sought. His cousin's interest in Arabella was tied to Gabriel and almost certainly to the suit for the titles.

But, how? How could she possibly be connected?

Whatever the link, it was impossible to miss the greater meaning: he, Gabriel, was personally responsible for every nefarious action Justin undertook that concerned the outstandingly sensible and mind-numbingly desirable female. If not for the suit, would Justin have even met the lovely Assyriologist?

More importantly, had his cousin forced his attentions upon her in her own home? Even if she had inadvertently encouraged him, Justin was animal enough to take a delicate situation and make it unwholesome.

For that, one day, Gabriel would beat the shag-bag bloody. He pounded the brick wall and welcomed the pain.

****

Glenda Warwick, Lady Winslow, was anything but happy. When she had arranged for a moment in which Justin might sway Arabella into a kiss, she had not envisioned force or that Arabella might be afterward so visibly upset by the exchange.

Between gasps for air as she sat propped up in her bed, she watched Annette pick through the tray of biscuits Arabella had brought up before leaving again to brew a fresh pot of tea.

"Arabella does not understand how a gentleman might seize an opportunity," her friend murmured. "She is too innocent for her age."

"How can any unwed lady be too innocent?"

Annette shrugged, then pushed the plate away and stood. "You have been too sheltered as well, Glenda. You were married to a man who did not appreciate you as he should have done, and thus you have a very limited view of relations between lovers. You cannot understand the exigent circumstances under which they operate."

"But Justin and Arabella are not lovers. That is the point."

"But they could be. Soon. That is precisely the point. Unless," Annette paused, "you wish to live on the streets?"

A fine point, indeed. She had to sell her daughter for her own comfort, but she was beginning to doubt the sale would be beneficial to all. Earlier, Arabella had seemed undone. Even so, she hadn't accepted the viscount's proposal. Instead, she had riveted her attention upon Brynley, as if his had been the only important opinion in the room.

"Arabella must not marry Brynley."

"He is completely unsuitable," Annette agreed. "Happily, he has not offered, and after finding Arabella in Justin's embrace today, he will not. Mark my words. He is over-proud, that one."

"Or regularly proud, I should imagine."

Annette picked up her gloves. "I am off. De Veer has made it a point to insist I be there to entertain this evening. Husbands are ever the trial. Do try to rest, Glenda, and resist the impulse to overthink the matter. Manning's affections are the only ones on proffer, and he will do very well by your daughter. That is all that matters."

Glenda wished she could still believe that.

Chapter 15

"His lordship is in the stables, polishing Shu's saddle," Reggie said pointedly as he set down a mug of his famous Irish coffee on the scarred table next to Peter's hand. "Second time today."

Peter lifted the steaming cup to his lips. He blew on it, his bright aquamarine eyes narrowing against the swirl of whiskey fumes. Coughing, he wiped the moisture away with the heels of his palms. "Why? What has the weasel-cousin done now?"

Reggie sank into a chair across the plank of oak, on the side of the rough-hewn kitchen table nearest the fire grate where flames danced merrily. Over the blaze, an old black cauldron of soup boiled, filling the room with the scents of onion and beef.

"Maybe not just the weasel this time," Reggie commented slyly, rotating to give dinner a quick turn with the cracked wooden spoon that hung from a hook on the wall next to the pot.

Careful to center the overlarge utensil so the drippings *plink*ed into the copper pot below, he was delighted to see his cryptic words had caught his second son's attention.

"Give over, old man. You know you can't keep a secret to save that wrinkled hide of yours."

Reggie leaned across the table and quaffed Peter in the head. "That's enough out of ye', and don't be gettin' too big fer yer britches."

"Yes, sir," Peter muttered.

Reggie nodded, appeased. It had been many years since the boys had been under his direction, but it was gratifying to know they still respected his authority, even as grown men. They were fine gentlemen, too, though alike as chalk and cheese, and the worry they could cause an old man was not to be dismissed lightly.

Darting his hand across the table, he ruffled the angelic curls upon Peter's head, barely grazing a lock as the boy instinctively ducked to the side, just as he had done while in short pants.

"Mind your own head, Reggie," Peter grumbled, shaking his curls back into place. "With all that wild gray hair, you look like some kind of hermit escaped from his cave. Someone who hasn't eaten in a month."

"Yes, yes," Reggie grumbled but smiled.

"That means you're too thin."

"I got ya', boyo. I was not born yesterday, so I don't understand the Queen's English. Do ye' want to hear about how Gabriel has been bitten by Cupid, or don't ye'?"

Peter snorted coffee through his nose, then sputtered. When he stopped coughing and waving his hands, he said, " 'Stung by Cupid,' not bitten. Meaning injured by the point of his arrow. Cupid doesn't bite. He's not a feral wolf."

"*Pff*! Lot you know about it."

"One always knows one's enemies." Peter took another sip as his expression became more serious. "I knew that woman was going to be trouble. She is entirely too perfect."

"Is she?" Disquiet rumbled along his fingers and over

the back of his neck.

Peter was quick to shake his head. "No, not in that way. Though her charms are evident, I have no interest in pursuing her. She is perfect for Gabriel, however. That is what I meant." He paused, his fingers wrapping around his coffee cup. "Odd, though. I'm not in the least attracted to her. She's really quite fetching." Then he shrugged. "In any event, there will be no accidental slips of the fencing blades on this matter."

"Or any other."

"I'm not arguing."

The two men sipped their beverages in companionable silence for a few moments. Then Reggie stretched out his aching leg. The knee had never quite recovered from an injury garnered in the war. On rainy days, of which there were too many, it felt as if knives ripped apart his bones.

"Gabriel needs to offer for her, of course," he finally murmured, foregoing the lilt he put on and took off as he liked. He held up his hand to preclude the argument Peter would make. "Hear me out. As baron, and possibly earl very shortly, should matters go his way, he requires an heir. Lady Arabella is of good family, and they seem friendly enough. Moreover, women who love Assyriology are not easy to come by. Best of all, though, by marrying her, Gabriel would roundly thwart the weasel in whatever nefarious plan he has concocted."

"An admirable goal, as there's certainly skullduggery afoot." Peter's finger circled the edge of his empty mug. "What if she won't have him?"

"He could compromise her."

Peter snorted. "So much for instilling morality into us." He gazed at a small crack in the wall and sighed. "I object to forcing a person to the altar. It is bad enough women so often trick a man there with sweet words and honeyed nights. Friends should not suggest such deception, most especially when there is risk to a fine woman's reputation in the balance. I may abhor Society, but Arabella is the one who has to abide by its rules."

"Morals and rules are fine things. I'm talking about pushing the heart where it intends to go anyway," Reggie argued. "Gabriel's problem has always been too much deliberation. He was in a bad way over the lass this morning. You would agree with me if you saw him. And, if it is the lady's welfare that makes you hesitate to drop a word in Himself's ear, even you must realize something needs to be done before she falls victim to Justin's schemes."

He sat back and waited, letting his words do their work.

Peter frowned menacingly in response, betraying again the graceful sweep and long lines of his features that bespoke centuries of aristocratic blood. Whoever Peter's father had been, he must have been a nobleman, which perhaps explained Peter's dislike and distrust of Society, Cupid, and marriage.

Reggie opened his mouth to say so, but a slamming door interrupted their conversation.

"I see Himself is back," he murmured. "Not a peep now, unless you plan to help me?"

****

Peter sipped his drink and considered Reggie's arguments. While he had little use for Society, there was something kind and charming about Arabella Warwick that put her outside the normal shallowness of her class. She was easy to be with. She wasn't demanding. She had a quality about her that almost screamed a willingness to be enthralled by new things. He could understand Gabriel's enchantment, even if he didn't feel ensorcelled himself.

It helped, perhaps, having seen them together, the way the world evaporated out of existence for them as they pored over boring old symbols. Still, he hadn't imagined Gabriel might wish to marry Arabella. Now, he was considering it.

"Where are you, old man? Do I pay you to butler or to sit around gossiping?" Gabriel peeked his head into the kitchen. "Where are my staff? And you," he added, glaring at Peter. "Don't you have anything better to do than sit around quaffing my beverages? What happened to your own townhouse? Given it to some especially satisfying actress, have you?"

"Your staff cower elsewhere, away from your angry slurs. I take it you've polished a hole through Shu's saddle. Second time today, was it?" Peter asked, keeping his voice light.

"Damn it, old man, can't you refrain from mucking in my business for one day?" Gabriel glared at Reggie before throwing himself into a third seat. He dragged it close to the fire and stuck out his hands to be warmed.

"You are my business, lad," the old man replied, fetching another cup.

He set a heavy ceramic mug before Gabriel, then used the kettle to refill Peter's drink.

"Hmm," Gabriel mumbled. He took a long sip, then plopped his cup down upon the table. "I visited Lady Arabella today for afternoon studies. I found her in the kitchen."

Quickly, he recounted all that had occurred, his fists

clenching upon the tabletop and a hard glitter lighting his green eyes.

"Justin was willing to risk more for his cause than I am for mine," Gabriel growled, punching his fist down softly upon the scarred surface of the table.

Suddenly, he flung himself out of the chair to pace to the door, running his hand through his mane of black hair and scowling at the beaten floorboards.

Peter sent a glance toward Reggie, who was smiling like a loon. He took a sip and waited.

"I am well aware of my growing regard for Arabella." Gabriel threw himself back into his seat. "I just barely managed to leave our morning session without showing her exactly how Gilgamesh went about winning the women of various towns to his cause. Then, afterward, I reconsidered my admirable restraint." He paused, tapping his fist down upon the table three times. "I had intended to steal a kiss this afternoon. I thought I might disabuse her of the ridiculous notion she's developed that I am interested in her only so I might study her copy of the *Epic*. The reprobate beat me to the line." He brought his fist down again, harder this time, and flinched. "I am too late."

"And why would she think that about the *Epic*?" Peter demanded with asperity. "Given that a perfectly legible, hand-printed copy rests upon your shelves?"

"Yes, I realize her misunderstanding is also my fault, but in the beginning, when she suggested as much, I thought it more expedient if she considered my interests to be purely academic. How was I to know I could even trust her, let alone I would…come to care for her?"

How indeed.

"And, frankly, I'm not certain I do trust her because

there's still Justin's interest in her to work out and whether she is knowingly involved in whatever scheme he is hatching."

"Do you believe her to be complicit?" Reggie asked.

Gabriel shook his head. "I don't, but I cannot put aside the possibility it might be true. I have a duty to my future heirs to secure the titles that should be theirs. I cannot afford to disregard any single qualm." He paused. "For certain, Arabella needs to marry, for her mother's sake, if not her own. Her requirement is objectively real." He ran his nail along a deep groove in the table's surface. Then he added, slowly, as if testing his words, "Therefore, despite my misgivings, and although Lady Winslow harbors an unfathomable dislike for me, I am considering offering for Arabella."

A look of intense satisfaction washed over Reggie's face, all his wrinkles relaxing into contented folds.

Peter winked at him. "Our father thinks you should compromise her."

"For God's sake, lad!" Reggie exclaimed. He leaned over and knocked Peter on the head again. "You have the tact of a bullfrog."

"Even less." Peter rubbed his scalp. He hadn't moved quickly enough. "Regardless, Gabriel, the old man makes a good point, though I hate to admit it. Arabella's days of freedom are fast ending. Justin has just committed to his intended course of action. We know this bounder, don't we? Once he moves, he is like a bullet loosed from a rifle. He does not change direction. He does not deviate. He has set his eyes upon the lady, and he will obtain her through any means necessary, even by physical force. More than a kiss might be at stake."

"Over my dead body," Gabriel whispered hoarsely.

"I don't believe he would quibble over your demise, do you? In any event, your cousin was right about one thing. Act, or don't act, but you no longer have the luxury of long deliberation."

"Sometimes, you have to do the wrong thing to do the right thing," Reggie said solemnly. "It is either you or the weasel for the lady. There is no longer a third choice, if there ever was."

With that, Peter could no longer argue. It just remained to be seen whether Gabriel could.

Chapter 16

The next morning, Gabriel entered the Winslow library earlier than normal. He found Arabella slumbering over her notes, her cheek pressed to the back of her hand. A few escaping tendrils of hair caressed her neck, a long, graceful stem rising from the lace of her gown. All he wanted to do was to tangle his fingers within her riotous, pinned-up curls and swear his life to her forever.

He no longer doubted what he felt or what he was prepared to do. He only doubted speed or compromise was necessary. Careful deliberation had won many a war for him in business, scholarship, and life. It had become part of his nature. Though in no way averse to action, he usually chose to move swiftly and surely only once he had evaluated the best path forward.

Since he had met the extraordinary bluestocking, he found himself jumping when he would have crept. His mind, capable of focusing like the point of a blade, had turned around her person rather than the price of silk, Gilgamesh, or his dastardly cousin and the title suit. Her laugh, her perfume, her bright quips, and the sparkle in her eyes haunted him when he was elsewhere, urging him to act. In her presence, he became obsessed with her Titian-like flawless skin, rosy cheeks, golden lashes, and parted petal lips.

He would have to marry her if he ever wanted to study effectively again, never mind pay attention to trade.

Gabriel sat down upon the adjacent chair and cleared his throat. She stirred but did not wake.

"Arabella, please. You are destroying me utterly," he complained.

Those fabulous jewels fluttered, half-opened, but even that was enough to catch him like a fly in amethyst.

"Gabriel?" She sat up and shook her head and then covered her mouth with the back of her hand as she yawned widely.

His heart skipped a beat. It was such a singular response to an ordinary gesture, he didn't quite know what to do with himself.

"Your, um, hair." He gestured with a finger to his temple and performed a curling rotation as he tried to ignore the impulse to drag her to the floor.

She reached up, shot him an embarrassed smile, and took out the pins. The full, lustrous cascade toppled. Not a part of him moved, not even his lungs, as she quickly twisted and pinned the riot back into some semblance of propriety.

He had never been so physically uncomfortable in his life.

It wasn't lost upon him that, having fruitlessly wished for a woman who might enjoy scholarly pursuits as much as he did, when found, he could think of nothing but closing the blasted books.

"I sympathize, my lord," she said as her hands dropped again to the table.

"Do you?" he muttered.

Arabella smiled, her lips pink from where she had been biting them. "When you frown as you do now, I realize how galling it must be to wait upon my availability to study the *Epic*, especially since your translation of it has the great possibility of establishing your reputation as a leading Assyriologist. Your reputation, in turn, will determine the approbation and funding you receive, two items necessary if you hope to follow in Rawlinson's footsteps and undertake your own excavations."

"I can fund my digs," he retorted, stung.

"Well, perhaps you don't credit just how expensive such things can be," she said, as if he were an idiot with an ego in need of a gentle hand. "One needs a king's ransom for such things, so investors are required. You will not feasibly be able to obtain those without the approval of the museum board."

Arabella looked so serious that, despite his unsettled humor, he found his lips beginning to twitch. He leaned back in his chair. "I assure you," he drawled in a gentler tone, "no such requirement drives me."

She looked set to argue but instead hesitated before agreeing. "Of course, my lord."

The pity in her eyes annoyed him all over again.

"You have misinterpreted a great many things."

Gabriel took a deep breath, intending to disabuse her of the notion he had helped develop, that his interest in her started and stopped with the *Epic*, when she lifted her arms to pin back a fallen length of hair. Her breasts lifted with the movement. Unbidden, a groan escaped his lips in place of the words he had planned.

She stilled at once. "My lord, are you ill?"

On top of Reggie's ill-conceived advice, her untutored sensuality nearly undid him. He gritted his teeth, determined to get the hell out of the room before he did something incredibly stupid.

The only thing stopping his flight was the tightness

of his trousers.

Arabella's cool hand clasped over his forehead, the lace trim of her sleeve batting at his lashes. "You do seem a bit warm."

He bit his lip hard, hoping the pain would help keep his hands from dragging her closer. The perfume of her, the tender scent of sleep and warmed gardenia, crept over him like a fine mist. With a dawning sense of horror at his lack of control, he reached up and trapped the hand leaving his forehead. Drawing it down to the level of his lips, he placed a long, searing kiss upon her palm.

She gasped. As her eyes rounded with shock, her hand trembled. He was not the only one swaying now.

"My lord?"

He dropped her fingers as if they were made of fire and nearly jumped across the room. Deliberately, he kept his back to her while he attempted to cool the proof of his ardor. He stared out the window but had no idea what he looked at. An entire circus might have performed juggling acts, and he was too blinded by lust to notice.

He needed to think about disgusting things. Worms. Cockroaches. Bloated corpses. Justin's face after he had cornered the parlor maid when they were fourteen. He winced but was rather relieved the last did the trick. His trousers gained an inch of breathing room.

"I must apologize, my lord," she said. "I...I know I was too familiar with your person. I assure you I meant no harm. I was merely concerned."

When he could manage, he faced her again, only to find her blushing to the roots of her golden hair. "It is I who should apologize," he muttered stiffly. "Arabella."

"Yes?"

Gabriel opened his mouth to explain but sighed

instead.

How could he begin to describe how everything was too complicated right now? He had his cousin in his sights at last. He had his duty clearly mapped and for once teetered on the verge of fulfilling his obligation to his familial line. Nothing could get in the way of his impending success, and already she was getting in the way. She demanded so much of his attention, though she didn't ask for a thing.

No, he could not approach her yet. Later, after the court date, he could woo her as he wished, with a clear conscience. He could court her as she deserved, with delicacy and charm, even if she proved to be a conniving jade in league with his cousin.

If he could not adequately pledge his troth to Arabella now and still focus upon his duties, then he could not touch her, because however could he possibly stop once he had started?

There was time. The suit would be heard by the end of next week. Surely, if he was vigilant, he could keep Justin at bay for at least that long. He could keep his ardor in check, as well. He wasn't seventeen, after all.

Compromise her, indeed. Blast Reggie anyway, for setting such a tantalizing idea in his head!

"I am not one for kisses anyway," she whispered, distracting him from his train of thought.

"Excuse me?"

"Kisses. You are thinking I am angling for you to kiss me as we had started to do once…twice…so very long ago, but I am not, at least…" She paused, then said quickly, "I had a schoolgirl image in my head of how romantic kissing must be, but the reality is far different, is it not?"

He had no ability to respond to that statement.

She sighed. "Ignorance is debilitating because it fires the imagination in ways that are unhealthy." She paused again. "You needn't pretend a passion for me, my lord, and you need not worry I shall trouble you in that way. It is only a lingering romantic image that sometimes pops into my head and makes me think, er, kissing you…um, well, might be nice. Habit, really."

"I see." He did not see at all.

"And you must not worry about the *Epic*. I am very aware our time together is growing short, and I know you must sense it too, brilliant as you are."

That snapped him out of his stupor. "Short in what way?"

She shrugged and picked at a loose thread on her embroidered skirt.

"Justin?"

Her gaze met his, and again he lost himself in the depths of those violet pools. There was such regret there. It called to him.

"May I speak bluntly?"

He nodded.

"My mother's condition is worsening. Her doctors recommend a change in habitation. London's air is quite toxic, it seems."

"Yesterday afternoon was upsetting. I found myself quite upset, for one."

She nodded but seemed unable to continue the line of conversation she had started.

However, Gabriel could no longer ignore the question that pressed against his brain. His heart. "Arabella, is your mother's situation the only reason you tolerate Justin's attentions? Has he promised you funds to

130

help her if you marry him?"

"How mercenary you must think me."

"Not mercenary, no. Please, I need to know why you continue to tolerate the man," he said, no longer bothering to be polite. And why should he when there had been so much blunt talk between them anyway? He needed to hear the answer from her own lips because it was one thing to assume but another to have it spelled out.

"I have a requirement," she finally admitted.

"But do you have affection for the…?"

Dandified, goat-headed, cretinous, boot-licker is what Gabriel wanted to say. Instead, he clenched his fists hard until he thought his fingers might break and said no more as she simply stared at him, then at her lap.

He thought she might have shaken her head in the negative, but it was such a small gesture he couldn't be certain.

He could say no more. To press her or reveal his feelings would mean he trusted her like he trusted Reggie and Peter. With Justin's presence in her life, he couldn't, not quite, no matter how much he wanted to. His gut told him she wasn't complicit, but there was still something so fishy about the entire situation that just by sitting near the smell she had acquired a certain malodorous stench herself.

Odiferous maybe, but as he gazed at Arabella and her innocent, open, trusting mien, he could not doubt the lengths he would go to forgive her any treachery.

Frustration rose and choked his throat. For the first time in his life, Gabriel wanted desperately to destroy something as an outlet for his irritation. Unfortunately, glancing about, he could only see Kismet, the map, and the *Epic*, none of which could reasonably be thrown or ripped to shreds. He was about to turn away, to gaze out the window again while he tried to compose himself, when a sudden thought struck.

"Have you already decided to wed him?"

Arabella's lips fell open, and her eyes widened, but she did not immediately deny his words.

Before he knew what he was doing, he had crossed the room and lifted her from the seat by grabbing her arms. "Have you already accepted him? Is it already too late?" It took all his effort not to shake her.

"Oh!" She swallowed, her eyes just inches from his own. They were filled with so many emotions he couldn't read a single one. "As I said yesterday, I am not yet ready to do so." She raised her fingers to his chest and pressed them to the linen. "Your heart is racing, my lord."

He swallowed and swore. Then he reached up and touched one of the curls on the side of her face. The scent of gardenia teased his nostrils.

"Arabella. Sweet Arabella," he rasped, his voice breaking on her name. "How you tempt me to the limits of my own moral code! Do you have any least notion how dreadfully difficult these study sessions have been for me?"

"Is my company so painful for you, then?" she asked lightly, although her gaze skittered to the side.

Gabriel's laugh was ragged. "Painful? I am in agony. I could bear it, I suppose, if not for the fact my cousin is given open license when I must steal so little."

Her head tilted as she studied him. "You need not fear Justin will usurp your place. You must realize you were correct when you advised me he has no interest in the *Epic*."

Gabriel inhaled deeply through his nose. The epic

misunderstanding about the *Epic*, again. He needed to explain. He couldn't.

"This is unbearable," he whispered.

As her face contorted, she remarked, "To think I have always admired blunt talk. I cannot fathom it now."

"I am fairly certain you do not fathom it at all."

Steeling his shoulders, hoping he might discover the words to explain how, yes, he had sought her room that first evening simply to find a way to foil his cousin's plans, but from that moment to this, his greatest interest had been in Arabella herself.

"Please, do not be undone. I will not let Justin usurp your place. If you just give me a bit of time…give me today to consider. I will find a solution by tomorrow. I promise."

"How?" he growled, gripping her tighter. "How, with this paltry, delicate frame, will you prevent Justin from taking what should be mine?" He shook his head and swore softly under his breath, releasing her. He needed more time as well.

She had asked for a day to find a solution, which suited him. He needed the hours to fight his demons or to lose her. Perhaps he had been wrong to think he had time.

How was it he had managed to fill the depleted coffers of his estate; wrangled and won against the most cutthroat nobility, businessmen, and scholars; and built a reputation both respected and feared, but a slip of a woman unmanned him so that he was unable to speak?

How had he come to be the hapless assistant he pretended to be?

Chapter 17

Stepping down from the carriage a few hours later, Arabella threw the fare into the hired driver's hands. As the man cried the horses onward, the wheels threw small, pinging stones. Some of them dotted her dress.

She took a deep breath and fluffed out her pink twill skirt. Her fingers traced the sprinkles of lime-green flowers dotting the bodice and extending down the front like a waterfall. It was an old gown made for her in her earlier years, so the chest was now too tight, and her breasts nearly overflowed the neckline. She peeked a look downward to ascertain the fabric still covered her properly before assessing the imposing grandeur of Gabriel's home.

It was unexpected, this immense, pristine swathe of wealth. He had implied money was not a concern, but nothing had prepared her for the monolithic piece of architecture.

The Georgian residence was as large as a row of Grosvenor Street townhomes. Made of gray stones with three rising stories, its windows quite pleasingly symmetrical, the building maintained a light and bright appearance despite its heavy construction. The oversized double entrance was pedimented with flanking pilasters. A dentil cornice was carved into the front façade, with decorative quoins at the corners.

Happy red and pink flowers in large stone urns

banked the stairs and ran periodically along the base of the wall, an unusual feature. That she noticed the decoration and architecture was a testament to how nervous she was.

She inhaled deeply, both appalled and excited by her temerity. By all rights, she should never, as a single woman, alight in front of a man's quarters to visit him, unchaperoned. Her ruination would be total should anyone discover this piece of folly, or if Gabriel outed her, as he most definitely should.

Yet, she trusted in his discretion. The realization calmed her a little.

Releasing the breath she held, she quickly mounted the stairs. Before she could knock, one side of the double-door swung open. A man of some years stood in the frame, his wild gray hair a flurry like feathers, his face thin and cragged like a skull. He wore a ferocious scowl. A plain shirt was untucked at one corner. His unbuttoned jacket and vest hung over stained pants fitted into expensive Hessian boots.

Suddenly, he smiled. "Welcome to Pheasant Ridge, Lady Arabella." He reached forward and grabbed her by her gloved hands before dragging her inside. He gave her no time to question how he knew her identity or even whether she was brave enough to enter. He waved at the retreating carriage and closed the door.

"Oh," she exclaimed, attempting to soothe her flittering pulse. "Please excuse the intrusion, but I am—"

"Bonnet, if you please, as Himself isn't fond of them, and I'll send ya' back to him quick," he said smoothly, holding forth his hand. "He's just reading in the parlor. Change of scenery, you know."

She stammered a reply, then set about removing the

hat and handing it to him. With surprising dexterity, given his creaky appearance, he placed it upon the mantel. He looked at her gloves appraisingly, then clucked his tongue and shook his head.

Fluffing her *coiffeur* as best as she was able, Arabella turned at the sound of boots clipping down the marble-floored hallway. A moment later, Gabriel strode into view, his head bent as he read from a book. His expression remained vague when he lifted his gaze until it sharpened upon her. He blinked and stood perfectly still. The book snapped shut between his long, graceful fingers. From a distance, she could not read the title.

He was casually dressed in tan pants and a white shirt open at the neck, clearly not anticipating company. His black hair was ruffled rather than slicked neatly back, lending his strong features an almost boyish appeal. The black Hessian boots were dustless, as pristine as the façade of his home. Despite the casualness of his person, he appeared far more intimidating than she could ever remember him having looked before.

"I'm Reggie, by the way," the gray-haired man said as she and Gabriel stared at each other. "*Tch*. No matter. I'll just be off then. Don't mind me. Nothing interesting to see here. Lemonade in the garden since the sun is shining? Capital idea."

He sidled off, but Arabella only barely noticed.

"What has happened? Why are you here?"

When Gabriel reached her, he slowly raised his fingers to her jawline, perhaps testing her skin to see if she were real, his touch as light as butterfly wings.

She shook her head, careful not to dislodge him, but he dropped his hand anyway.

"Come." He took her hand and wrapped it around his

136

arm as he deposited his book upon the mantel next to her bonnet. "Unless there is an urgent matter requiring my immediate attention?"

His eyes glowed green like the trees in the sunlight. She managed to shake her head.

Without another word, he escorted her down the hallway and through a parlor possessed of scrolled parquetry floors. Heavy French doors stood open to catch a breeze now that the day had shaken off its bad weather.

Instead of the fussiness of the current decorating style, all the room's surfaces were clean and crisp. There were few *objets d'art*, although plenty of books upon the shelves and tables. Dark blue painted walls had been left unpapered, and lines of white molding carefully defined geometric areas. Portraits and landscapes in jeweled tones had been hung so the eye both rested and jumped to the next. Unlike many homes Arabella had visited, the paintings didn't compete with each other. Intricately designed in the same tones as the artwork, lush Persian carpets crossed the floors, adding warmth, as did the overstuffed chairs and couches.

These were rooms in which a person could breathe. Her shoulders dropped and her pulse steadied, until she shot Gabriel a glance and rediscovered his imperious and commanding air had not been a figment of imagination. Instantly, her insides began wiggling about again.

"Come, we will take a turn about the garden, and you may explain to me just what has brought you here," he said, his voice even as the beautifully polished wooden floor.

Once through the parlor doors, they exited over a grand stone patio and into the garden below. Her feet crunched on small gravel, and she realized yet again she was strolling the grounds of a wealthy man's home. The tiny stones were white and pink, something he must have paid dearly to have imported. Their endless expanse curved through the manicured hedges, around a pool with statuary, and up to a gazebo at the distant end.

There were gardeners too. Three bobbed about near them. Women's voices rang out, servants probably. Because this wasn't the center of London, room existed for a stable, the particular smells wafting on the breeze. A large fenced paddock stretched to her far right. It wasn't quite a country estate, full of sprawling acres, but it had to be a sizeable piece of land for all that.

Suddenly, the full force of her impetuousness assailed her as everything her gaze beheld told her the truth about the easy-going, scholarly assistant who promenaded beside her. He held command quietly, but Baron Brynley was lord of this manor and everyone in it, of that she could not doubt. She had become used to thinking of him as a friend, as someone she could trust, someone who made her life more interesting. He had become an object of her desire, but built on an approachable terrain. She had never thought of him as a rich, powerful, intimidating man.

Arabella looked back at the house, the gracious breadth of the patio, and found herself wobbly. The lord who ambled beside her was a stranger, a formidable stranger, to control all this. Something hot and full pooled in her belly. Quickly, she pulled her fingers from his arm as if it burned. Stepping back, she mumbled her apology.

"I'm sorry, my lord. I am intruding."

"You are not."

She glanced up at him again. He smiled. It was a kind smile, the one to which she had already become accustomed.

"I am afraid I am."

"Arabella. You are most welcome." He offered her his arm again. Something moved in the depths of his eyes. "Walk with me on this glorious day. I want to see the sun shine upon your riotous curls and your reflection in each budding flower. There are roses up ahead, a whole mess of them. The smell is divine. You will appreciate their heady fragrance."

Without quite realizing it, she was strolling again, holding his arm. They promenaded for a few minutes before he said, "Perhaps we should discuss what matter has brought you here? It must have been some reason of import to carry you so far. Peter calls this place 'the back of beyond,' although I think he exaggerates simply to irritate me. Of course, he is successful."

He was trying to put her at ease, she realized, and the effort soothed her. It made him her Gabriel again and less grand.

Swallowing, she said, "I came to tell you I have reached a decision."

"Have you?"

She shot him a look, but he was gazing at some flowering bushes off to his right.

"Yes." She paused. She had come here determined to say the next words, but they were difficult nonetheless. Still, fair was fair. He had given her so much of his time and attention. She owed him, at the very least, some sort of exchange.

Gathering her courage, she continued. "We have skirted propriety quite a bit in our dealings, which is understandable for scholars such as we are, but I am afraid I must positively traipse upon respectability to convey my next sentiments. Although, I suppose I've already done that just by coming here."

His eyes glittered, but he didn't reply. There was nothing comforting he could say in any case.

Gabriel stopped when they arrived at the roses, a wonder of heady scent and color. In any other moment or any other time, Arabella would have stood captivated by the flowers and the way they arched over the pebbled path, cocooning them. Instead, she could hardly draw breath for the potent combination of the baron's nearness and the awareness of the loss she must suffer when she said what she needed to say.

"I do not mind a little impropriety, Arabella." Gabriel coaxed her with a smile when the silence lengthened too long. "I am an excellent secret-keeper, I promise you. Surely, anything you have to say to me now cannot be so terrible, can it?"

"There are certain truths more unpalatable than terrible." She glanced at his left ear rather than meeting his gaze. "One of those unpalatable truths is that I will soon have no further need of the *Epic*." She paused and took a deep breath. "I intend it should be yours."

Her words seemed to stall him. Then, gently, he lifted his fingers and ran them along her cheek again. "Tell me."

She gulped. He was forcing her to look at him. There was nothing else for it.

"You have given me invaluable service with the knowledge you have shared. If I could, I would study Assyriology with you for the rest of my life, but that will not be possible." She stopped again. "I see no course for it but to marry Lord Manning," she finally blurted.

Gabriel's gaze hardened as it held hers captive, but

his fingers remained delicate flames upon her skin.

"He will not allow me to continue studying," she continued in a ragged whisper. "I am certain of it."

"Have you discussed any of this matter with him?" he asked gruffly.

"No, but…"

Dropping his fingers, he angled his body away from hers and stared toward the house. Arabella waited. When she finally began to turn back toward the patio, Gabriel pulled her close.

"Do not run off. Let me think."

Instead, all the words she needed to say for her own sake tumbled from her lips.

"If you do not accept the *Epic*, Gabriel, I feel certain the viscount will deny you access, and once we are wed…" She inhaled another deep breath as she strove to say the terrible words. "He will have control over everything that is mine. However, he does not have such power yet. I may still give you the means of accomplishing your life's goal. I beg you to accept because knowing you will succeed in translating this priceless treasure will give me a sense of completion and satisfaction."

It would be about the only sense of satisfaction she was sure to enjoy for the rest of her days.

"Will it?" he asked, voice grim.

"I will rest content, knowing Justin will not be able to steal your dreams, yes. I am relieved someone deserving will own the *Epic*."

"How kind you are."

His words were sultry, mocking. Heat traced her chest and cheeks.

"Despite your welcome denial this morning, I am

aware how mercenary my motivations are," she retorted. A short silence followed her words. "Well then," she continued more briskly. "I suppose I am just as glad to have this out in the open between us as well, especially after yesterday."

His jaw looked like granite, and his eyes were hard too.

"You must see I have an obligation to care for my mother?"

"As my parents died when I was a young boy, I have little experience of the necessary sacrifices," he responded gruffly. He turned his attention toward the sky, his gaze fixed upon the fluffy clouds.

She could not read his expression, though a tiny spot ticked in his cheek. When he turned back, he reached over her shoulder and plucked a pale pink rose. Carefully, he threaded it through her hair before extending his arm again, which she took.

Propelling her onward, he said, "I am surprised by your offer."

"Gratified?" She peeped up at him.

"One would have to be. I suppose it means you consider me a more-than-adequate assistant to your studies, that you would grace me with so priceless a gift."

"You don't seem pleased."

"Hmm."

"You despise me," she stated baldly when the silence pressed in upon her.

"No." He paused in his steps, so she stopped too. "But answer me this: am I wrong in believing you would show my cousin the door if not for your mother's condition?"

"As a man, you must resent the very idea a woman

would agree to wed someone whom she does not like, simply for money. But…yes." Guilt clogged her throat.

Gabriel inclined his head in a way that was neither agreement nor disagreement but some combination of both. "I suppose I do not like the idea in general, but in the specific, I am very grateful for your honesty." He studied her, and suddenly his expression was tender again, his jaw unfirmed, his green eyes bright. "I understand you have little with which to bargain or make a way for those you love in this world. But like you, I would ask for a day before addressing, perhaps, a solution to both our problems. One that does not require you to marry my odious cousin."

"A solution?" Arabella brightened. "How can that be?"

With his intelligence, surely he would find a path out of the muddle for her, one she had overlooked in her desperation.

"Let us just say your generosity with the *Epic* has given me an idea, one with which we might both live." His face relaxed further. "Will you grant me twenty-four hours in which I might consider the matter more fully?"

"I would grant you anything," she promised rashly.

He groaned but smiled. "Not anything, Arabella, for I find myself too close to taking advantage of such a vague and all-encompassing accord."

A flight of birds took flight within her chest, little bubbles of happiness winging about, though she wasn't even sure yet whether she should consider a path out of misery.

"Good. That is settled then. Come. I will have Reggie escort you back to Mayfair before you are missed. In an unmarked carriage." His lips twitched again. "Can you avoid falling into trouble until tomorrow, do you think? Perhaps stay abed with a good book and an attack cat ready to defend your honor?"

Arabella was afraid to breathe, afraid to dislodge the affection written upon his face. For the first time in a very long time, she began to hope.

He raised her fingers to his lips and placed a kiss upon them. He held them there for longer than he should as if he could not bear to part contact.

Gratitude for her promised gift of the *Epic*, or something more?

As Reggie dozed against the corner squabs and the carriage bumped along the road, Arabella consoled herself with the knowledge she need only wait a day's worth of hours to find out.

Chapter 18

"Do pay attention, Arabella," her mother snapped. "We need to discuss how you might salvage the situation this evening with the viscount. *If* it is to be salvaged after yesterday's debacle."

Lady Winslow perched upon her bed, propped up against a wall of feather pillows. Dressed in a cerulean robe that complimented the soft blues and whites of the bed linens, a tea tray upon her lap, she held the delicate saucer and cup between graceful fingers as she sipped the hot beverage. Her face was wan, as if yesterday's attack had sapped all her energy and her only source of replenishment had run dry.

At a tiny table to the side of the bed, Lady de Veer and Arabella shared a plate of cucumber sandwiches. Lady de Veer picked up one of the small crustless wedges and bit into it delicately.

"Leave Arabella be, Glenda. The girl is in love. What harm will it do to allow the viscount a small doubt, so long as she remedies it quickly?"

"I'm not in love with the viscount."

"Of course not, dear." Lady de Veer reached over and patted Arabella's hand. She threw Lady Winslow a conspiratorial glance. "I remember my first kiss with the viscount's father. I, too, mooned about for days, although my love unhappily did not translate into marriage." She shrugged. "Well, life will work out better for you and the earl's son. There is no one standing in the way of your bliss, and the groom is anxious enough."

"Too anxious," Lady Winslow announced suddenly.

"Mother?"

Knotting the bed linens between her fingers and looking unaccountably guilty, Lady Winslow bit at her bottom lip.

"Mother?" Arabella again prodded.

Lady Winslow flushed crimson. "We arranged it. The kiss, I mean. Annette and I agreed if you could just be shown a small, a very small, sampling of what the marital state might bring, you would be far more contented with the viscount than you have appeared to be thus far."

"Oh, what a discreet partner in crime you've turned out to be, Glenda," Lady de Veer snapped, tossing the remainder of the sandwich onto her plate.

It skipped off the porcelain and plopped to the floor.

Arabella grasped at the table. If she had not been seated, she would have fallen with the turning of the earth. "You-you set me up…to be compromised?"

Suddenly, she was on her feet, the motion rocking her cup of tea. The contents slopped over the sides.

"The two of you?"

"The three of us, if you include the viscount," her mother admitted tremulously. "It was his idea."

"Don't put this all upon his shoulders." Lady de Veer turned toward Arabella. "The poor man realized you refused to see him in a proper light. He only wished to turn you to his favor."

Arabella had no idea how to respond.

"He was only supposed to kiss you lightly, and we were right down the hall, mere footsteps away, just in case he became, er, inflamed. If I had thought, for even a moment, he would use force—"

"Nonsense! He didn't force Arabella to anything. Tell your mother such terrible slurs upon the viscount's character are misplaced."

"You wanted me to be disgraced so I would be forced to wed him?" The cucumber sandwiches Arabella had eaten rose and blocked her throat.

"Don't be ridiculous. I merely thought to nudge you a bit. In private, so your reputation was safe. I'm not as silly as you seem to think me," Lady Winslow retorted.

Arabella stared at her mother, then hurried to the window. If she could have flown out of it and away, she would have. The two women she thought cared for her most had actually conspired to force her into marriage. As if she wasn't already being forced by circumstances, love, and duty. How was she to deal with this information?

Behind her, the two argued about fault and intention. Arabella forced her attention away from their words, desperately seeking to calm herself before she said something she shouldn't. She searched the garden outdoors. The sun was lowering in the sky but still shone brightly over the wild-grown hedges so shadows like teeth and claws raked up the unmanicured lawn to bite at the side of the building.

It felt a great deal as if those shadow teeth were ripping into her chest. She took a deep breath, and then another. At least she now understood why Lady de Veer kept pushing the viscount at her. The woman still held a *tendre* for his father.

What was Lady Winslow's excuse?

"Mother," she finally said, turning from the window, "have you considered, in all your scheming, that Brynley was likely to become a witness to your little nudge? He was expected, after all. Were he the type, he could easily carry tales to ruin me. I am fortunate he is discretion itself."

"There is no need to sing his lauds," Lady Winslow snapped, then sighed. "In any event, when you marry the viscount, everything else will wash." She paused. "*If* you marry the viscount." She peeped at her daughter. "I truly am sorry, darling. You were so upset afterward. I-I hadn't considered the viscount might be…forceful. If he was—"

"Really, Glenda, it isn't as if he tried to pin her down and have his way with her. I feel I must defend him. He offered to make it right, so he must feel, and I have to say rightly so, Arabella encouraged his offer of marriage and likely his romantic overture as well. Quite a few advantageous unions have been brought about by the afterward preceding the main event, if you catch my meaning."

"As always, it would be hard to miss," Lady Winslow declared.

Arabella paced back across the room and threw herself into the chair again, aware her mother watched her.

"Moreover, you cannot deny the boy may have felt pressured by our ruse to approach Arabella more, um, precipitously than he might otherwise have done."

Lady Winslow muttered, "Perhaps." She sighed and looked down at her tea tray, but when she tried to lift it from her lap, the makeshift table shook so hard the contents upon it shifted.

Arabella grabbed and righted it at the last moment, narrowly avoiding a mess. Carefully, she placed the server upon the dresser. Her mother had eaten very little of the consommé Lady de Veer had brought over from her cook.

Her chest constricted.

"He will make Arabella an excellent lover and husband," Lady de Veer declared. "You worry this subject too much, Glenda. It grows tiresome."

"He has slugs for lips."

The words were out of Arabella's mouth before she even recognized she intended to say them. Further guilt weighted her chest as Lady Winslow's expression melted into sorrow.

If only she could, just once, hold her thoughts!

"Oh, Arabella, you are being preposterous," Lady de Veer declared, waving her hand.

"Is that what you think, darling?" her mother asked softly. "Truly? Or is it because the viscount doesn't have as much of an interest in your *Epic* as he pretends?"

"You noticed?"

"I'm not a completely befuddled old woman."

Arabella examined her mother again, so tiny in her lawn nightgown and caped robe. With the heavy tray gone, she made such a small bump in the sheets that if her head were detached she would have gone completely unnoticed. Lady Winslow's pale blue eyes watered, but the concern that filled them bothered Arabella more than the insipient tears.

Her anger fled, leaving her strangely bereft and exhausted.

She loved her mother. It was not hard to forgive her actions, crazy as they had been. The woman was desperate. They were both desperate. Lady Winslow didn't know that Gabriel would help them find another way out of their current predicament. He had to.

In the scheme of things, Justin's slug-lipped kiss

could be nothing but a fleeting disgust, rather like eating parsnips, which she despised. It could be nothing so long as she never had to kiss him again.

By the time she rejoined the conversation, her mother was past her qualms, agreeing Arabella must attend the Stapleton ball that evening in the hopes of patching up the rough spots with the viscount. Rather than argue, feeling almost numb from the revelations, Arabella flopped into her chair and picked up her cold tea. In one long swallow, she downed the contents.

If she had been hoping the brew would work some sort of magic, she was disappointed.

Lady de Veer finally stood and smoothed her gloves. "I must be off. Arabella, we shall come fetch you at half eight. Kildare and Manning will accompany us in their carriage. I do so appreciate arriving at an event upon the arm of a gentleman. De Veer never seems to understand a woman's need for escort. Well, that's men for you. Now, although it is a costumed affair, many will come in plain dress, so you needn't worry. I'll bring an extra mask for you, which will suffice. Oh, and I shall send my maid to tie your strings and finish your hair. She's quite a lazy thing and all enflamed over the cook's helper, who is quite beneath her station, but there you go. The heart is unpredictable." Lady de Veer glided through the doorway.

Suddenly, she gave a little scream and backpedaled into the room again. A shadow loomed. It crossed the portal, then resolved into the figure of a well-dressed male of tall proportions and wide shoulders who filled the width of the doorframe.

"Brynley!" Lady Winslow gasped from her bed.

"Gabriel!" Arabella exclaimed in delight.

Lady Winslow frowned and telegraphed her a pointed look.

"Good evening, ladies."

He bobbed his head. His gaze sought Arabella's before deliberately slanting toward Lady Winslow. Then, he tested the shadows at the corners of the room.

"Forgive the intrusion, but the front door was ajar, which concerned me. Is all well?"

"Brynley," Lady de Veer acknowledged. "Glenda, do you require my presence?"

Lady Winslow shook her head. "It is fine, Annette. We will see you later."

When Lady de Veer had gone, the baron tossed a small smile in Arabella's direction before approaching the bed.

"Please, excuse my presumption, Lady Winslow, but I've come to present a rather pressing matter."

"There is nothing so pressing it cannot await the morrow," Lady Winslow snapped as she sank back into the pillows. "Besides, I have my hands full preparing Arabella for the Stapleton ball this evening."

"The Stapleton ball?" Gabriel repeated.

He looked at Arabella, who shrugged.

"Apparently, my presence is required."

"Indeed." Lady Winslow turned her basilisk stare upon her daughter. "Arabella, do go ready yourself. I will converse with the baron and then seek my rest. Brynley, I shall meet you in the library if you insist upon conversation, which I must tell you, I find most ungentlemanly. If you would be so kind?" She gestured toward the door.

With a quick bob of his head, he took his leave.

"Mother—"

"Get dressed. We shall discuss the matter later."

Not wishing to over-excite her mother, she slid out of the room. Once in her own bedchamber, Arabella sat upon the edge of the bed and stared at the door, trying to imagine the topic of the conversation below.

She nibbled at the side of her nail, caught on the knife edge of dread and excitement.

Chapter 19

Lady Winslow reluctantly fluffed out her robe, wishing she might stay abed instead of facing her greatest fear. She could barely tie the belt around her waist, her fingers shook so mightily. She tried to take a breath and failed. The next inhalation was easier, proving her difficulty was not her illness this time.

That was to be expected. Facing the past was for stronger souls. She would have gladly left it where it lay, decrepitating and ignored.

Perhaps the only surprise was that Brynley had decided to seek redress for old grievances so late into their acquaintance. She had been expecting his knife at their throats long since. But maybe that had been his game. He had toyed with them, eased them into a sort of comfort, so his revenge, when enacted, would be much more terrible.

And, it would be, Glenda acknowledged with a sinking stomach, because like it or not, her beautiful, sweet, innocent Arabella had come to care for the instrument of their destruction. Brynley had played them all like pieces on the chessboard from the very beginning. Even that first evening, it had already been too late.

How very like his father he was proving to be.

After wrapping her long braid into a bun, Glenda stuck in some pins to hold it all in place. She was a long way from elegant and intimidating, but at least she was relatively presentable. She gathered what courage she could find within herself, a little surprised by how much of it there was.

Arriving at the library door not ten minutes later, she hesitated yet again, caught on the point of fleeing. If Arabella had just agreed to the viscount's proposal yesterday, then maybe Brynley's revenge could have been avoided. With the venerable Kildare and Manning titles publicly behind them, revenge would have been foolhardy.

Perhaps he would simply take the ring, the one tangible item she could give him, and leave them all in peace? Perhaps he only wanted that part of his father left in this world?

Now, who was being the foolhardy one?

Refusing to knock upon her door, she drew herself to her fullest height and simply opened it instead. Brynley leaned upon the ledge of the cold hearth, the burning candle next to him throwing a halo around his head. The flickering flame danced shadows and highlights over his chiseled features but left his eyes as bottomless and black as a dangerous well.

The polite man of tender expression and helpful deportment, the man who had pored over Arabella's dratted book and rapturously drawn figures and lines upon maps, was gone.

In his place stood the man rumored to squash his enemies with no more qualm than many had stepping upon an ant.

A shiver rolled up her spine. Her fingers shook, but she closed the door behind her. She was surprised to spy puzzlement in his expression, but then the emotion fled. Left in its place was icy, glacial calm.

"Well then," she murmured. "I have come, as you insisted."

"Please, sit," he said, motioning to the chair.

"I prefer to stand, thank you. I do not need to be dictated to in my own home."

Suddenly, he stood beside her, his speed in crossing the room impressive.

"I do not mean to order you about, Lady Winslow," he murmured as she instinctively shrank from him. He held out his arm slowly. "I merely thought you would be more comfortable if we talked while you were seated."

Her face heated with embarrassment. To cover that, she picked her way to the couch. When she was seated, he took the chair next to her.

"Do get on with it, Brynley. There is no point in drawing this out."

"Agreed. You seem to be aware of the subject I wish to discuss."

"Arabella," she agreed in a voice that sounded too much to her ears as a plea.

That would not help. He was not the sort of person who would be bent by abject entreaties to emotion.

"Indeed. Well, I have hardly been circumspect in my desires, although your daughter remains singularly unaware. I think, however, she is beginning to realize my feelings on the matter."

Glenda's heart sank.

"May we skip to the point where you tell me whether you intend to fight me?" he demanded.

It was the worst thing, then. It was everything she had feared.

Gasping silently, she cast a glance down at her white knuckles, frail against the deep blue of the dressing gown.

The robe was worn in places, mended in others, and it was just one more reason she cursed the man she had once loved with all her mind, body, and soul. Her husband, John Warwick, Earl of Winslow, had driven her to this moment as surely as if he were still alive and wielding the carriage reins. He had been a weak and foolish reprobate, and she missed him still.

Taking a deep breath, she forced herself to meet the demanding gaze. In the stern nobleman before her, encased in dark burgundy so rich it looked almost black, she saw nothing of her husband's brand of reckless abandon. Brynley's control spoke more of logic than desire.

Perhaps he could be reasoned with if emotions would not move him.

Glenda cleared her throat. "My lord, I entreat you to leave aside your intentions. You've shown Arabella kindness. Surely, you must have come to respect her, to realize her heart is…" She searched for a way to address the unaddressable. "What you wish will destroy her, and she is innocent of any wrongdoing. Do not punish her."

He appeared surprised, his eyes rounding before narrowing again as if he had not anticipated a refusal of his terrible proposition. Had he expected her to jump at any humiliation for the chance to fill their purse?

"Destroy? Punish?" Though his tone was mild, a tiny tick fluttered in the corner of his cheek, and a hard flame lit in his pupils. "I believe I am insulted. Whatever you think of me, Lady Winslow, you should remember I have willingly kept your family's secrets, any of which might have ruined both you and your daughter. I believe I have approached this matter honorably, which should be enough for you." His lips tightened. "In any case,

Arabella would want for nothing under my care. I can promise that." He paused and then said grimly, "Moreover, mine is a better offer than any other you will receive, I assure you."

"You think…" Her voice cracked with emotion, and she shook her head wildly.

He could not be reasoned with, after all.

"Can you not just leave us to our own affairs?"

The green of his eyes grew pale with suppressed anger. He jumped from his chair and paced to the window, his fists clenched at his side. Although there was little to see in the dark of night, he stared out anyway, rigid and offended. Waves of tension rolled from him even across the room. Finally, he turned.

"You believe Justin will be your savior. You are wrong. Even setting aside my strong belief Arabella would prefer my offer to his, you should know the louse is riddled with debt and hasn't a farthing to his name."

"Slurs do not become you, Brynley," she replied sharply.

"Regardless, I speak the truth. Let me be frank. He cannot save you. You may have heard I have lodged a suit to recoup both my uncle's and my cousin's titles. Without funds, without an outward façade of nobility, how is that reprobate to help either of you, now, when you are at the end of your abilities?" He shook his head, the anger seeming to drain from him. "You are naïve, and that naiveté will doom your daughter to a hell of which you can have no concept. I am offering you, her, another way out."

"I don't believe you."

Shards of fear suddenly cut at her skin because actually, she was terribly afraid she might. They had all heard the gossip surrounding the court case, but the rumors of Brynley's advantage were largely dismissed. The suit could be nothing but an empty gesture by a baron desperate to prove his antecedents better than those of his cousin. Still, although the titles mattered, if the viscount was without funds, without ancestral lands, they were indeed lost.

He drew in a long, audible breath. "Your first impression of me was troubled," he allowed. "I understand, and I am willing to offer you whatever assurances you might require, Lady Winslow, but one way or the other, I intend to have Arabella."

Glenda surged from the couch. "I will never allow it! You are no longer welcome here, my lord. Leave this house at once, and do not come back. You have very much overstayed your welcome with this-this…"

Her lungs constricted and collapsed.

Not now! She closed her eyes and fought to control her breathing. Not in front of him. Yet, with growing horror, Glenda recognized the signs. If she could only calm herself, there was air. It rushed all through the room. All she had to do was to settle her mind and body.

She clutched for oxygen, but her lungs came back empty.

Brynley's *coup de grace,* finally administered, laid his intentions bare. Glenda had feared just this eventuality from the moment she had found him seated with Arabella upon her bed. He would ruin them by taking her daughter as his mistress.

She wheezed, bending double.

The ring that had belonged to his father would go with Arabella now, a symbol of all that had been wrong between their families, a golden emblem of the baron's final, inevitable win. She had thought by allowing Brynley the time with her daughter, he would fall enchanted enough to forgo his revenge. Instead, he had merely come up with enough information to ruin them even if Arabella should reject his offer.

The room began to spin.

Arabella would never reject his offer. A mother knew when her daughter's heart had been captured. A mother knew when her daughter would believe there was no other choice left to them anyway, which there wasn't.

A blue film covered Glenda's eyes. She barely realized the baron was attempting to open the buttons of her robe and high-necked sleeping gown. She tried to raise her fingers to stop him, but even when he slit the collar with a small hunting knife from his pocket, she could not manage over her body's desperate essays for breath. Her legs gave out.

"You must be calm."

He grabbed her up in his arms as if she weighed no more than feathers before laying her upon the couch. Then, his fingers rubbed her temples with surprising gentleness.

"Breathe."

She couldn't resist. She couldn't push him away. All her efforts centered upon inhaling. As the minutes crept by and his touch remained gentle, she finally began to relax. She caught a full breath rather than the partial, and then another. She focused her lungs upon the rhythm of his massage, an extraordinary kindness she did not understand at all.

When she had recovered sufficiently, she grabbed his wrist. "I…will…be all right now. You…will find…your way…out."

He looked as if he might say more, but instead he simply stood, nodded politely, and took his leave.

Things were at a pretty pass indeed when it was up to her enemy to offer aid. She fought to breathe evenly. She had no idea what to do if the baron's words were correct. Where was the viable path toward a secure future if the viscount was impoverished?

With a sinking heart, Glenda realized perhaps there wasn't one.

Chapter 20

Gabriel left the library and paused by the hall mantel, lost in thought. He now had more questions than answers. At base, they all seemed to revolve around one central, unbelievable fact: Glenda Winslow was absolutely terrified of him.

He saw it in her eyes and in the way she instinctively shrank from his touch, though to her credit, she had tried to hide her reactions. It was more than the *contretemps* in Arabella's room the night of her soiree. It had to be. Though he had often been accused of being cold and controlling, no one had ever blasted him for instilling dread within the female heart. Such would be his cousin's domain.

Yet, if Lady Winslow feared him, why had she allowed him access to her daughter? Her convenient fit had forestalled any questions he might have asked.

In any considerations of his own future, he had never once imagined being denied a parent's blessing. His marriageability had long since been taken for granted. He had fully expected Lady Winslow to sob with gratitude at being saved from penury and an early grave. Having screwed his determination to the sticking point and expressed his desire to wed Arabella, he was quite flummoxed now by being rejected.

He could offer marriage to Arabella directly. She was of age to make her own decisions. Past it, even. After all, it had only been an ingrained politeness to seek out Lady Winslow first.

Gabriel wrinkled his nose. Now, having jumped precipitously, he had revealed his cousin's financial straits. Justin could no longer be considered a viable option. That narrowed Arabella's choices to just him, an overwrought, uptight, lowly baron who cared too much for Assyriology and not enough for normal pleasures.

He didn't want to be a requirement. He wanted to be a desire. Yet, weren't his wants a selfish thing, next to Arabella's need for a roof over her head, food in her belly, a mother alive, and salvation from whatever horrors Justin would certainly unleash? *Yes.* His reflection in the mantel mirror answered for him. His need for proof of affection was ridiculous. His qualms about his title suit and Arabella's potential involvement were silly.

She needed him to act, but her sick mother was against him. He was stymied, and it rankled.

There was another option. He could offer to purchase Arabella's copy of the *Epic*. He examined his reflection and smoothed down his hair as he weighed the potential and the risk.

Carefully, he folded the idea through his mind, seeking out the rough edges. Women of the Winslows' station could never simply accept funds from a man not their relation, but they could sell their possessions quietly. He had more than enough funds to ensure Arabella would be comfortable for a long, long time.

Indeed, he could offer so much he gave her the choice of her own future. It didn't have to be a baron or the streets. It could be a baron or nobody at all. Risky but a gamble worth making.

Crooking his neck, he eyed the long staircase.

Arabella rested in her room on top. He could grab his hat from the mounted side table, or he could walk up those stairs and make his proposition to her.

****

Arabella had meant to return to her room temporarily, a mere nod to her mother's dictates, before sneaking back and apprehending Gabriel below as he sought to leave.

Once in her bedchamber, she had made the mistake of sitting upon the bed to wait before descending. The pillow had looked so inviting she had laid her head upon it to pass the time. It seemed only an instant later the smell of vanilla and fir tickled her nostrils, dragging her from her dreams. Strong, powerful hands turned her gently onto her back. Instinctively, she reached out and touched fine-woven linen.

Lips parting in a silent gasp, she allowed her fingers to spread over his hard muscles, the grand width of his shoulders.

Opening her eyes, she met Gabriel's deep green ones, hazy now. Hungry. The features of his face were stone. He looked feral and hard, like some leonine creature poised to pounce, waiting until he was sure of his prey. He belonged in the *Epic*, in days when men were made of the stuff of heroes, able to battle enemy forces with both physical strength and intelligence.

Like Gilgamesh, Gabriel could climb the adventurer's path, seeking something others did not even see. If only she could join him on his journey.

Her back arched, seeking contact with his torso as need flared within her. How had she thought him safe, even bookish?

"I don't want to hurt you, Arabella," he growled. "Intentionally, or unintentionally. My control, it fails me, finding you thus, all warm and soft and sleepy." He stroked her cheek gently, and she shivered beneath that small caress.

"You won't hurt me. I'm not afraid." She reached up to clasp her hands around his neck to draw him toward her.

He came willingly but then pulled back at the last moment. She groaned.

"No, we…we cannot. Not yet."

He moved backward, but only the very smallest of distances. How much easier it would be if he were to take all decisions from her, even this last one. The burdens that dragged her down were so enormous she longed to slip out from under their punishing weight. Whether for an idyllic moment or a longer time, even if mere illusion, she wanted his strength to help carry her load.

More than that, she just plain wanted him. From the moment they had met, he had fired something within her, lit a fuse that burned slow and bright. It hurt, the flame.

"Please," she whispered.

She squirmed beneath him, lifting her body as she clung to his wide shoulders, rubbing the length of him like Kismet against the bed linen. He was still so close it was an easy thing to do.

Lightning speared through her and then pooled in her lower belly and beneath. Hot caramel sweetness and acid need radiated through her veins.

"Listen to me, Arabella. I have done the right thing and asked your mother's permission, but I was denied. That leaves me only one option, and to-to make love with you now…"

"I want you to show me, Gabriel. I need you to show me."

164

He shook his head, looking pained. "I am trying to free you from compulsion, not add to it."

"Don't you desire me even a little?" she begged, unashamed to be asking because the hot need whipped her to do so.

Gabriel groaned. Then suddenly he was there, his lips hard upon hers, seeking, tormenting, driving the need inside her hotter still, although she had imagined his kiss would calm her turbulent blood.

In the taste of his lips' first bruising, she felt the full force of his confusion and his own need. Reveling in it, her hands moved upward to wrap in the silky blackness of his hair, trying to pull him even closer to her. But he resisted. A mewl of displeasure crossed her lips because somehow, she needed…

More.

As if the universe had tilted upon its axis, her desperation, rather than increasing the pressure of his kiss, instead gentled him.

"Shh. Easy," he murmured, his breath against her lips. "Open for me."

As his mouth softened, hers followed and rounded, then parted to allow his tongue access. He used it to stroke her own, toying, swirling, first nesting here and then flitting there, until she almost screamed as his instrument of torture, wielded like a feather-tipped sword, drew the very breath from her body.

When he ended their kiss, he pulled away abruptly and jumped to stand. Breathing raggedly and audibly, he turned away. She brought her hand to her lips that still tingled and pulsed.

"How does that compare with my cousin's kiss?" he demanded, rotating back. In his sternly held chin and glittering glass eyes, fire raged.

The blood pooled between her legs again, a wanting that thrummed with insistence.

Instinctively, languorously, she smiled and stretched, delighting in how his gaze moved like a dark wave over her body. Peeping at him mischievously from beneath her lashes, she murmured, "Far less like slugs, my lord. More like butterflies, and warm burnt butterscotch, and the deepest of crimson wines."

Her tongue snaked out to touch her upper lip as she savored the lingering flavor of him and tested the fullness that remained from his touch.

Gabriel groaned. Then he suddenly laughed, a harsh, ragged sound. "You slay me." With a sigh and a shake of his head, he sat next to her on the bed. "Push over."

She did, but not before leaning across and grabbing his hand. Brazen enough, now that he had finally kissed her, she held his gaze while her tongue traced the cuneiform symbol for "heart" across his palm. When his fingers convulsively closed, she laughed softly, releasing her grip before falling back upon the pillows.

"Arabella, what you want…it is impossible. If I ruin you, I must marry you, and I cannot do so when your choosing is constrained by necessity. Later, when you have options, I will rush you to an altar. I cannot ruin you."

He was everything she had ever wanted and never dreamed of meeting. Tall, dark, and handsome, but he was more than that too. He was trustworthy; she knew it to her core. He was protective. He didn't want to hurt her, so he didn't want to touch her. Yet, he desired her because a kiss like that *couldn't* lie.

Her body told the truth as well. Though she hadn't

known this level of desire could exist, she had to resolve the needs within her. Even if he didn't stay past the next few moments, the memory of more kisses and whatever came next would carry her through the rest of her lonely life.

It was such a relief to know he didn't have slugs for lips.

By some grace, he was here, on her bed. Maybe the *Epic* seduced him, or maybe the same hunger that drove her pressed him to court their mutual destruction. It didn't matter. The pain of his parting could await tomorrow.

Let him be confused by her actions. He had kissed her finally, with lips so fine, and soft, and hard, and delicate, that all she wanted was for him to do it again.

****

On his palm burned the cuneiform symbol, a house with a cross in it, tilted to the side. The symbol that meant "heart" could be extrapolated to mean "love." Lightning flashed from his toes to the ends of his hair as she traced the mark. He squeezed his hand into a fist, but the fire-writ message did not die.

Confronted with her spread golden curls, strong curves, and those limpid violet eyes, Gabriel knew only a far stronger man could have resisted her. He was not so valiant. Only his mind remained obstinate, reminding him with each pulsebeat she was an innocent of good name, virtue, and family.

Ruthlessly pushing down the fierce desire she ignited, he said, "We need to be sensible about this, Arabella."

She smiled, an innocent smile with wanton edges. "I don't want to be sensible."

"Then what do you want of me, damn it? Do you

want to see how far you can drive me before I simply destroy you and be done with it? Don't you understand what such an action will do to us in time?"

"If there would be more kissing, then I consent. Ruin me, Gabriel. *Please*."

Even his blood stilled. He couldn't move. He couldn't breathe. He couldn't think. There were only her words swirling in his head and her invisible mark upon his palm.

"I want you, Gabriel," she continued softly, "and I think you want me."

"You don't understand what you're saying," he rasped when finally he could find a voice. "You cannot know what you are driving me to do."

She smiled. "You're right, of course. I haven't the vaguest notion of what comes next, not really. Women are kept far too sheltered. But I trust whatever it is, you will do it well. You'll show me what to do in turn, won't you?"

His sharply drawn breath and soft curse were all the warning he gave her before he swooped, released from his strange ethical paralysis by her words. This time, he had no intention of pulling away. There was no need to stop because she wanted him, and he would make it all right afterward.

Her mother be damned. His conscience be damned. His fear and common sense be damned.

The symbol for love burned even hotter. This was an inferno, a lightning-strike, the interior white blaze of a bonfire so hot it melted metal, let alone flesh.

As the soft down mattress gave way beneath their weight, he felt as if they were more than sinking into a bed. He pulled her up simultaneously, up and up; his hands twisted in her glorious hair. He tugged out her pins, delighting in the gardenia perfume that flooded his senses, all while he kissed her everywhere he could reach.

Finally, he forced himself to pull back. She groaned with frustration, and he smiled as he bent to trace more kisses along the sensitive skin of her neck, across her shoulder bones, and down to the valley covered by the simple fabric and lace.

When the dress proved too much of a hindrance, he growled and moved his mouth over the linen to wrap around the fine point within.

His eyes closed, and the bed swayed.

****

Arabella thought the world would explode.

Violent sensations chased up and down her limbs, and her whole body quivered as she called his name and held her fingers against his head like it was the only thing keeping her in line with the spinning earth.

As the fabric of her dress grew damp, the wet cool against the fire of her skin, she mewled again, shivered, and moaned as one possessed.

Gabriel. All she could think was his name, and the pain and the longing were so intense she might just die of it.

****

Each cry from her sweet lips made him harder, and he already felt as if his body were carved of jade. Never had he felt so strong, so essentially male. It was what she did to him, her open responses, the way her nipple hardened to a little bud beneath his tongue.

He moved his mouth to her other breast and it likewise quickened, and for a moment he was in her body, feeling the things he did to her.

When he pulled his mouth away, she opened her

eyes, so heavy-lidded it was a wonder they could open at all. In those purple depths, a wanting reflected to match his own, along with a faith that humbled him even as it angered him beyond reason.

She trusted him. He was about to betray that trust.

To warn her and let her know her confidence was misplaced, he brutally rent the now damp fabric from neckline to hem.

"That is what I will do to you, Arabella. I will tear your body apart, and I will fill it. Just as this gown will never be one whole piece of cloth again, there is no going back," he growled, running his hand over her curves.

"Do it," she whispered.

He wanted to cry. There was no way to resist her, no way to say no.

Deliberately he tore the shift so she lay there, naked, upon the tatters. A part of him knew she must object to such treatment. He hoped she would be terrified. If she shrank from him just a little, modestly tried to hide her unfamiliar lengths from his lascivious gaze, he might find the willpower to stop. Already her innocence flayed him like a whip.

Instead, she lay panting, silent, watchful. Delighted. His hands reached out to grab her, to stroke that flawless skin, the curves of which jutted and rolled so any man would find himself touching her, even if the man were dead ten years.

"Will it hurt?"

The prick of tears at the corners of his eyes startled him. "Aye, it will hurt," he replied simply enough, defeated.

"Will you tell me before that part? I don't want to miss the other parts out of fear of the pain." Arabella held out her arms.

She was singular. She was an original. She was simply extraordinary.

Groaning, he swooped down again to catch her lips, to set the fire raging even higher as his hands found her hips, pulled at her buttocks. Then gently, like the butterflies she had compared his lips to, he allowed his fingers to find the golden, moist center of her longing.

"Ah!"

Her hips arched against his caress. His lips fluttered over her breasts, tracing lines, as his fingers gently moved against the white, hot heat of her.

When her world exploded into a million pieces, he knew he couldn't last a moment longer.

Cursing his impatient body even as he freed himself from his pants, he pushed between her legs to the very portal of her womanhood. Slowly, ever so slowly, he glided in on shimmering dew, gritting his teeth at the amazing tightness of the passage. His shirt stuck to his body as if he had run a mile under a summer sun.

When he felt the obstruction to his progress, he halted. He could still go back. Her maidenhead had not yet been breached.

Before he could tell her, she took a deep breath and then wrapped her hands about his neck, surging upward while bearing down upon his length. As he impaled her, he caught her small scream between his lips, swallowing her pain as he used his greater strength to keep her still.

"Shh," he whispered against her tongue. "I've got you."

He thought he might well die of the waiting. His heart beat faster than he could imagine his body could bear, but despite every instinct that urged him to move, he held very still until slowly, gradually, her muscles loosened around him.

"My love," he whispered, kissing her neck again, stroking every part of her he could touch.

Under his questing fingers, he was relieved to find her velvety pink nipples again budding to rose points. Her body undulated against his as she instinctively sought another release.

It was his undoing. With a giant roar, he spilled into her with unending spasms until he was completely drained, limp, and heady with momentary satiation. Caught on waves of pleasure, he stilled, flew, and then floated away.

Collapsing beside her, he was held in bliss he had never known. If perfection could be captured in an infinitely small space of time, he imprisoned it.

Then he was rampant again, alive and ready, as her body, still connected, twisted against his.

He opened his eyes.

"I love you, Gabriel," she said quietly.

It wasn't only his manhood full nigh to bursting.

His skin wrapped too tight and feeble to contain his explosive joy.

Chapter 21

The evening shadows were lengthening into true night by the time Gabriel managed to bestir himself. Even then, for many handfuls of minutes, he could only lie still, stunned by his good fortune. Within his arms, he held the most gorgeously sensual female that had ever been born. Except the proof of her innocence had clearly been felt, and the blood of it visible upon her sheets, he would never have believed her unused to bed sport. Like a siren, she had lured him to his doom.

Not that he minded. His gaze roamed over the soft incline of her pale pinked cheeks that bore too much a pallor of indoors. When they were married, he would have her outside for days in the sun, reading and playing and doing all of the things he had never done. Years ago, Peter had convinced him to build a secluded grotto, complete with a deep fountain, wide benches, and succulent plants. It was time to make use of the space.

They would need a special license to wed. He pressed a small kiss to Arabella's forehead. While he had hoped to woo her with honeyed words and delicate gestures, to be certain of her feelings when eventually they did marry, she had already said she loved him. Those words were more than enough to settle his silly qualms about duress.

At this juncture, they had to be enough. He had already ruined her, after all.

"Come, Arabella," he murmured, dancing his fingers

through her glorious hair as he attempted to stir her into wakefulness. "It's going on ten, and we should not be caught thus entwined."

"Ten?" Her eyes sprang open as she jolted upright. "Oh, no, it can't be! I have to get ready for the ball."

"Must you attend?" he demanded, dragging her back to the pillows.

When she nodded, he sighed. "Well, if you must, then so must I. Now that I am to be your husband, I have the legal as well as the moral right to protect you from Justin's plotting."

Arabella sat up again, slowly this time, the long strands of iridescent curls covering her from Gabriel's eyes. "Husband?" she exclaimed, smiling. "How long have I been asleep?"

Gabriel smirked, then laughed. Propping himself up on one elbow, he said, "You are correct. I fear I haven't even had the delicacy to ask you for your hand, Lady Arabella, but perhaps that's because I've been so busy taking all the other sweet parts of you instead." His gaze swept the length of her, from her naked top to her sheet-wrapped bottom.

Arabella was no longer smiling.

Quietly, she demanded, "Do you imagine your actions here require you marry me?"

"I would hope they do. A better man would have waited until after the vows were said, but I might at least correct my impetuosity." When her eyes grew large, he reached out and pushed a strand of hair behind her ear. "As I mentioned earlier, though I fear you neglected my words, I have already asked your mother for her blessing. She refused me, but the ground has been laid. Our actions here merely confirm we should wed with haste."

The tenseness in her shoulders relaxed.

"Now that you mention it, I do recall something said to that effect." She shook her head. "How did such a startling bit of news slip by me?"

He chuckled. "You were focused on more immediate topics. Speaking of…"

Gabriel reached for her, but she jumped from the bed, oblivious to her naked state. He wasn't. The long lines of her waist, the lush curves of her hips, breasts, and buttocks, set him sweating as he resisted clambering after her.

"Why did my mother refuse you?" Arabella asked, gazing about, presumably searching for a robe. "She knows better than anyone I need to marry." She paused and assessed him from the corner of her eye. "I'm sorry."

"I am not offended, certainly not after this." He gestured at the bed and settled into a more temperate state, despite her nakedness. "Any concerns I might have had regarding your affections are no longer relevant. We will have a happy marriage," he stated confidently, "and if overcoming a few pesky concerns like poverty and ill-health coincide with our desires, so much the better."

Arabella tipped her chin, but her forehead crinkled.

"I'm not certain why your mother objected to my request, but I will resolve the matter. Later. After she's rested."

"Rested?"

Uncomfortable, he admitted, "Unfortunately, she was overtaken by a tiny breathing episode as we spoke. No, don't worry, she's fine now," he added quickly, as Arabella's eyes grew large as plates. "I cut the collar of her sleeping gown."

"You what?" She rushed back toward the bed. "I

must go to her. Stop looking at me, will you, and help me find a robe?"

"Stop looking? You'd have to blind me, I'm afraid."

Arabella huffed and tried to yank the sheet from his grasp to wrap it around herself, which she almost managed until Gabriel reached out and pulled her down onto his lap instead.

"Shh," he whispered, holding her until she stopped trying to pull away. When she settled, glaring, he added, "You don't need to hide your beautiful body from me, and you don't need your robe. Your mother was fully recovered when I left her. I swear it. She will be sleeping. Your worry is unnecessary. Please. Do not be distressed."

It was a few more moments to convince her, but when finally her shoulders relaxed again, Gabriel did too.

He ran his hands over the soft skin of her arms. When she leaned in and pressed her lips against his, he sank into the kiss. Inexperienced, by starts too intense and by stops too light, Arabella nevertheless used such sweet torture to make him hard again and ready.

"Again?" she whispered, trailing her fingertip down his chest.

"Again and again, every night you want me for the rest of our days." But when her fingers trailed downward, he caught her hand, turning it over to place a kiss upon her palm. "Except right now, because you will be quite sore for a while, although this will have been the only time you'll have experienced actual pain."

"I'm not so sore," she teased.

"You will be. We have our whole lives ahead of us for pleasure, Arabella. I am more than happy to lie entwined, but gently. Platonically, as it were. I do not wish to ruin our future pleasure in any way."

Suddenly, her smile dropped. "Do we, Gabriel? Have our whole lives ahead of us? Do you mean what you say? And even if you do, how can we marry when to do so might kill my mother?"

"I've been considering the matter. If we are wed by special license, we can lessen her anxiety about the planning. Furthermore, I expect the court to grant me the Kildare title, possibly by next week's end. That will soothe Lady Winslow's doubts, I'm certain."

Arabella bit her lip. "I don't believe it is a question of title."

"My only real concern is Justin."

Guilt flashed across her features as she studied the bed linen. "I'd forgotten all about him. I haven't played very fair, have I? Leading him on." She shook her head, her golden curls bouncing the candlelight. "He will be hurt when he discovers I will not wed him."

Gabriel gritted his teeth. "Do not waste tender feelings upon that viper."

"How can I not? I am the one who misrepresented my affections."

"He is the king of misrepresentation. He is capable of many things you could never imagine, all of them more horrible by turn. You must not trust him."

Arabella nodded, but he wasn't reassured.

"I am deadly serious, Arabella. If Justin catches wind of our plans to wed, he is certain to disrupt them. He wants something from you, something I cannot fathom."

He looked at her pointedly, hoping she might confess, and equally terrified she would. But Arabella merely raised a delicate eyebrow and glared so that he quickly reviewed his words.

"You are perfect, especially for me. Just not perfect

for him." Gabriel paused. "Has he touched upon any subjects with you that were...unusual, or that might explain his interest?"

"Not at all, unless the fashions of Society can be considered unusual. He says he is interested in the *Epic*, but we both know that's not quite true." She sighed as she pulled away from his embrace and rose from the bed. "I am committed to going to the ball tonight, and my mother must not be made to suffer any further setbacks just now. Will you truly attend?"

"Yes."

"Wonderful."

Gabriel didn't believe he imagined the relief in her voice.

"The viscount and his father will accompany Lady de Veer and me so that I won't be alone with Justin. There is nothing to fear. Now, if you wouldn't mind grabbing a shift from the top drawer and that corset," she said, nodding her chin toward the dresser, "and lacing it so tight I can't draw a decent breath, I shall be much obliged."

For a minute, he contemplated denying her but thought better of it. Tomorrow, he could meet with her mother again. They both could. Arabella was right. If they pushed Lady Winslow into another fit so soon after this last one, they risked her very life.

He fetched the items and watched hungrily as Arabella's beautiful skin disappeared beneath the linen. When she placed the corset around her waist, he drew her laces so tight, she gasped.

"Should I loosen them?" he whispered, nipping her ear with his teeth.

She mewled and swayed into him in response. As her

backside brushed the most sensitive part of him, he laid his forehead against her crown and took a deep, steadying breath. How long did it take a woman to recover from her first bout of lovemaking? Why didn't he know the answer to this all-important question?

"Come," he said, voice gruff as he gently pushed her away from his body. "Let's fasten your gown. Then, you may walk me to the door, pointing out which stairs creak so we won't risk waking your mother."

Quickly, they finished dressing, watched over by the cat who seemed unfazed by their antics. As Gabriel stood in the open doorway, Arabella took care to light a long burning candle within a tall glass hurricane.

"For Kismet. He's afraid of the dark."

Gabriel laughed but then suddenly stilled. Slowly, he looked around the hallway as the hair upon the back of his neck stood up. Someone was watching them.

Expecting to find a furious and outraged Lady Winslow emerging from the shadows, his gaze instead encountered nothing but empty air.

It must be the cat. He rubbed the tickle from the back of his neck. It was no wonder the ancient Egyptians worshipped felines. They were uncanny creatures at the best of times and positively spooky at others.

He smiled at his own imaginings. He was overtired and anxious and newly given to megrims. Once he safely wed Arabella and removed her to his home and protection, he might finally be able to sleep through the night once more.

As he had proved, over and over, this house was far too easy to break into.

Chapter 22

"Damnable, conniving, double-crossing, bob-tail bitch," Justin swore, pouring himself another tumbler of gin. It was his third within the half-hour, and his father frowned.

"Yes, so you've said, and no one is arguing with you, but do you think it wise to imbibe so freely at present? We leave within minutes to collect the gel, and we can't jeopardize all our plans just because Darkie beat you to the finish. We must be ready to strike." Robert Manning stuffed another dried apricot into his plump mouth and sucked greedily at his fingers.

"Father, must you?" Justin demanded, disgusted.

"It's going to be a long drive, stuck with three simpering women. Annie, I can stomach, especially when she's naked and on top of me, but the presence of the other two will require I forego such diversions."

"Then I thank heaven for their attendance. I do not wish to watch you swive that loose bag of jelly. Her age and reputation render her beneath your standing."

"She will have her uses this evening; you will see."

Justin slammed the lid back on the crystal container with such force the clear ringing tones sent up a vibration among the other decanters on the tray. There were few books on the shelves to muffle the sound, as literary pursuits were not the Kildare habit, not to mention such tomes cost a great deal of money to acquire and preserve.

When their debts mounted excessively, it had been their habit to sell the volumes off piecemeal, and so far as Justin could tell, no one had missed a single treatise. The sad part was, the decanters would have to go next.

"I tell you, Father, I refuse to marry that piece of baggage."

"Perspective, my boy. Our plans yet hold. You searched her room after the lovebirds left, and you found nothing, so we still need her, but not for much longer, eh?"

"I found bloodstains on the sheets, bloodstains I should have put there!" Justin fumed.

"And you're certain you searched every nook and cranny for the ring?"

"Yes, yes, of course, I did. Her every drawer, robe, dress pocket, and box. All revealed nothing. Over this past week, I have also combed through every room and every object in that house. I cannot imagine where they are hiding the blasted ring, but I tell you, Father, if we do not find it quickly, we will have to risk fabricating the seal from memory." He downed his drink, then set about refilling his tumbler. "She will wear Darkie upon her skin now like a stench that won't wash. I cannot bear it."

His father helped himself to another apricot. "Your emotions are needlessly turbulent, for if you would just cool your head, you would quickly realize Lady Arabella's spoliation works to our favor. By marrying her now, you will steal from Darkie the thing he loves most." The earl paused. "The timing, actually, couldn't be better."

Justin's simmering anger receded enough so he might be able to maintain the necessary façade. His father was right, as always.

In a matter of hours, success should be his.

He tossed back another drink and straightened his collars. Lady Arabella would pay for her lightskirt ways.

She would pay in very painful ways indeed.

****

Arabella was nigh on hysterical, although she strove to hide it. After spending the most glorious span of hours with Gabriel, she had come back to her room to find her candle out, the hurricane tilted, and her bedcovers pulled back to reveal the dark stains she had taken such pains to hide.

Someone had seen the evidence. Someone had been in her room, but if not her mother, then who?

"I'm certain Kismet knocked into the glass, extinguishing the flame. There is no need to excite yourself, darling," Lady Winslow replied mildly. "I assure you no one has been breaking into bedchambers to douse flames, especially as we have no servants."

Lady Winslow turned but suddenly veered and reached for the lintel.

"I'm fine, I'm fine," she said, waving Arabella off.

"No, you're not, Mother," Arabella replied, trying to hide her panic under firm resolve. "You must lie down."

"I shall, right after I see you off." Her mother sat down heavily upon the end of the bed. "Let me just rest here a moment. I am grateful to Annette for taking you out in Society when I am so clearly unable, but her tardiness is frustrating."

"Not today. I don't even wish to go." Except she did, suddenly, now that Gabriel would also attend.

She turned to her mirror again and pinched her cheeks. The pink that blossomed was becoming. For once, she did not appear tired, despite the time she had spent in paradisal exercise between the sheets. Instead, she felt unusually invigorated.

Lady Winslow wheezed, and Arabella quickly pivoted upon her stool, though there was nothing she could do to help her mother.

"You can't breathe for me, darling," Lady Winslow said softly.

"I can try."

"Do not bite your lip when you worry."

"Yes, Mother."

"Common air is priceless when you cannot get enough, is it not? But come, I see that Annette's girl fastened your laces and gown, but whyever didn't she do something more with your hair?"

Arabella's stomach suddenly righted. She had forgotten Lady de Veer had promised to send a maid. The girl must have been the one who had disarranged the room. Relief washed through her. How silly to have imagined Justin had come calling, only to skulk about upstairs.

After quickly running a brush through Arabella's hair, her mother pinned it up in a simple style. With a last pat, Lady Winslow asked, "Darling, you do still have the ring your father gave you? The one with the mythological figure?"

"The griffin carved into that unusual yellow stone?" Arabella adjusted her spectacles and pinched her cheeks once more. "The one for which the pawn refused to pay more than pennies because it has so little value?"

Lady Winslow crossed toward the fireplace again, then traced her fingers over the ledge and moved an inexpensive ceramic figurine of roses. "Yes. I'm sorry, darling. I know how fond you are of the piece, but I'm afraid we require even the small amount it can fetch."

For once, news of their penury didn't unduly bother Arabella. Gabriel would see to setting right their fortunes. It was a wonderful benefit of marrying a man she adored, this sudden ease over their financial condition.

"Might I give it to you tomorrow?"

Her mother laughed, a happy, light sound. "Oh, certainly, you wouldn't want me to see your secret hiding cache beneath that loose floorboard there," she said, eyes sparkling, as she pointed toward the board in question.

"You knew?" Arabella demanded, smiling as well.

Lady Winslow shrugged. "I am not, as I remind you often, quite as vacuous as you think me."

"I am only grateful you have not gotten it into your head to rob me of my cache of dried flowers and pieces of lace."

"I am the dastardly sort to do so, that's true." Her mother made a face that looked silly.

The two of them laughed together, and it lifted Arabella's spirits to see her mother so.

Turning back toward the mirror, she considered her aged-lace gown, the very one in which she had made her late debut into Society. Having daringly decided to forego the fichu, she worried about being on display, though the neckline was high enough not to garner scandalized glances. There was a look in her eyes, however, a sort of feverish expression, and maybe something hungry, that made the dress more risqué. Lady Winslow hadn't seemed to notice. Perhaps no one else would, either.

Perhaps Gabriel would.

As if reading her mind, her mother suddenly blurted, "Promise me you will not go off with Brynley, should he attend."

Arabella started with surprise. "Brynley? He doesn't usually frequent these events, you know."

"Neither do you. Promise me," her mother repeated.

She hesitated but then choosing her words carefully, said, "Fine. I promise not to go off to the library and pore over some dusty old tome with him, all right?"

"You absolutely must not. He has proved he will not offer marriage, even when caught in a compromising position."

Despite her resolve moments before, she couldn't help objecting. "But he has." She paused, bit her lip, then blurted, "He has asked me to marry him, and I intend to accept."

"What?" Lady Winslow visibly paled as she clutched at the mantel.

"You needn't act so surprised. He told me he talked to you about it earlier, but you refused him for some mystifying reason."

"We spoke, yes, but I thought…was that what he was offering? Marriage?" Lady Winslow shook her head, confusion evident upon her face. "But I thought…surely, what he meant was…I…" Her mother's mouth opened into a round "o" before her eyes suddenly narrowed with suspicion. "And how have you learned what passed in the library only a short time ago?"

It was Arabella's turn to lose her words, not having had much practice in deception. For a moment, she considered lying but swore softly under her breath instead. "Gabriel came upstairs to tell me what had happened. To ask me to wed him."

"Brynley was here? In your room?" Lady Winslow screeched. "And you are using his given name?"

"Mother."

"No, no, Arabella, you must listen to me," Lady Winslow cried, suddenly aflutter. "Brynley is not honorable in his intentions, no matter what he might have told you. You must have nothing else to do with him," her mother begged, charging her daughter and clasping her hands.

The urgency in her voice was mirrored in her eyes. Lady Winslow was afraid. How bewildering.

"Mother, you are over-reacting. Perhaps you did not understand. He means to marry me," she replied, careful to keep her voice calm and reassuring, and most of all, to enunciate clearly.

"He means to destroy us!"

"That's nonsense, Mother. Gabriel, er, Lord Brynley, is the most tender-hearted, trustworthy man I've ever met."

"He is a villain!" Lady Winslow cried. She dropped Arabella's hands and stumbled to the fireplace where she stood, gripping the mantel. "Are you in love with him?" she demanded, face turned away.

Arabella's hands jerked upward. She clasped them together at her waist instead. "I am," she admitted softly. "I hadn't even realized it until today."

"Oh no." Lady Winslow exhaled roughly. She took a deep wheezing breath as she leaned her head against the ledge. "No, no, you mustn't be."

"Mother…"

Arabella approached her carefully. Lady Winslow raised her head. She wore a look of deep despair and panic, as if everything they possessed was being fed to a fire.

"You do not believe he is evil. Fine," Lady Winslow whispered. "But believe this: the man is like your father

186

in the worst regard because he cares only for his desires, and those desires, be they cards or business dealings or Assyriology, will always take precedence to the woman he marries. Do you understand me? He will leave you alone, your heart shattered, unwilling, and unable to go on until your only prayer is for release, either your death or his. That's the only place marriage to a man like him will take you."

Stunned, Arabella blinked. "Father hurt you badly, I know…"

"He nearly destroyed me." She looked down and then up again. "You were a child. You did not see or understand the way it was when he touched me, or the way my entire being focused to a tiny point when his lips brushed my skin. Love?" Her voice warbled. "I think the word too calm to describe what I felt for John Winslow, even unto the day he died. Even," she admitted slowly, "until today."

In the silence that followed, the sound of a carriage rolling to a stop in front of the house reached into the room. If Lady Winslow noticed, she gave no indication.

"I loved him," she continued in a ragged whisper, "but I hated him too, and even though the love didn't die, not exactly, the hate grew beside it, intertwining until I couldn't tell where one emotion stopped and the other started. I felt myself splintering, caught between adoration and loathing. I turned bitter. I became someone I despised. It was only you, Arabella, and seeing your pain at my turning into some shrew that enabled me to push everything I was becoming aside." She paused. "Do you remember visiting Bath when you were five?"

"Vaguely," Arabella replied, curious despite her mother's upset. Lady Winslow rarely spoke of her

187

husband, except in the most general of terms.

"We were there, taking the waters. One afternoon, as I strolled along the forest path, I came across your father making love to another woman. Right there, not a few paces into the trees, they had laid a simple blanket. Pedestrians promenading on the mall below might have seen them. I thought my heart would quite literally break. Later, he told me he had seduced her only because she had promised to stake him for that night's game, which, lord help him, seemed cause enough for the man. Before that conversation, however, I had taken up his pistol, intent upon returning to that cursed blanket. I would have killed him, Arabella, had I not happened upon you with your nurse, perambulating in the sun-filled streets."

"Mother."

"I saw the sun glinting off your impossible hair, and I knew I couldn't hurt you by killing him. I couldn't leave him. I couldn't stay with him. I couldn't do much of anything, so I decided to simply…survive. For you. But the only way I could do so was to build a wall between reality and…and the world, I suppose. I ignored those facets that distressed me and focused only upon the positive, happy parts of my life. You. My friends." She paused and then laughed. "Lord help me; it was easier once he was dead."

"I'm so sorry, Mother," Arabella replied, her heart tearing for the woman who clung to the mantel with trembling fingers.

Taking a deep breath, Lady Winslow continued gently, "This love you are beginning to feel for the baron will destroy you, Arabella. Even were he an honorable man, which he most assuredly is not, the only passion he feels is for his books and his business. He is incapable of providing you with an equal love, for his nature is too cold. Wed to him, over time, his uncaring will crush your soul, day by day, until you are flattened into nothing, just as I was. That is the only result when a woman loves a man in unequal measure." She paused. "On the other hand, should you marry Manning, the two of you might quite companionably get through life."

"Companionably?" Arabella was shaken more than she would like to admit by her mother's vehemence.

"A lack of passion in marriage is a stabilizing force, darling." Lady Winslow wiped her eyes with her fingers.

"Even so, I don't think I like the viscount," Arabella said slowly. "There is something not quite right about him."

A peremptory knock sounded at the downstairs door.

"There are things you don't know about Brynley's family, his father…" Her mother's gentle eyes fumed, and she shook her head as her lips thinned. "There is no time now, but I beg you to believe Brynley is not who you think he is."

"Gabriel has never tried to hide his motives, Mother. I am well aware he requires my copy of the *Epic* because translating it will make his reputation. He has never tried to pretend otherwise, and I understand and support his need." She paused. "It is not love on his part." Her admission burned into her own brain, her own heart. She tried to shake away the terrible avalanche set to bury her. "But I do believe he holds me in high regard nonetheless."

"Arabella, you must heed me."

There were footsteps in the downstairs hall. They were male and heavy.

"If the viscount strays, ignores you, or treats you like

a pet, your heart won't shatter. If he looks at you with careless indifference, you won't wish for death. The smell of another woman's perfume will not suffocate you. His disinterest in your opinions will not slay you. To marry Brynley, however, given what you feel and what you admit he does not, even were he an honorable man, which he is not—I repeat, which he is not—is to subject yourself to a torture beyond endurance. I know. I faced it. And only by the grace of Heaven did I survive."

Each word struck deep within Arabella. She had told Gabriel she loved him, hadn't she? And he had said nothing back. In the height of ecstasy after making love, she had not noticed overmuch. Now, with her mother's words in her ears, her perspective on her suitors shifted as her prior joy turned to dust.

The winds of logic had effortlessly blown her happiness away, and in its place, remained barren, empty spaces too blighted to refill.

Chapter 23

Though it was only the distance of a few blocks, the trip to the Stapleton fete crawled. Seated beside the viscount, grasping the mask Lady de Veer handed her, Arabella tried not to break. Her spine and shoulders were stiff from holding herself upright against the ruts on the London roads; every bump aimed to send her flying onto the viscount's lap.

Her mother might for once comment favorably upon her rigid posture.

Matters weren't helped by Lord Kildare's presence. He sat opposite her and seemed to delight in accidentally bumping knees. An expression rode his face she didn't understand, as if he were about to savor a delectable bite of ambrosia. It disconcerted her.

"I notice, Lady Arabella, you wear no rings," the earl purred, inspecting the length of her as if she were a platter of very nice beef. "Surely, you must have one or two?"

Arabella glanced down at her gloved fingers. "I don't particularly care for rings, my lord. They weigh down my hands and prevent me from writing clear strokes."

"Why, what an odd thing for a woman to say." He laughed. "I thought all women were jewelry-mad."

"We are wrong sometimes, my lord." She resisted another pull toward the viscount's lap.

Lady de Veer caught her eye and scowled, then trilled in a way that sounded forced. "What I believe Lady

Arabella means, my lord, is we are not the avaricious creatures men believe us to be."

The earl sent her mother's friend a pointed look. She laughed again.

Silence lengthened.

He cleared his throat, fiddled with the bow at his neck, and scowled. Finally, his leg bumped Lady de Veer's.

"Oh yes!" she exclaimed. "Right. Er, um, tell me, my lord, about the lovely stickpin you wear. Quite stunning. Has it meaning?"

The earl pressed his lips together and simpered at Arabella. His fingers touched the stickpin on his lapel. "I did wonder when one of you pretty things would take notice of my stunning ensemble."

He was dressed in the guise of Henry VIII, complete with feathered hat, draped skirt, and hose. He also wore an excessive amount of jewelry and a great many rings. Strands of pearls fell from his chest to waist. His most noticeable accessory, however, was the blood-red cabochon ruby stickpin centered on his lapel. The stone spanned the width of a man's thumb. It was surrounded by diamonds so that the size of the central gem appeared doubled. The crimson gem was engraved, although Arabella couldn't make out the design in the dim carriage interior.

"You are familiar with ancient things," he said, removing the pin carelessly and tossing it across the small space to Arabella. "Tell me, what do you make of this design?"

Arabella took the piece and examined it, aware of how expectantly both men watched her. "It is not something an Assyriologist would recognize, my lord," she replied, handing it back. "The engraving looks like a snarling sheep, a device with which I am unfamiliar."

"Snarling sheep?" Justin demanded, rearing back and scowling.

The earl appeared annoyed as well, but Annette laughed merrily, and if the sound rang untrue, no one commented.

"Well, yes." Arabella swiveled to face her suitor. He was dressed as the sun, clad in a golden-thread suit that blinded her whenever she beheld him. Still, as always, his garments exacerbated his chiseled features and the flop of auburn hair. "That is what the device looks like to me."

"It is most obviously a griffin-demon," the viscount corrected. "You insult the emblem of the Kildare line. Snarling sheep, indeed."

She bowed her head. Inside, she seethed. How dare he sound peeved? After all, she hadn't been the one who had asked to see the blasted piece of jewelry. It didn't even appear genuine. The stones lacked depth and sparkle, and the construction was certainly lighter than she had anticipated. She wouldn't be surprised if it was but a poor paste copy.

A rut in the road jarred her into him. She gritted her teeth. "The light is poor, my lord."

"Does the carving remind you of anything?" Justin pressed. "Perhaps you've seen a similar, even if not exact, design elsewhere, on a bracelet or a ring?"

"I don't believe so, no."

"Something like it, surely? On a ring?"

"No."

He appeared to want to shake her, though she couldn't imagine why. She was the one forced to bear his company.

Arabella stared down at her lap again, but not before she saw the earl exchange a glance with his son.

When the carriage slowed to a stop, a sense of deliverance swept through her. Outside the window, the bright lights of the Stapleton house cut the night. Once inside the spacious hallway, Arabella quickly escaped her escorts and chaperone by seeking the retiring room. She darted off to the right. Most retiring rooms, she had discovered, lay in that direction.

Relief swallowed her as she disappeared from their sight by dashing behind an overburdened potted palm. From there, she was able to view the mass of glittering, chirruping guests as they passed through the main hallway, enroute to the ballroom that lay at the far end.

Scrutinizing those assembled, setting her gaze high as Gabriel was taller than most, she tried to pierce the masks of the gentlemen. Few were arrayed in standard evening kit. Most outshone the women in the garishness of their costumes. Would the baron also arrive, skirted and almost bare-chested like Lord Mellon, who had crisscrossed sashes to form a spindly sort of shirt?

The thought briefly amused her until it didn't.

Perhaps it might be better if he didn't show. Despite her desperate need to see him again, her mother's warning rang within her brain. She couldn't deny the future was likely to be as Lady Winslow had painted it. Would she grow bitter, as her mother had when a deep, abiding love failed to grow within him? Could friendship and a shared physical union make up for the lack of that ill-defined emotion?

Yet, not all hearts could be equal, so someone must always, of necessity, be besotted more or less.

These were matters Arabella had never pondered

before the choice between the viscount and the baron had presented itself. It was a debate that had immediate consequences. How had a poor scholar like herself come to such a pass?

"Here you are, my dear. Whatever are you doing, skulking behind the potted palm?"

The viscount, eyes gleaming, handed her a glass of Champagne. He appeared a bit winded, as if he had been searching for her all over London instead of merely within the Stapleton home.

"I thought the bubbly appropriate. After all, you are rather a wild creature tonight, *sans* fichu. Did you imagine I hadn't noticed? And here you are, waiting for me, away from prying eyes."

She took the glass he offered, unsure how to reply in return.

"I must confess, Arabella, I hold out more hope for an interesting wife than I had previously imagined possible. What daring you possess, to be certain." His pale golden contemplation roved her bodice, focusing upon her chest as if the lined lace was transparent glass. Arabella wanted to cross her arms, but she forced her spine straight instead. She refused to give him the discomfiture he sought.

"I doubt my lack of fichu is all that daring, given the Duchess of Brighton's ensemble."

She took a small sip of the bubbly liquid. It teased her nose, and she wrinkled it.

"True, but I am a man of impeccable taste, my dear, as I will teach you in time. Understated elegance is always preferable, and her costume, while audacious indeed, is blowsy in comparison to your modest one."

"I'm so glad you think so."

Trying to do so unobtrusively, she took a careful half step back.

"Leave a man to his imagination, and leave him wanting, such is the siren's song."

Justin drew nearer and reached out to stroke the skin along her throat with the pads of his fingers. She shivered and backed up another step, but the potted plant prevented further movement.

"My lord, please," she snapped.

He smiled, his lips thinning as his eyes narrowed. "*Tsk, tsk*, my dear. I am to be your husband. Surely, if I anticipate the banquet a bit by tasting the display, no one will mind overmuch."

"If you think to compromise me, my lord, think again. I will not be trapped by you a second time." She ducked under his arm and twirled away. "And," she added, lifting her glass to him in salute, "I would not anticipate overmuch if I were you. No one likes the man who drools in the dish."

His hand fisted at his side.

"Have your fun, Arabella." His lips spread into an unpleasant smile, one which did not reach his eyes. "Your hours close in upon you."

He stalked away. Although she could not say why, the hair stood up along her arms. Perhaps it was his confidence in the face of her clear antagonism.

Slowly, she set off toward the dancing couples, glad of the press of people around her. She was suddenly apprehensive of resting alone for reasons she could not adequately name.

Arabella deposited her glass upon the edge when she reached a table and slipped into her feathered mask. Draining the liquid in the hopes it would lend her courage, she ambled into the open. Spotting a wandering waiter, she changed the empty flute for a chilled, fresh one before her attention was drawn across the width of the room. Lady de Veer hung upon Earl Kildare's arm as she laughed gaily into his face. Apparently, she had no fear of what the gossips might relate to her husband.

The older woman gave every impression of being besotted, although why was a mystery. The earl was fat, balding, stocky, and mean. There had been an edge to every word he had uttered within the carriage confines, despite the superficial pleasantness of his manner. What could she see in him when her husband was an intelligent man, occupied with governmental service, and of a salubrious, quiet nature?

As if sensing her regard, Lady de Veer glanced her way. Raising a hand, her mother's friend waved her over. Arabella spun away and pretended not to have seen. It was not the lady she sought to avoid, however. It was the earl and his discomfiting regard.

****

"Why, I've never!" Annette de Veer clutched the earl's velvet sleeve for support.

"You've never what? There can't be very many things about which you might truly say that." Robert guffawed.

She gasped, spilling a few drops of Champagne as she tilted the glass in her surprise. "Robbie! How dare you say that to me?"

He laughed again before his gaze dove across the room. Following his regard to the opposite end of the ballroom from where Arabella perched, she beheld Justin, just crossing the doorway.

Robert nodded at him, and he nodded back as if they

197

shared some silent communication.

"The question one must ask oneself is, how dare you?" the earl purred, drawing her full attention again. "How dare you continue living as such a caricature? Why, you must realize anyone who matters thinks you little better than the blowsiest of hedge-whores?"

A buzzing rose between her ears. She shook her head to dislodge it.

"What? R-robbie," she sputtered, "why would you call me such a terrible name? Y-you told me you didn't believe those…those baseless rumors."

"Well, what a lover declares when he's about to blow the grounsils is usually different from what he declares to himself." His eyes flattened and glittered meanly. "You should know that by now, having engaged in more than your share of pulley-hawleys. Stale sheets are what you have, my dear, and I'd have had to be blind not to see it."

She could only blink at him. She opened her mouth but couldn't find her voice.

He dropped all pretense of civility as he added, through a smile both cold and precise, "Rest assured, old girl, it was passion of a kind. Of course, any man could literally screw a horse, so long as it was standing still and dusted with a sweet-smelling powder, so perhaps you shouldn't take too much pride in my acquiescence to your charms, such as they are."

Annette suddenly sympathized with Glenda Winslow. Although she tried to breathe, her lungs would simply not accept air. She could only stare. The ballroom spun like a top as she tried to comprehend the joke.

"I don't understand. Why do you jest like this?"

He leaned lower so that his eyes lay on level with her own. "No jest at all, Annie. Did you really think a woman of your years could hold a man like me? I tell you now, plain out, I never wanted you once I'd had you. I wed elsewhere with great enthusiasm all those years ago, and I kept away from you because I had forgotten your existence entirely. But then, well, I rethought the matter as I saw the advantages to our union."

"And discovered you did love me." She caught his arm. "Robert, I would forgive you anything; you must know that. I know you love me. I just don't understand why you are saying all these cruel and hurtful things now."

"I am saying them, Annie," he retorted, wrinkling his nose as he carefully disengaged her grasp, "because we are through. If you don't want your heartbreak bandied about, I suggest you take a carriage home. Now, perhaps you should leave before people begin staring. Immediately."

"A carriage? But I came with you."

"Then it is rather a good thing your husband just walked through the doorway. I suggest you seek him out, for once, and ask for his escort home. Plead a headache, if you like. You've certainly given me one with your incessant caviling."

Tears threatened, and she sniffed them back. When a small sob found its way between her tightened lips, she pressed a gloved fist to her mouth to stifle it.

"Go," he said softly, "or I will make your foolishness public for all to see. I will survive the gossip. You will not."

Not knowing what else to do, Annette strode away. She stood as tall as she could and pasted on the best smile she could muster as she drew her pride around her like a shroud. Although she couldn't stop blinking back tears,

Judy Lynn Ichkhanian

she could make an exit as well as anyone. She had, after all, had a bit of practice.

Annette was halfway across the room when she stopped. Turning on her heel, she marched back to the earl and whispered, "For the record, your breath smells like dead worms, and your stomach is as attractive as a bloated, decaying stoat. My kindly nature bid me overlook the villainy of your person, but now you have displayed the corruption within your very soul, it is my great pleasure to inform you that you couldn't give a woman an orgasm if she were already brought ninety-nine percent of the way there first by some strapping lad in livery." With an elaborate curtsey, she hastened from the room in search of her husband.

It was nothing that couldn't be forgotten under the strong arms of a virile coachman.

The ache in her chest did not lessen.

****

"I see you gave the old girl her walking papers," Justin muttered as he sauntered over to where his father stood, lapping at the Champagne, girth overflowing his waistband.

"We needed her gone, didn't we? I told you I would arrange it."

He could almost feel sorry for the old gel, given the voluble exchange he had witnessed.

"What if she takes Arabella with her?"

"She won't even remember the chit's existence."

Justin inclined his head and clapped his father on his back.

Everything was going according to plan.

Chapter 24

Gabriel's leg jiggled up and down as he wordlessly urged the coach to travel faster. Taught from youth to present a still and emotionless façade, he was helpless now to stop his agitation. Something didn't feel right, which made no sense at all. He had left Arabella's bed convinced happiness was stuck to him with strong glue, but suddenly he was filled with a premonition of disaster.

Perhaps it had only been Peter's news, imparted just as Gabriel was set to step out his front door. They had posted far and wide, from the lowest levels to the highest, that good coin would be paid for any news of the earl and his son. Today, forethought had borne fruit.

"He's a villager and a drunk," Peter had said of the man who had come to him for his reward. "Still, the fellow admitted readily enough to poaching, and there's no doubt about his description of the two men who tried to run him to ground like some fox. Your uncle and Justin were visiting their country estate. The man overheard them discussing a woman named 'Arabella.' And blood. Worse still, they were seen in the village afterward, obtaining a special license from the priest."

The conversation left Gabriel uneasy, so it was with a sense of relief when he finally spotted the lights of the Stapleton townhouse ahead. The street was awash in parked carriages, carriages leaving, and carriages arriving. When his vehicle snagged again in a snarl of traffic,

Gabriel could stand it no longer. He opened the door and jumped down.

"Be ready to leave when I need you," he instructed the driver over his shoulder, already rushing toward the overflowing townhouse.

Darting his way through the jam, narrowly avoiding a horse with a murderous look in its eyes, he ran up the stairs and through the rooms, stopping only to slip into his half mask and utter polite regards to his hosts. That done, he went in search of Arabella.

He couldn't say why he felt so certain she needed his protection tonight. It was ludicrous, really, with Society there to safeguard her. Still, his gaze roved everywhere, and his heart beat faster than was normal.

"Why, Lord Brynley, what a charming costume; although unmasked as you were when you arrived, it was easy to glean your identity. Who are you meant to be with that particular plaid across your waist? A wild Scotsman, perhaps?"

He didn't recognize the woman. All he knew was she wasn't Arabella.

"I am Gilgamesh, ancient Sumerian warrior-king. Please, excuse me."

He strode off, searching the crowd. The costume addition had been very last-minute, painfully inaccurate, and a nod to convention only. Plus, he had thought it might make Arabella laugh. He would do a lot of silly things to hear her laugh.

It took several long minutes to find her in the gloom behind a potted tree. Though her toe tapped in time to the music, she did not seem particularly happy. There was a tenseness to her shoulders that had no place at the glittering party. Slowly, he exhaled, then rounded behind her. Bending over her shoulder, he whispered, "I understand a goddess is lurking about in the ferns. Naturally, such rumors interest me."

"How typically male of you, to ignore respectable females in search of the fantastic." Arabella snorted. She kept her body averted. "How is a woman to compete when there are goddesses mucking about in the world?"

"The goddess of Erech is no competition of yours," he said fervently, and meant it.

Arabella giggled. "Ah, but will the hirsute interloper, Enkidu, he of the wild and wary strength, challenge you to battle upon my behalf?" Arabella laughed again and turned, her pansy eyes sparkling with delight.

Champagne bubbles he hadn't drunk sparkled wildly in his chest. She was gorgeous. In a room filled with over-dressed and over-bejeweled women, she stood out for her simplicity. The mask dimmed her violet eyes, but their color proved their amazing quality by remaining visible through the mess of feathers. Her lips, pink rosebuds, were parted gently, and it was all he could do not to lean in for a kiss.

"You cannot know how I long to slip my hands around your waist and pull you to me, Arabella. Having seen your curves uncovered, I find I am annoyed now to find you so hidden from my sight."

"Then you are not a man given to jealousy?" she asked provocatively. "You would prefer I walk around in my naked skin, even though other men might ogle me?"

"Oh, on the contrary. I am very, very possessive of that which is mine."

"I think I shall always be yours," she said, though her smile dimmed, and it seemed as if a shadow crossed the wilted pansy of her eyes. "I see no help for it. So, come," she added, rallying, "will you invite me to dance so all of Society can admire the High King of Sumer and the bluestocking who adores him?"

His mouth twisted. "Do you realize no one at this gathering has the least idea of my identity?"

She reached out and touched his chest with her finger. The linen shirt, vest, and jacket he wore did nothing to prevent the burn her fingertip left upon his skin.

"The length of plaid and your royal air should have identified you, but no matter. You are a man of mystery, my lord, and all the more enticing for it."

"Since when have you become so accomplished a flirt?"

She giggled. "Since this moment. Since a couple of hours ago, when a dastardly devil entered into my home and seduced me in my bedchamber."

"Or was seduced by you," he retorted.

His hand snaked to the small of her back, lightly, gently, but he just managed to refrain from pulling her body into his. They were behind a palm, yes, but they had not been rendered invisible.

"I should like to dance."

It was beyond him to refuse a request made twice.

Moments later, they were on the floor, joining the mass of other couples waltzing about the room. He knew he held her too close, spoke too little, and offered too much expression on his face. He didn't care. Holding her was joyous.

He had barely been able to focus upon the cuneiform before him for wanting to touch her just so all those hours studying together. Now that he had her warm flesh under his hands, he couldn't imagine ever studying with her again unless she was naked and sitting astride him.

No. He would never get any work done that way. Who cared? What was the whole of Assyriology next to her?

He drew her closer, so close they bordered upon obscene. She melted into him, giving no thought to her own reputation. Then, some old harridan to his side practically shouted to another, "And they say she is almost engaged to his cousin, Manning, who is around here, somewhere. That young buck better watch behind him."

The words were like ice flung upon his head. It was enough to break the sensual web they had woven between them. Carefully, Gabriel maneuvered Arabella to a more proper distance.

"Apropos of engagement, have you considered how to tell your mother we'll be wed? What? Why are you pulling from me?" he demanded as she tugged at his hands.

Those beautiful violet eyes suddenly filled with shadows.

Cursing under his breath, he searched the room, only to determine they were some distance from the exit. He couldn't question her with half of Society looking on, but the path was long to travel without garnering remarks. "I will dance you to the door," he said under his breath. "We'll talk once we're outside."

When she nodded, he took advantage of a surge in couples to twirl her directly toward the opposite corner. Once there, he grabbed her gloved hand and pulled her through the onlookers and down the hall. When they reached a long corridor, he knocked upon a closed door, and when no one answered, he opened it. The interior was dark, but the room seemed empty enough.

"Let me find a light."

He dropped Arabella's hand and stalked toward the mantel, where he soon found the implements necessary to strike the oil lamp sitting upon it. Moments later, a soft glow illuminated the small antechamber, little bigger than the furniture within. Ledgers were piled upon the surface of a desk, some open to reveal neat lines of figures. Two hard chairs and a small settee against the wall completed the space. None of the furnishing were decorated or of the same quality as the rest of the fittings within the house.

The estate agent's office. It would do for privacy.

"Come in and close the door. It would not be politic to be seen here," he said as she remained standing in the doorframe.

Upon her face rested an expression that twisted something in his chest. There was confusion that had no place existing, not after their time together in her bed.

There was something worse. He would swear it was regret.

"I…" She reached up and massaged her throat as if to free words stuck there.

"Come. We will sit and speak of whatever is troubling you," Gabriel said, reaching forward in a beckoning motion. "You must know you can trust me with your thoughts."

Still, she hesitated, biting her lip, her hand upon the lintel. He was just considering hauling her over to the couch when she decided to close the door.

Sitting upon the settee, she slipped off her mask and held it in her lap. "I may have been premature in my acceptance of your kind offer."

"No."

"No?"

"No, you were not premature, and no, I will not release you from your promise. We are affianced. There," he affirmed, joining her upon the small seat, "now I've reduced your missish fears to rubble, I find I have an urgent need to kiss you." With his thigh pressed to hers, he could excuse the huskiness of his voice. It was a wonder he could speak at all.

She veered away, but then leaned into him as if he were the magnet and she the metal. Her chin tilted up, and he wasted no more time in lowering his lips to hers.

It was like coming home. It was as if he had known the feel of her mouth against his for his entire life. It was comfort, and sweetness, and a yearning fulfilled.

But then, unexpectedly, she pulled back, just as his hands tried to draw her closer.

"Wait," she whispered, her gloved fingers curling against his chest.

He brought them to his lips, resting there a moment. It nearly destroyed him when she pulled her hand free.

He carefully placed his palms upon the flat of his upper thighs. "All right. Tell me why you've changed your mind when your body cleaves to mine. Tell me what this is all about."

Her hands trembled in her lap. He waited.

Finally, she said, "Someone was in my room between the time we left it and the time I returned from walking you to the front door. I think…" She swallowed. "I think it must have been your cousin. I had hoped it was only Lady de Veer's maid, but Justin is too different tonight. Harder. Uncaring." Her lashes flitted up and then down again. "He must have seen the sheets."

"The sheets?"

"Er…yes." She turned her head to the side, and Gabriel smiled.

He allowed his thumb to stroke gently along her cheekbone. He hoped this was the extent of the problem. "I'm sorry for the pain I caused. It is a biological inevitability for a woman, I'm afraid, but it will be better from now on, more and more so as your body becomes accustomed to mine."

She gazed back at him. "Yes, well, the pain was irrelevant, and it was over before it began. The pleasure made it worth it, in any event." A deep blush stained her cheeks.

"Then, what? Why do you turn from me when I bring up marriage? Because Justin saw the sheets and knows we've been together in your bed? Good. By tomorrow, after we have spoken with your mother, you will be mine officially. Enough so, at any rate, I can keep him away from you. Fiancés do have some legal rights, although I will not rest comfortably until we are properly wed. And if he talks?" He shrugged. "I don't believe he will. I hold too many secrets he would not wish disclosed. He would think twice before besmirching your reputation."

"I believe you are overlooking Justin's fairly intractable pursuit of my hand," she murmured. "Additionally, my mother greatly favors his suit."

"Then she is gravely mistaken in her assessment of where your future should lie."

She bit her lip, appearing uncertain.

For an instant, he debated with himself as he pushed down panic bubbling up from his belly. He hadn't expected to be met with her resistance at this point in their relationship.

"Arabella, there is much I haven't said plainly that

will convince your mother to deny the cad entrance. I've related to you some of the reasons I believe Justin's interest in you must be illegitimate. Chief among those factors is that the man requires an heiress, which you are not. He and my uncle are courting destitution, which I told your mother earlier in no uncertain terms. Furthermore, as you are aware, I am challenging their claims to their current titles. What you don't realize is my evidence is unshakable. The earldom and its lesser titles are my birthright, and when I have them, Justin and my uncle will be left with nothing but their questionable wits." He paused. "They are cornered men, and cornered men are dangerous, however hapless they may appear. You are right to stay far from my blood relations, although wrong to worry about gossip they might spread."

He didn't want to elaborate further about the nastiness of the upcoming trial or even about the competition that had always existed between him and his cousin. Some details were simply too unpleasant. Above all, he feared she might come to believe she was just another prize over which they fought. Thoughts like that could ruin a happy home.

She lowered her head.

"Even if you cared for Justin, which I don't believe you do," he continued gravely, choosing his words with care, "he is not a viable choice."

Arabella finally glanced over at him. "My poor mother."

"I will protect you both now."

She nodded but then shook her head. "Gabriel," she began, then sighed deeply, as if drawing pain from a deep well. Her eyes sparkled with unshed tears. The panic and sorrow within them were like quicksand, sucking him down.

"No," he denied. "It is not possible that you are still considering that pod snapper. You do not even like the dolt."

"Gabriel!"

Deliberately, he closed his mouth; his lips stretched into thin, tight lines. When he spoke again, he had regained some control. "You made love with me earlier this evening like a woman possessed. You admitted to holding strong feelings for me. What more do you require?"

"My mother will never accept you, Gabriel. Trust me when I say she is unshakable in her stance. A union between us will only exacerbate her illness. I cannot risk her health, not even for my happiness, assuming I could be happy with you, which is no longer clear."

"You sound uncertain of what should be an unassailable fact."

Suddenly, he was filled with outrage. How could she doubt they were created for each other? Who else on the entire earth could appreciate her passions for Assyriology as he did, and who else was strong enough and rich enough to take care of all the plaguey nuisances of her life so she could pursue that passion? It was almost too much to bear.

She squirmed, and he feared she meant to rise and leave. Ruthlessly, he tamped down upon his ire and breathed deeply through his nose, forcing a calm he was far from feeling.

"I shall have to prove your happiness to you in the only way available to me, Arabella. With time. In any event, the matter cannot be adequately addressed now."

She swiveled her head away again, and took a

voluble, quavering breath.

"What may be determined is a way out of your predicament," he said, standing up slowly and striding over to the desk as he sought for some inkling of how to handle this unexpected development. He flipped through the ledger, his eyes unseeing. Finally, he rotated back to her. "We shall have to cushion the news of our engagement, perhaps tell her only once she has benefitted from the air abroad."

Gilded pansy eyes widened in question. "How could I—we manage that?"

"Quite easily. I shall give you the money to send her to Nice. No," he added, when she reared back, "I mean no disrespect. I understand your hesitation, but I have a plan."

"I cannot accept money from you," she retorted immediately, "not if I wish to remain a lady. Surely, you are aware of that?"

He leaned against the desk. "You can if I give it to you by purchasing your copy of the *Epic*." He held up his hand to forestall her interruption. "I appreciate you would gift it to me, but I cannot allow myself to accept something of such value. A sale serves both our purposes. Shall we say, two thousand pounds?"

"Two thousand pounds!"

"Yes, I think the *Epic* is worth that. There's a very limited supply, after all." He paused and added gently, "You will be free of your obligation to marry anyone you don't wish to. Including me."

It took all his willpower to include those last words. He let them hang there, an anvil in the air poised just above his head.

"You can live comfortably, albeit simply, for the rest

of your days. You might even join your mother in the south of France if that is your desire."

He could lose her. He watched her face carefully.

Still, there was no other viable course if she was determined to object to a public engagement to him now.

Though her mouth opened as if she would protest, she closed it quickly enough. What he hadn't expected, what made no sense at all, was the expression of sympathy that drew down her eyes at the corners.

"Thank you, my lord. I accept your generous offer."

There was something about her smile. He frowned and tried to puzzle it out.

"You must know I hold every expectation this arrangement proves to be nothing but a ruse," he blurted, despite his best intentions. "I am hopeful in a few months you will choose to marry me. That is," he added, trying to feel his way, to assess what she was thinking in that fabulously complex brain of hers, "it is my hope, but not a requirement of the transaction. The choice will be yours, I promise you."

She nodded, her smile still quivering in place.

"Tell me what you are thinking," he demanded.

"I think," she said softly, "you are a wonderful man, heroic and strong. Any woman would be lucky to have your regard. I fully appreciate the honor you do me, Gabriel. I will never forget it." Her eyes sparkled. "Now, if you will excuse me? I should collect Lady de Veer. I've a bit of a headache, and I'd like to go home."

Something was very, very wrong.

"I'll call upon you tomorrow, and we'll complete the transaction in front of your mother, so she understands there is a reason you have suddenly come into funds. And, if you need more, Arabella, you must never hesitate to ask me. Do you understand?"

She rose and wrapped her arms around him as if comforting one bereaved. He put his head next to hers, holding her close, inhaling the smell of gardenias from her hair.

In the next instant, she was gone, and he was left all alone to brood.

Chapter 25

Arabella made a beeline for the front entrance, only to learn that Lady de Veer had already departed in the company of her husband.

It was just as well. Her mind was almost blank with confusion, and surely Lady de Veer would have pried secrets from her in such a state, which meant that Lady Winslow would have known everything about two minutes later. Above all else, she could not upset her mother.

She returned to the women's retiring chambers as she considered her options. When she spotted a stool before the long mirror, she perched upon it and stared at the reflection of her flushed face. Her thoughts whirled.

Gabriel's offer to purchase the *Epic* was inspired. The sum he offered was far too exorbitant, of course, but not unreasonable, given his scholar's needs. His generosity was a blessing. Lady Winslow would be able to relocate to a more salubrious climate, and she, Arabella, would no longer need to endure the viscount's company. She should be relieved.

Unfortunately, his solution did little to mend her fast-breaking heart. Certain truths still remained. She had told Gabriel she loved him. Had he felt likewise, he certainly would have said so. She supposed it was a credit to the baron's innate honesty; he had not even tried to lie.

His honor only increased the ache pushing down

upon her chest.

There was no way around his lack of abiding affection. Her mother had been right. If she married Gabriel, every moment of every day for the rest of her life would be spent realizing how lopsided their relationship was. Like Lady Winslow, she would always wonder why she wasn't enough to hold her beloved's interest. She would worry Gabriel would fall in love with someone else. How had her mother endured such agony? Having made love with Gabriel only once, the thought of his becoming enamored of another was enough to crack her spine and pull the soft parts of her belly through the shards.

He had given her a way out, with his offer to purchase the *Epic*. For him, to free him from the obligation he felt because he thought he had ruined her, as well as for her mother's situation, she was obliged to accept his generosity.

She would take his money and run, leaving the country and all the memories she had never thought to make far behind.

The decision made, Arabella wove a path through the rowdy crowds to the front entrance. Before she could ask a footman to fetch a cab, Justin was beside her.

"Lady de Veer has gone."

"Yes, I know," she mumbled, attempting to divert her gaze for fear of what he would see within her eyes.

"We will escort you home, as you cannot remain, unchaperoned. My father is already waiting in the carriage."

His voice was oddly devoid of emotion, but Arabella ignored her disquiet. He grabbed her elbow, and she tamped down on her instinct to pull away. Unless she wanted to make a scene, it was best to allow him to maneuver her through the doors and down the steps. Home rested only a few, short blocks away. Lord Kildare might not be the best type of chaperone, but surely he could be counted upon to act as one in these circumstances?

Once in the carriage, she fluffed out her skirts as the vehicle immediately sprang forward.

"You seem pensive," the viscount murmured as she sought her balance.

He sat too close on the banquet, crowding her. In the dim light, he looked wickedly handsome, too handsome, as if perhaps he had been fashioned from clay and painted with flesh tones. An almost manic glitter sharpened his eyes, but for all that, he seemed lifeless. There was a sheen to his skin as well, like oil upon the surface of the Thames. She was unnerved by these aspects of him, though she tried not to be.

"I'm disappointed by your lack of costume, my dear," the earl suddenly said.

He ogled her chest, which did nothing to lessen her anxiety.

"As the Lady Manning, you will be required to show yourself off to better advantage."

Arabella drew in a long breath through her nose, unable to respond to such improper advice.

"My son tells me you are a spirited filly," the earl continued. "I don't see it. Too bad, as it is such a pleasure to break such a nature in private."

"Father."

"Just giving the girl the lay of the land." Robert smirked.

"You're frightening Lady Arabella with your

insinuations, Father, and we've not yet left the block."

Justin exchanged a look with the earl that Arabella could not interpret. Then he reached down and pulled a basket out from beneath the seat.

"You must have imbibed too freely, Father. Luckily, I've brought provisions."

The earl exhaled as he leaned his head back against the cushion. "Capital idea. I could do with a bite."

Justin leaned into Arabella and whispered, "He's had too much wine, I'm sorry to say. I have sandwiches to sop up the alcohol, but he won't eat unless we all do. Think you could force a few bites?"

She examined the viscount again. He seemed sincere and not quite so manic anymore. Perhaps it had all been her fevered imagination that had caused her to be uneasy.

"I would love a sandwich," she said loudly.

If eating would help the earl regain equilibrium and propriety, she was all for it.

The viscount handed her two halves of salmon laced with hardened Devonshire cream on crustless bread, along with a napkin. "Thank you," he mouthed and smiled.

Arabella nodded and took a tentative bite, surprised by how delicious the snack actually was. She hadn't realized she was even hungry, but within moments, the entirety had been consumed.

"The salmon comes from the Kildare estates in Ireland," Justin commented agreeably, eating a piece of his own. He handed her another half, and then uncorked a small carafe of white wine. "The Riesling is sweet, but I love the taste of it after the fish. At this time of the evening, I find it difficult to stomach anything stronger."

Taking the small silver cup he poured, Arabella

sipped while the men conversed in low tones, ate, and drank. For a moment, she wondered if it was wise to give the earl more liquor, but then the thought floated away from her.

She took another taste of the delicious beverage. The cup grew heavy in her hand.

****

"I hope I haven't given her too much," Justin murmured.

Arabella's head lolled against the plush velvet squab, her lips open. When she listed too far to the side with the movement of the carriage, Justin laid her across his lap. She looked so innocent. He had the oddest sense of wanting to protect her from his designs. He chalked it up to nerves. After all, these next hours would drive the nail home into her coffin, but if she slipped while he hammered his cause, she might yet escape.

That couldn't happen.

"She'll live."

"It was you who wanted her for grandchildren. How far now?"

"Not long."

"The priest knows his part?" Justin asked, aware he had already done so several times this day.

At that moment, the carriage slowed before making a wide right turn.

"Relax, Justin. In five minutes, the doctor will examine her. In ten minutes, you'll be wed. In eleven, you can bed the chit, should you be able to wake her." The earl shrugged. "Might be easier to get it done while she's sleeping, though, especially if the doctor agrees Darkie did the deed. You've got needs, after all, and if you can't swive her the regular way, there's the back door. Sleeping women don't put up a fuss when you stick things where they don't think they should be stuck."

Justin winced. "Really, Father." He frowned. "I'm not going near her until I'm certain she isn't carrying Darkie's seed. There can be no accidents, no soft-hearted feelings in the midst of passion. I refuse to allow his bastard to become my heir."

Justin studied his bride again, noting her perfect nose, the long lashes that hid such luscious, jewel-like eyes, and the fullness of her figure that stopped just short of wantonness. He would wait a month, maybe six weeks, to be certain she wasn't with child, and in the interim, he would find other ways of pleasuring himself with her body that did not lead to accidental congress. It seemed a waste to kill her before he needed to.

He pulled the forged letter and the special license his father had acquired from his pocket as the carriage ground to a halt. "I've got Lady Winslow's permission, outlining how her daughter bedded me and then refused to marry. It looks genuine, I think. Is the doctor here?"

"I'm certain he is. Once he swears to the priest Arabella is a virgin no longer, the good father will marry her to a corpse without further question."

"It never hurts to be prepared."

They waited as the coachman pulled out the steps and fastened them to the doorframe.

"I don't suppose you'd share?" his father asked.

Justin looked away from his bride in time to see his father lick his lips. He stared at the sleeping female as if she were a plate of apricots, and he without a meal that day.

"Let me manage getting an heir on her, Father, and then we'll see."

"You're a good son, Justin. I'm awfully glad you didn't die like the others."

An unreasonable welling of gratitude coursed through him at his father's words. It felt wonderful to be so appreciated.

It felt even better to realize in ten small minutes, the game would be his.

Chapter 26

"What do you mean, she isn't here?" Gabriel demanded as he confronted Lady Winslow in her library at eleven the next morning.

After a sleepless night and an uneaten breakfast, he had rushed to the Winslow residence to exchange a bank draft for the *Epic*, fully intending to kiss Arabella into compliance if necessary. Instead, he interrupted a frantic Lady Winslow, who was searching behind the draperies as if she might find her daughter there.

"The words are plain, Brynley, and I am certain you possess intelligence sufficient to comprehend them," Lady Winslow snapped, wringing her hands.

"You don't understand. We made specific plans to meet here this morning. She has promised to sell me the *Epic*," he replied, attempting to keep panic from his face.

Here he was, dressed to the nines because he wanted Arabella to see he was more than a mere scholar, businessman, or even what his present title suggested, and she wasn't here to see any of it.

Why wasn't she here?

Last night and this morning, his hands kept folding around her softness, a habit they had been quick to acquire and been unable to break. His body cleaved to the memory of how she had spooned into him. He missed the feeling of her skin pressed to his and the scent of gardenia filling his nose. Heck, he was even feeling kindly about

Kismet, her dreaded attack cat. In short, he was simply done for as an intelligent creature unless and until she was his to hold, every night for the rest of his days.

Gabriel made to pass Lady Winslow, out the library door and up the steps to Arabella's bedroom, convention be damned, when the woman's words stopped him.

"Arabella never came home last night."

Fear iced his blood as he recognized the import of the trembling speech. "Pardon?"

Before he could ask anything further, Lady de Veer brushed into the room, her eyes strangely red-rimmed and her face puffy, as if she had been crying.

"She is not at my home, either," she announced, looking sallow in her yellow gown. Turning to Gabriel, she added, "This promises to be a scandal of the highest order, my lord. I'm certain we must throw ourselves upon your mercy and beg you not spread this news any further than this room."

"Lady de Veer, where is Arabella?" He drew in a long breath because his voice was shrill.

She shook her head. "I don't know. I departed the party early, with Lord de Veer. It was…an uncomfortable evening for me. I wasn't thinking." Suddenly, she burst into tears. "I'm sorry, Glenda." She grabbed her friend's hands. "I had to leave. I had to!"

Another wave of ice slithered through his veins as he understood more than he wanted to. "How did Arabella leave the ball?" he asked tightly.

Annette shook her head.

"I feared she was with you," Lady Winslow admitted, her voice so low he had to strain to hear her. "The viscount, then? Surely…" She slumped.

Before she could touch ground, Gabriel managed to

scoop her up. He carried her to the small couch.

"Oh, Glenda. Please, forgive me," Annette wailed, sinking into a chair and fanning her face.

"Unchaperoned?" Gabriel turned on Lady de Veer. "You left her to those two snakes?"

"The viscount will do right by her," Lady de Veer whispered, but her voice didn't seem very certain.

"Oh, Annette. Not like this, Annette." Lady Winslow began wheezing with each breath. "Not like this."

As her breathing grew shallower, Gabriel cursed and ran his hands through his hair as he paced. Finally, he grabbed Lady de Veer's arm and dragged her through the doorway.

"Escort me out, Annette," he said bluntly, foregoing her title.

It was doubtful Lady Winslow even noticed. She was hunched over, trying to draw air. He couldn't help her. Not now. Not when he was afraid he would scream at her like some madman.

In the hallway, he released Lady de Veer's arm as if he held a bouquet of roaches. "Now tell me everything. I know you are sleeping with my uncle, so spare me the evasions, and relate to me how you could have left my intended bride in that monster's clutches."

She stared, a rabbit against the fox, then lifted her chin. "Very well. You know the broad part of it. I loved the earl, and he wanted Arabella for his son, he said. I pictured a happier time in the future, one big family once my husband had gone to his grave. I thought Robert would marry me. I envisioned Glenda coming to live with us. All of us so contented," she replied mournfully.

"What happened?"

She sighed, and tears filled her eyes again. "He said

the cruelest things to me, things no woman should ever have to hear, let alone from her beloved. He quickly disillusioned me about who and what he really is. He told me to leave with my husband, and indeed, at the time, I couldn't have remained." She looked up at him. "I fled before I made a laughingstock of myself. I didn't think. I...couldn't."

"A plan impeccable in its cruelty." Gabriel cursed. "Did you ever consider Justin meant to ruin her?"

She lost the tiny bit of color she held. "Oh no," she cried, raising her hand to her mouth. "No, no, no. He means to marry her, surely?"

Gabriel could stand it no longer. His voice shook as he grabbed her arms. "Why? Why is everyone so desperate to see them married?"

"B-because he's the only answer."

Gabriel released her, and she took a step back. "You're wrong. I am the only answer. The only road to her happiness in any event. You've all been sold fool's gold." He blew out a long gust of air.

"Then, if you care about Arabella, if your motives are pure, what will you do now?"

He shook his head. "Go after her, of course, although I suspect it is already too late. I'm certain he'll have married her by now, by special license."

"And if she's married?"

But Gabriel had no answer for that.

His insides had turned to stone, and all he could do was hope he caught them before that event.

Chapter 27

The sun shone brightly, and the birds chirped like mad carolers when Arabella awoke.

Vague images of peril had haunted her sleep, and now, what should be splendid, seeing Gabriel standing there, was marred by the rage wafting from him in palpable waves. In the flurry of the storm in which he was surrounded, he was carved of hardened steel. The only part of him that moved as he stared at her was his upper lip, which curled with disgust.

She opened her mouth, but no sound emerged through her parched throat but a scratched, gravel caw.

"Shh, love, save your energy," the viscount chirped in a manically bright voice next to her ear, startling her.

He lay a handbreadth from her body.

"After all that delicious play last night, you must be exhausted. Never mind Darkie, who has kindly come to wish us well upon our marriage. Come, Arabella, do kiss me yet again."

He grabbed her hair and pulled so she could not move away, then leaned over and pressed his slugs to her lips. Though she instinctively turned her head until her scalp stung, he still managed to catch part of her mouth. Laughing, as though delighted with her spirit, he fell back, but not far. Not far enough. She could feel his arm pressed against hers, which made no sense.

It made no sense at all.

"Wha…?" She tried to gather her thoughts and her ability to speak.

Gabriel and the Earl of Kildare stood only a few feet from the bed. Though Gabriel glowered, the tic in his cheek beating like an erratic heart, the earl smiled like a fat, jokerish fool.

Quickly, she closed her eyes, certain she must still be dreaming, but when she opened them, she was speared by Gabriel's forest-green stare, the expression upon his face hard and frigid. He was all brittle ice shards, chipped from the frigid Thames in winter. When his gaze slid down the length of her body, she followed and gasped.

She was undressed to her shift, all but naked. The sheets were tangled around her knees, and the only nod to modesty she wore was Justin's well-placed leg across her body. The viscount's hand ran under her neck, over her torso, and toyed cruelly with the side of her breast under her arm, pinching her like a crab.

"Ah!" she cried, rearing up and pushing Justin away.

He rolled to the other side of the bed. Grabbing the sheets, she tried to stand. No sooner did she feel the wood beneath her toes, but her legs gave out, and gravity won.

"*Tsk, tsk*, darling, I told you that you expended too much energy last night. Poor thing outdid herself. Such energy when she is lying on her back, although we prefer to be dogs, don't we, darling?" He propped himself up on one elbow. "Perhaps you'd best take yourself off, Darkie. This is my honeymoon, after all, and you are most definitely not invited."

The most unbelievable part of the nightmare to which she had awakened was how Gabriel abandoned her there without uttering a single word.

"Gabriel," she cried, just as he passed the door.

He stalled, and she thought he would turn, but he stiffened his already straight back and vanished from her view. A few moments later, she heard his quick tread upon the stairs, fleeing from her as if she were yesterday's vice.

Someone was heaving. Distantly, she realized the sound issued from her own throat.

Justin laughed, slapping his palms against the bed. "Did you see?" he demanded gleefully. "Did you see, Father?"

"Well done, my son, well done. He'll not recover from this blow for a goodly time, let alone by week's end. Ah, but fortune is smiling upon us."

"She is indeed. Even the timing of his arrival was perfect, just as the drugs wore off. Oh, to play that scene again!"

"What is happening?" Arabella cried between heaves.

Gabriel's eyes. His eyes had said goodbye.

Inside her chest, a deep cavern cracked open, a ragged tear she thought she might never be able to close. The emptiness that filled the void rose to drown her. She swayed and moaned.

"Stop your racket, Arabella," the viscount ordered. "You sound positively insane, not to mention ugly. Come now. Do not force me to lose the goodwill I am feeling."

The room spun like a top as Arabella attempted to sit up. At the same moment, her insides heaved again, this time with force. Reaching wildly under the bed for the chamber pot, she grabbed at the cool porcelain and pulled it to her. In the next moment, she was violently ill.

"Oh, that is so revolting," Justin exclaimed. "Father, she has sick in her hair," he whined.

"Now, son, don't get your trousers in a twist. It's just

the drug coming up. You know the apothecary mentioned we might expect as much."

"Expected or not, I am revolted. Arabella, see you are ready within the hour to return to your mother's home. We'll announce our news and collect your things, most especially a certain seal ring which you received from your father, yes?" Justin stalked to his dressing table, taking care to skirt a wide path around her as he did so.

In the large room, maneuvering was a simple matter.

"After those chores are behind us, why, we'll be free to return here and start our married life, which pleases me to no end. Now that Darkie knows about our union, there's no sense in removing to the country as I had planned originally. Things could not have worked out better, although, I confess, when that overweening cock-of-the-walk burst in through our door this morning, I experienced a moment or two of trepidation. Ah, well. That's behind us now."

The viscount's body was thin and taut, elegant in its way. He was casual about his nakedness, even the long thing hanging limply from a thatch of copper curls. If he had been a statue or a painting, Arabella might have admired his form, but her stomach turned over again, knowing he had touched her. He was beautiful, yes, but also repulsive, like a snake, or a toad, in a jungle.

She remembered his fingers weighing the side of her breast, the heaviness of his leg across hers, and was sick into the pot again.

When finally there was nothing left within her to spew, Arabella ran the back of her hand across her mouth. She looked up and locked gazes with the viscount through the mirror into which he was staring. Everything on his face was twisted with disgust of her and she was glad.

Perhaps this was not the scene he had envisioned after all; his new wife slumped over a chamber pot with sick in her hair.

"What have you done, Justin?" she asked quietly.

He seemed to flinch under her regard. "What was necessary, my dear." He paused. "But if you are wondering, then yes, we are truly married. A village priest performed the ceremony at midnight. Quite romantic. Then we proceeded up here to bed, where you slept off your over-indulgences."

"You drugged me."

He lifted his shoulders as if that was a minor point and faced her. "No matter. I simply expedited the conclusion. At any rate, as Darkie himself will testify, the marriage was well and truly consummated, although I feel I might confide in you, in private, just so there is no mistaking my feelings on the subject, knowing you've lain with that son of a whore, I cannot think of your glove as anything more than the most virulent of chamber pots."

"What?"

"Chamber pot. Your glove," he added, his eyes narrowed as he stalked a step closer. "You let that whoreson deflower you. You are dirty now. You are a pestilence, and I will not breed my heir upon your tainted loins until I am certain you are not already carrying Darkie's seed."

She stilled, barely breathing, at first relieved he hadn't touched her *in that way*, but then she realized what else he had said. "You were in my bedchamber."

"And saw the sheets, yes."

The expression on his face was mixed, so she could not pull all the strands and decipher meaning.

"Then, why marry me? Why go through all this—this

madness? I don't understand."

"Your understanding is not required."

For a moment, she thought she spied a softening in his expression as his gaze roved over her body.

"Do not fear too much, Arabella. You are fulsome enough. In a month or so, when I am certain you are not growing my cousin's bastard within your belly, I may well try to get an heir off you. You possess certain compensatory assets, which may, if you are a very lucky girl, balance your idiocy in lying with that stodgy, interfering dullard. Meanwhile, I suggest you resign yourself to the inevitable and pray I shall soon be able to overcome my squeamishness where you are concerned."

"Yes, pray, gel." The earl snickered.

Arabella shivered and clutched the sheet tighter to her bosom. Vomit was not as off-putting to some as she might imagine.

"Why?" She used every ounce of her willpower to keep her voice level. "Why did you marry me? Gabriel says you haven't any money at all. That you lied. What is it you want from me so badly you would force me to wed, even knowing I love another?"

"Love?" the earl hooted. He sputtered a bit and then laughed. "You fancy yourself in love with that devil?"

But Justin seemed less amused. If anything, his eyes narrowed, and the turn of his nose became more pronounced. "You truly disappoint me, my dear. Passion I could understand, perhaps a willing and able body, given your years and your reclusive nature. But love? Well. I suppose we may be able to use that feeling against him yet since he seems equally as enamored of you."

"Why?" she demanded again.

He sighed. "This is fast becoming tedious. Fine. I

married you to obtain your ring, the one your father won from Darkie's father in a card game. The ring has an ancient Kildare griffin crest etched upon it. Griffin crest, not a snarling sheep. It was the only object Darkie's father never managed to recover, even after he deliberately set out to ruin your family."

She put aside that information to be examined later; it was too much to piece out now.

"I won't give it to you. I won't give anything to you. With the last breath in my body, I shall thwart any plan you make." Her fists clenched. "And I shall seek an annulment or a divorce as quickly as I am able."

Justin's smile grew brighter and the earl chuckled, as if her threats amused them greatly.

"Ah, Arabella, I think I can get fine sons from you once I am assured you do not carry Darkie's seed," Justin murmured. "What fire! What resistance to the inevitable! But how will you thwart me when any image you present other than that of the happiest of brides will crush the last breath from your mother's lungs?"

Arabella tried not to let him see the hit, though it did not matter. His arrow had found its target with unerring accuracy.

Justin turned back to the mirror and fluffed his fingers amongst the locks of hair that fell upon his forehead. Through the glass, he continued to scrutinize her.

"In any event," he continued, smiling and checking his teeth, "you are mine now, my legal responsibility, and you no longer have a say in your own doings. There will be no annulment or divorce unless I initiate one, and frankly, there are far easier ways to rid myself of you when and if I choose."

Once again, his words struck dead center. What an amazing archer he had turned out to be, and she had never even guessed he could hunt. She had been a fool to have dismissed him as a fop.

"Furthermore, you will give me the ring, or I promise you, I will hasten your mother's inevitable demise. And," he added, holding up his hand, "before you tell me even I would never stoop to murder, might I remind you I have already drugged and kidnapped you just to obtain that cursed object? I forged a permission note from your mother for a priest of God to read. I am deadly serious, so do not imagine I would quibble over some negligible, proletarian morals." He sniffed audibly, scrunching his nose. "You stink. I must bathe and wash the stench of you from my skin. I'll send Alice, the maid, up with some water for your ablutions. Will you come, Father?" Justin asked, stalking naked to the door.

The earl nodded. "You must get your fastidiousness from your mother, Justin," he mumbled. "I'd swive her even now."

Arabella shivered and swallowed her scream.

Chapter 28

Peter sat with his elbows upon his knees as he stared hard at his friend and worried.

Gabriel had lost weight in the weeks that had passed since the Stapleton ball. His once angular facial structure now resembled a famine victim's copse of stacked bones. Even his wrists, where they shot from the unbuttoned cuffs of his half-buttoned shirt, were ropey with exposed muscle. Growth of beard and stubble lined his caved-in cheeks and strong chin, lending him a darkly dangerous look belied by his empty eyes.

His bedraggled shirt hung from his trousers without the slightest hint of vest, jacket, or neckwear. The man hadn't changed, or bathed, in days, not to mention his feet were bare and dirty, a condition that sent the maids into a frenzy of blushing and scampering whenever the baron worked up enough energy to slope about the halls.

There was some reason to worry. Not all closed doors led to an open window.

Now, seated across from Gabriel in his library, Peter searched for the words that would light a fire beneath his all-but-brother's feet. Surrounded by trunks filled to the brim with books, all of them ready for shipping, the lord of the manor, still only Baron Brynley after the trial that had cost a fortune and attained nothing, chugged hard liquor from a goblet. The glass had been clutched in the baron's hand for the past two weeks as if it were the only preserver capable of saving him from drowning.

Perhaps that was the reason he had lost the fight for the titles. Bottles of whiskey sank and didn't float. Though Gabriel had appeared for the oral argument, his garments pressed and clean, his conviction had been lacking. When the decision had been rendered, after Kildare had presented the ostensible Last Will and Testament of Russell Manning, he had simply bowed his head and slunk from the courtroom without another word on the matter.

His lack of defense had been damning to his offense.

Since then, Gabriel had exhibited energy in only one department: his departure. Even that had been conducted in fits and starts, as he refused all of Reggie's tempting meals and rebuffed attempts to speak about anything connected to Arabella Warwick.

Only once, the same day he discovered Arabella had wedded his cousin, had Gabriel mentioned her. In this very room, they had gathered to hear him order a draft be taken to Lady Winslow in the sum of two thousand pounds for the purchase of the *Epic*, and then they had been forbidden from ever mentioning her name again.

Not that he and Reggie regularly acted upon orders, but his all-but-brother had looked so undone they had decided, for once, not to prod his bleeding sores.

In any event, the daily journals did enough poking for them. News of Justin's marriage quickly titillated Society, especially given a certain dance at the Stapleton ball the same night the nuptials had been performed, where the bride had been seen to press tightly against Brynley rather than her actual groom.

Then, not a week later, the improbable will, complete with the authentic seal, had been brought to court. Unable to prove it a forgery, the baron was assessed exorbitant costs while his relatives danced upon his defeat, all of which the papers related in horrifying detail that mixed fact with wild speculation.

Peter was still speculating. He had seen the will, and the seal was real, on that they had all agreed. It was identical to a wax imprint Gabriel found stowed among his papers. The parchment on which the will had been written was of suitable age, and the ink correctly faded. Even the signature appeared authentic. Despite all that, Peter had no doubt they had been roundly hoodwinked by the richly dressed lobcock and his gundiguts father.

The dailies, however, had rejoiced with the earl and viscount. Order had been upheld. As always, the rags failed to print the right side of the news.

"Gabriel, I've had enough of this nonsense. You are behaving like a fool. Leave here and follow that damnable *Epic* to wherever it takes you. Go uncover your Bilgeland. Find your keys to eternity. I'll handle all the business while you're gone, and I'll find out how those vermin forged that blasted will. Your hanging about this place like a damp bat has become most enervating. I object. *Strenuously*."

Gabriel half-raised a brow. "Dilmun, not Bilgeland, you lout," he corrected in an anemic tone.

Peter's pulse quickened. It was the first time in too many days his friend had bothered to correct one of his deliberate errors.

Gabriel raised his glass to his lips once more, discovered it empty, tipped it over to be certain, then sighed. He tilted his head back and closed his eyes. "Let it lie, Peter. I've lost everything. Allow me to lick my wounds in peace, won't you?"

Judy Lynn Ichkhanian

Peter leaned so far forward he almost fell out of the chair. "Is it so easy then, to give up your belief in your fate, your destiny? Are you so weak you crumble under the tiniest bit of adversity?"

Gabriel curled his lip.

Peter ran his hands through his hair as he tried to think of another goad, which likely didn't improve his coiffeur since he was certain it already looked as if he had combed it with a fork. When he worried, he tended to mess with his hair.

"You're a selfish old fool, aren't you? What do you care about Reggie or me? No, we must all slap about like secondary characters in a play, not an ounce of sense or emotion between us except as it concerns your life. Well, I'm done with it, all this tip-toeing around so as not to overburden your delicate nerves. Poor Reggie is in his bedroom, crying every night, and me, I'm wasted, trying to hold it all together while you mope about and give the maids a fright. I'm done, I tell you. Look, I'm shaking with the strain."

Peter held out his hands. They did tremble, though he was forced to enable them to do so.

For just an instant, he could swear Gabriel's mouth twitched, though he did not open his eyes. It was a mere quirk of the corners of his lips, almost a smile. Still, it was progress of a kind.

"I don't believe for even a moment Reggie is really crying. He'd rust if he did."

"Near enough to make it not altogether a lie," Peter insisted. "If you would step outside your head for even five minutes, you would notice he is no longer young and spry. Seeing you disconsolate has cut him deeply. If you can't heft yourself out of the morbs for your own good,

236

then do it for him. Hell, do it for me. I haven't been able to bed a single comely wench since this whole affair began, and I must tell you, the strain of celibacy is near to breaking my spirit."

This time Gabriel's eyes opened and his lips really did turn upward. His smile was a bit sheepish. "I hadn't realized I risked attack by all the willing maidens in England, denied a place between your sheets."

"*Their* sheets. I rarely bring them home."

"Never bring them home."

Peter shrugged. "We are not all so fortunate to find a female who is both comely in face and spirit." As Gabriel's smile tightened and then disappeared, Peter hesitated.

"So, Reggie was right yet again, blast him. This moping has little to do with the title, and everything to do with Arabella, doesn't it?"

"Don't," Gabriel snarled.

Peter leaned forward. "Is Arabella really worth losing your life, your dreams, your ambitions, when she chose elsewhere?" He deliberately articulated the name he had been forbidden to say.

"I said, *don't!*"

Without warning, Gabriel launched himself across the space, fists raised. Yet Peter was prepared, having expected and hoped for just such an attack for days. Women could speak their disagreements and concerns in carefully constructed phrases. However, men needed to rumble physically to dissipate their woes.

Gabriel rammed him in the belly, driving him backward into a table that toppled. Peter pushed back once he found his footing. Gabriel swung his fist. Peter ducked and punched upward.

The two men grappled and then rolled around the room, exchanging blows that neither bothered to check. They had had a wealth of experience together in such pursuits, and they were evenly matched. Furniture fell, and trunks overturned. Books littered the space like fallen leaves. Ceramic cache-boxes crashed into pieces, and a careful stack of wood scattered.

Peter barely paid attention to Gabriel's pounding fists as he focused upon returning as good as he got. It was just such a relief to be taking action instead of quietly worrying, he grinned. Gabriel wasn't quite smiling, but that might be because his cut lip spurted blood.

The sound of struggle must have roused Reggie, who rushed the door and swung it wide. "What in heaven's name?" he roared.

At the sound of his voice, they both froze like the boys they had once been.

"Get off each other. *Now*," Reggie ordered in a voice that booked no argument. "Separate corners!"

When they had complied, Gabriel groaning now that he must feel the results of the blows because Peter suddenly could, Reggie added, "Good. I'll be back in a moment with a couple of steaks for those black eyes you'll be sporting. And don't you be thinkin' you won't be given' me a fine explanation for these shenanigans," he added, slipping into a light brogue. He hobbled away, leaving the door open, but not before throwing Peter a wink.

By the time Reggie returned, pushing a cart laden with food, Peter huffed in a corner, his ribs aching. He rubbed his head where it had connected with a trunk of books. He groaned loudly, hoping to make Gabriel feel guilty, but his all-but-brother didn't seem to notice as he lay upon the rug, his shirt sleeve pressed to his lip.

"I've got a lovely tray of hearty broth, some fresh and crusty bread, and a crock full of sweet butter. Oh, yes, and those steaks, but you boys can wait to wear those until after you've stuffed your gullets. I swear, my heart can't take much more of this behavior. And I won't be cleaning any of this up, so you two, get yourselves off the floor right now and get to work," Reggie ordered.

Carefully, he dragged one of the lighter chairs over to the fire. Then, he set right the folding table they sometimes used to eat their dinner. While Peter and Gabriel righted tables and chairs, restacked books, and tried to sweep the shards of porcelain into a pile, Reggie sat and helped himself to one of the bowls before tearing off a chunk of the round loaf.

After shoving some books under a table with his foot so as not to have to shelve or box them, Peter glanced toward Gabriel, and shrugged. Gabriel nodded, and they made their way toward the soup bowls. The baron moved with an alacrity that had previously been missing. When he pulled up a chair, all the remaining tenseness in Peter's shoulders eased.

"Were you really in your bed crying?" Gabriel asked Reggie before biting into a hunk of buttered bread the old man handed him. He winced as his lip split open upon the sharp crust but continued to chew.

"Sobbing until the maids thought I'd brought my pillow into the bath," Reggie affirmed with a wink.

Gabriel actually chuckled, and the old man looked suddenly lighter.

"I'd like to get some sun into these old bones. Maybe dry out those pillows of mine. We haven't gone anywhere warm in a dog's age, and I'm thinking your idea to head to the desert is a good one. Change of scenery would be nice."

Gabriel stopped in the midst of spreading butter on another hunk of bread. For a moment, he looked down at his bowl, then sighed. "That was the plan. But you're right, the both of you. I cannot mope about any longer. I've lost, but only dreams. Dreams aren't real, are they, and certainly no adequate reason to invite further defeat?" He nodded suddenly. "Yes. All right. In a week's time I should be ready. Let me get some affairs in order and we'll go."

"Good man." Peter helped himself to the butter before his friend ate it all.

Reggie's stash came from his Irish cows, and the cream was the most delectable stuff on the entire planet, even if he did say so himself, which he most decidedly did. He took a big bite and let the sweet churned dairy melt against his tongue.

As they ate, they discussed the trip's details and what matters Peter, who would remain behind for a few months, would tend to. The glow of the fire glinted off their spoons, the happy clink of cutlery against casual stoneware filling the silences when talk ceased.

Finally, after tilting his bowl to get at the very last drop of soup, manners informal when it was just the three of them, Gabriel pushed his plate away. Already, color rose into his friend's wan cheeks, the soup and bread doing their work far better than the whiskey had.

"Gilgamesh, beware, we are coming for you," Peter murmured as he raised his glass of cider. "Although, frankly, I am more interested in seeing your harem."

Gabriel smiled, and if there was something a little forced about his expression, Peter chose to ignore it.

Chapter 29

It was no use. In disgust, Arabella threw down her pen and stretched her hand to exercise her cramped muscles. She couldn't concentrate on writing another cuneiform symbol from memory because Assyriology had lost its appeal.

She had nothing left to translate anyway, now that her mother had sent the *Epic* onward. Instead, she had spent her time revising the English language into symbols she had already translated, encoding love messages to the man who clearly was glad to be rid of her.

That Gabriel had kept his promise to purchase the *Epic*, despite what he must believe to be her betrayal, was gratifying, albeit unsurprising. As compared with her husband, who had promptly forgotten his promises where her mother was concerned the moment he had collected the silly ring, the baron's word had proved true. His generosity had been a gift. It was also a secret she and her mother shared alone. Neither of them had seen fit to apprise Justin of the transaction as they ought to have done.

The *Epic* had been Arabella's. The money from its sale was hers as well, and what had been hers was now legally his. It was a potentially depressing situation even her mother had instinctively understood.

"I've put five hundred of those pounds under your floorboard," Lady Winslow had whispered to her daughter during one of the rare moments Arabella had been able to escape Justin's hearing.

A cup of spilled tea had never been so welcome.

"While I have every hope you will have a happy marriage, I know too well how a woman feels when her husband, er, misbehaves," Lady Winslow had added. "If you need to leave Justin, do not hesitate. Take the money and run. I will follow with the rest when I am sure he will not follow me."

It had been a rare stroke of logic displayed by the woman who regularly preferred happy dreams. Arabella supposed her charade of a willingly-eloped, radiant bride had not been as convincing as she had hoped. Still, her mother would retire to the south of France in a week because of Gabriel's largesse. She would be safe. She would be able to breathe again. That was not nothing, though it was no longer enough.

Though Justin had bothered Arabella little, except to insist upon her presence at Society events during the evenings, she recognized she was in terrible trouble. Her life trembled at the edges while she was too numb to do much about it. It was strange to think not so long ago she had considered relocating her mother to be her largest concern. Now, what she feared most was death: either the living kind, born of too many days passed upon the knife edge with her dictatorial and mercurial husband, or the real one that might come for her soon, also thanks to her husband.

She sighed again and looked around the room she had been given. It was powder blue and crème, but it showed wear around the edges. Gabriel had been correct in that too, as he had been in all else. There wasn't an extra shilling to be had. Everything went into maintaining the minimum façade of wealth, although Justin seemed unreasonably optimistic his luck would soon change.

Perhaps it would, she considered tremulously, as her fingers touched her stomach. Such a change, though, might well destroy her.

Always regular as clockwork, her monthly cycle was now a good week late. It might mean nothing, but it might mean she would be using the five hundred pounds earlier than she had anticipated. Any guilt she still felt over accepting Gabriel's funds was alleviated when she considered how that money might save his child.

If there was to be a child.

Because if she were pregnant, the babe would be born only to die unless she managed to act quickly. Despite Justin's assurance he would farm out Brynley's baby to be raised by others, Arabella didn't believe him. She was no longer so naïve, not when that child might one day threaten the succession of his titles.

A knock upon the door interrupted her musings.

"Do leave me be," she snapped in response, just as the door flung open.

"Your tone, Arabella, needs softening." Justin stepped into the glow of the light she had recently lit. He was dressed in golden silk and bronze, the colors, as always, exacerbating his good looks.

"I've a headache."

It was their routine. Every late afternoon he would find her and tell her what was expected of her that night. She would plead a headache. He would tell her she must attend; then she would bow her head and comply, because really, what did she care what she did or where she went, or even of whom the company consisted?

"Your presence is required. We're to go to the

Smithsons' home for a formal dinner. He's an admiral in the Royal Navy. Do try to impress him, because he's very interested in ancient ruins. For once, your hobby might prove rewarding."

"And what is to be your reward?" she asked, not really caring, as he crossed the room to lean against her dresser.

"Access to certain ports in Alexandria which have been blocked against non-military use. But now, with the fighting easing up for the moment, a new consortium I'm part of wants to start trading. I need the funds this venture will bring, so please, do be on your best behavior, won't you, my dear? No more sullen silences and long sighs?"

His eyes narrowed as he scrutinized her. She was dressed in a blue cotton dress that showed many signs of mending along the cuffs. It was one of her favorites and she often wore it when she planned to sit and study. But with her hair caught back in a simple matching ribbon, she recognized she looked younger than she was.

"You look quite fetching. Very beddable," he added as if confirming her thoughts. Suddenly, his expression darkened. "Have you had your courses yet?"

The question wasn't unanticipated. He asked it every day.

"I told you, it is too soon."

She lied glibly, wondering at how easily the untruths slipped from her tongue now, but she needed time, more time, to plot and plan and become accustomed to the idea of what she must do. To run would be to lose any place in Society she had ever held. Although it was not as dear to her as it was to some, the loss would not be inconsequential.

Justin flung himself from his negligent stance. He

grabbed her up from her chair and into his arms. In the next instant, he pressed his wet slugs against her lips, battering with his tongue against the teeth she clenched against him. As he pulled her nearer, she struggled to keep him away. The hands she pressed against his chest weren't much use, and her legs were trapped between the fabric of her skirts.

He bent her back until her spine felt as if it would snap. She did the only thing she could think to do. She bit his bottom lip. Hard.

"Ow! You little whore!" He stepped back and thrust her from him with such force she was hurled to the floor. Immediately, pain radiated up her back.

Justin dabbed at his lip, and his eyes narrowed when his hand came back bloody.

Too late, Arabella realized she should have allowed his small liberties, for the eyes he turned to her were filled with a frightening, icy rage. Before she could attempt to flee, he dragged her upright. His fingers pressed painfully into her arm. Taking careful and deliberate aim, he pulled back his hand and slapped her once across the cheek.

The earth tilted, and she would have fallen had he not held her upright. He pushed her from him, so she landed in a heap upon her bed. A mewling sob escaped her lips as she cradled her stinging face. Shock held her rigid.

"Ungrateful whore. I promise you'll soon welcome my kisses and beg for my touch. If you don't appease me, I may offer you to the grasping attention of lesser men. That would earn me good coin, I think."

It was a new threat.

"Y-you wouldn't!" Arabella sat up. She wiped at the tears streaming down her cheeks.

He considered for a moment. "I don't know. Maybe

not. I do want an heir, and I don't want one off a wife who is the catchall of every man's leavings. There's the pox to consider. On the other hand, now that I have the ring, you really are expendable." He shrugged. "It is something to think about, for certain. You will be ready to leave at half-eight."

"Justin," she implored, "you can't still mean for me to go? My face…"

"I'll send up some cold water to help with any swelling and some pancake powder to conceal the worst of any bruises. My stepmothers often used it after receiving my father's attentions. In any event, you are my property, to do with as I please, and you should be grateful I hit you gently, and but once. Let Society see the disobedient wife I've married, and let them judge you for it."

The truth, she acknowledged, rising silently and limping over to her dressing table once he had gone, was he was right. Society would condemn her, not him. He was a golden boy, and she was the bluestocking who had captured him away from the bevy of other Society matrons who had eyed him for their daughters.

Besides, it was always the female's fault, wasn't it, when aspects went awry in a personal relationship?

Arabella touched her cheek. The sting had been fleeting, her shock more enduring. Her pain served a purpose, though. It reminded her she needed to act.

If there was even a chance life was growing within her, she had a purpose. It wasn't the plan she had envisioned for herself, back only weeks ago when Assyriology had filled her every waking thought, but it was enough.

Her hand strayed toward her stomach as she prayed

the one time would have proved sufficient.

It was a long while before she remembered she needed to dress.

Chapter 30

"I don't know why I let you talk me into this, Peter. I'm in no mood for light chatter and obsequious compliments." Gabriel grumbled as he leaned back against the leather upholstery.

His new carriage was so well sprung he could barely feel the sway as the team of matched grays pranced their way down the narrow streets of London.

"Am I to believe, after such a lengthy period of seclusion, you aren't longing for scheming mamas to parade their horsy daughters before you?"

"At the very least, my back no longer aches as I haven't had to fetch a single reticule from the floor in weeks. But perhaps I'll send a couple ponies your way? Explain to the mamas that, even though you were born slightly off the branch, we're all a bunch of veritable paupers next to you? A good bank account can compensate for lack of proper birth."

"I was properly born. My mother swore the event ruined her figure too," Peter quipped.

"Then let us say instead, a healthy income compensates for lack of nobility."

"I'm noble enough, thank you. Why, didn't I send Sally Witting off three nights since without having my lusty way with her?"

Peter's eyes sparkled merrily in the dim interior, reflecting a passing streetlight.

"Only because she is already visibly rounding with another man's child and moony-eyed about her state as well."

For a moment, Gabriel's thoughts flipped to Arabella as they were wont to do anyway. Could she be rounding too? He ruthlessly clamped down upon the thought and buried it deep. What good would it do to ponder such a question since it would be impossible to know the father? Two men in one day. That was a feat not many ladies could boast.

He gritted his teeth and shoved the thought down again, down until it sank into the churning mass of acid swirling inside his mid-section.

Why dwell on something he couldn't fix? Tomorrow, he and Reggie would set off for Baghdad. All their many trunks and cases were packed. His clothing had been laid out. Most of the rooms were closed up, and the excess servants given their pensions. With only Peter staying in residence to oversee the estate and businesses for a short time, nothing but a skeletal staff was needed.

"So, you think old Freebody has a map?" Peter asked, turning the conversation to the sole reason Gabriel had agreed to attend the Smithson dinner.

"That's the rumor. If I can persuade him tonight, I'll follow him back and either draw up a quick copy or perhaps take the original if he'll sell it to me. A few hours of stultifying conversation will either land me with a partnership or leave me to explore at my own folly." He shrugged his shoulders. "Doesn't really matter which."

Peter didn't respond, so Gabriel turned to look out the window. They were not yet arrived due to the constant snag of London traffic. His fingers fiddled with his collar. It was too tight. It trapped and suffocated him, just as the carriage did. Just as the city did. The blocks and warrens of ceaseless activity had grown too small.

He couldn't wait to be away from everyone and everything that had gone wrong of late, not least the mysterious appearance of Russell Manning's will. The document, couched as a sober *mea culpa,* had cleverly explained away the Darkwood right to the inheritance. But would any man, even Russell Manning, willingly admit to such deceit? He had claimed to have hired a coachman to pose as a priest, thereby nullifying the sanctity of his prior union with Bertha Darkwood.

It had all been very neat, too neat, but even now, Gabriel couldn't bring himself to fight. Titles and family honor, be damned. All that mattered was he had lost to Justin. Again.

Outside the carriage window, drivers hurled insults at each other, interrupting his thoughts. Damned city. Too much noise, too many people, all of them clawing for some artificial supremacy that would end with their inevitable deaths. He wondered how they survived the boredom of their days without any real interests outside of their own importance.

"I wish to discuss your will," Peter said suddenly as if sensing the train of Gabriel's thoughts.

"Worried you won't be mentioned should I perish in the sands?"

"I won't justify such ridiculousness with a response. No, I wish you to consider that since your relatives have managed to hold onto their titles, and now that Justin has married…."

Gabriel growled.

"Their ability to obtain much-needed funds is limited to either locating some blind and utterly brainless heiress to wed your uncle or to inheriting at your death. I'd wager on your death, naturally."

"You believe me so benighted I do not realize they will try to have me killed, now they have conclusively established the pecking order?" Gabriel shook his head. "Your worries are unnecessary. As you are rich as Croesus, I have left the entirety of the unentailed portion of my estate to Reggie. I had the papers drawn earlier this week."

"Then I shall get the word out so you do not meet with any untimely accidents sooner rather than later. Of course, the entailed portion of the estate may be enough to cause them to act against you anyway."

Gabriel shrugged. "There's nothing to be done about that."

"No, I suppose not. It is a shame, though, that Justin's bride will rise and fall with his fortunes."

For a moment, Gabriel's response caught in his throat. Gruffly, he cleared it. "She made her decision."

The carriage lurched, then stopped. Gabriel pushed back the curtain and peered out the window into the dark streets. Shadows from the occasional light created a dance of grisaille-colored specters. Sighing, he closed the draperies.

Peter thrummed his fingers against the seat, the action belaying his calm façade. Instantly, Gabriel grew wary. Peter was never perturbed.

"Out with it. What has occurred?"

Peter quirked his head to the side. "Ah, well, since you raise the question…I find I must trespass upon an area you have declared off-limits."

"As if you haven't already."

"Not as much as I could. I have come to believe

Arabella may not have wed your cousin willingly."

Gabriel drew a careful, long breath through his nose, mostly to try to stop his heart from beating right out of his chest at the mention of her name.

"Let me finish. First, you must know she never liked the man. Such was obvious, in retrospect. Lady de Veer, whose feathers I sought to unruffle after your uncle's dastardly treatment, said as much last night. At great length."

Gabriel waved his hand as if to swat away the consideration. He didn't want to hear about Arabella. He wanted to forget her.

"I believed, like you, the lady had been convinced by her mother's illness to wed quickly. Foolish of her, true, I thought, but it seemed the obvious explanation. Annette, however, maintains your bluestocking was quite voluble in her dislike of the viscount. So why marry him? She was under no obligation because when you promised the funds for the *Epic*, you provided her with an easy way to avoid Justin's advances."

"Perhaps she did not trust my promises."

"That's absurd. Anyone who knows you at all knows to trust your word. Consider this: the earl unceremoniously excised Lady de Veer in public so she had no recourse but to flee the ball or be exposed by her own emotions. Her flight created an opportunity for your relatives to force Arabella before a priest."

Gabriel's stomach flipped, though he tried to still it. Hadn't he thought the same thing when he had discovered Annette's lucky absence?

"And," Peter added, holding up his hand, "don't tell me such deviant behavior is impossible. You know only too well it isn't."

Gabriel sat very still, his fingers biting into the window frame. He grabbed the wood with enough energy to make it crack because if he released it, he might just punch his friend to stop him from speaking.

"She's a woman. She's fickle. Her nature can't be trusted."

"Untrue, unfair, and unlike you to think so. Her preference was always for you and was obvious no matter how she tried to hide her feelings. Plus, as you've remarked, she disliked Justin's kiss, was aware he was short of funds, and you had already, by agreement to buy the *Epic*, saved her from the necessity of marriage to anyone, even your fine self. I am out of time as well, Gabriel. There's little of it left in which to talk some sense into you."

"And you choose now to press me with this? Now?"

"Yes."

Gabriel shook his head and let out the blast of air he held. "You didn't see her as I did, all sleepy and sugary, entwined with him. Damn it! The sight won't leave my eyes." He released the frame and raked his fingers through his hair, tangling the mass of it as he threw back his head. "I won't. The wise learn to accept defeat, and I have done so. And if you bring up her name to me again, no matter I love you like a brother, I vow I shall never speak with you again."

Peter smiled, his expression that of a cat savoring a recent mouse kill. If his response to Gabriel's threat was disconcerting, there wasn't time to pursue why, as the carriage finally rolled to a halt.

Peter gathered up his hat and pushed it onto his head. "Shall we go?" he asked jauntily, as if he had not just overturned Gabriel's carefully constructed balance.

"It is unimaginable that Society consents to host you." He stretched for his hat.

Peter just laughed, as well he should. Gabriel had never prevaricated about his belief: Society should welcome anyone capable of wresting the essence out of life, whether a person was born to wealth or had earned it himself. It was the modern view and gaining popularity. As the world turned to commerce and industrialization rather than farming, the narrow social restrictions broadened. Lesser titled nobility, like Gabriel, and even illegitimates, like Peter, were entitled to entry by virtue of their aptitude and pocketbooks.

"It's going to be an eventful evening," Peter commented, jumping down from the carriage first, "now the ice has been broken. Frankly, I can't wait to see what happens next."

Gabriel studiously ignored him and straightened his jacket. Tomorrow, he would be gone.

It couldn't come soon enough.

Chapter 31

"Ah, so good of you to come, Lord Manning, and what a pleasure to meet your charming bride. The two of you have been on the tips of everyone's tongues, haven't you? But, my dear, whatever happened to your face?" Admiral Smithson asked as he took Arabella's hand and peered at her solicitously under the too-bright hall lights.

"Loggias, don't embarrass the poor girl," snapped his wife.

She held out her hand to press Arabella's. Well, she would comprehend, wouldn't she, given her husband must parade a host of officers and their wives before her? That men could be violent was a secret kept from most girls, but not once they had become women.

"Ah, Admiral, without her spectacles, I'm afraid my wife has a tendency toward clumsiness," Justin explained smoothly.

"Yes, a door, no doubt. Or a garden rake. They do have a way of jumping out at a person," Mrs. Smithson agreed, "which is why I advocate keeping ours in the shed." She shot Arabella another sympathetic look and surreptitiously touched her elbow.

The little kindness almost undid her.

"My wife would not rest, Admiral, for her desire to hear your opinions on the layout of…what was it called, dearest?" Justin asked, utterly missing the sarcasm embedded within Mrs. Smithson's remarks.

"Dilmun," Arabella politely agreed. "Your opinions. I wished to discuss them."

She shot the admiral what she hoped was a smile, taking care not to pull her bruised cheek too far. She knew her part. If encouraging a dusty relic to wax rhapsodically about a place he would never seek was the price she was forced to pay for peace, then simulate she would. She had mastered the charade. Surely, she might continue to act until she could escape with her mother at week's end?

"Dilmun?" the admiral asked. "Why, nothing could please me more, my lady, though I must admit I am not the sole expert on Assyriology present this evening. Mr. David Freebody has recently discovered a map of the city's supposed location, drawn, you'll never guess, by one of his very own ancestors. You'd best hurry if you plan to extract information from him, however, for Brynley already has the man's feet to the fire."

"Brynley is here?" Justin demanded, taking a step backward.

Mrs. Smithson, obviously not a stupid woman grabbed Arabella's arm. She pivoted them away from the men. "Come, Lady Manning, let us go inquire into Mr. Freebody's wonderous map. I confess to some interest in ancient cities myself."

Arabella allowed herself to be led, not bothering to look back at her husband. She was suddenly light-headed and wobbly as Mrs. Smithson guided her to the main salon and the assembly of the gathered guests.

Gabriel was here? Here?

Her grip upon her hostess' arm tightened as the floor tilted, but she stared straight ahead, forcing her breaths just as her mother must do.

She found him immediately, standing next to the fire, deep in discussion with the man who had to be the famous David Freebody. Her feet no longer obeyed her. She could do nothing but stand and drink him in. Although she was distantly aware Mrs. Smithson was speaking, she paid her no mind.

When he stilled, she realized he had sensed her presence. It was impossible to believe she knew him so well, but she did. When he turned his head, his brows already drawn into a thunderous frown, she nearly smiled. Only his unmoving rigidity stopped her. He was a statue made of granite, unbending, unmoving. There was nothing in him to indicate he would favor any expression of welcome from her, even now, weeks after the last terrible time she had laid eyes upon him.

Trembling, she tried to will herself still. Uncannily, she was saved from her reactions by Justin's arrival. His proprietary arm encircled her waist. His other hand squeezed hard around the tender bones of her elbow. The pain snapped her spine straight and stopped her shaking. For the first time, she welcomed her husband's cruelty. At least she wouldn't humiliate herself and bring social ostracism down upon them all by running across the room, throwing herself at Gabriel's feet, and begging him to take her away.

Then, as she stared hard at him, drinking in every plane of his face, he simply swiveled away. He returned to his conversation as if her presence was of no account.

Immediately, her longing burst into an angry flame. How dare he believe the lies Justin had created? How dare he ignore her, as if now he had the *Epic*, she no longer mattered at all? How dare he not care a shred she might be carrying his child? Yes, the entire situation in which she found herself was her own fault, but never, not for a single moment, had she imagined he would be indifferent to her fate.

Her mother had been right. Marriage to such an uncaring man would have been a knife through her heart on a semi-daily basis.

Allowing Justin to lead her away from the relative safety of Mrs. Smithson's company, they made their way around the crowded room. It was a small and intimate affair, only thirty for dinner, with most making their way to various parties afterward. Arabella cringed, knowing they must come to Gabriel soon, yet, as if by design, as they circled the room, so did he. The three of them never came face to face.

As she rotated, Arabella did her duty and spoke with the admiral. She hoped she charmed him despite the icy fog that surrounded her like a shroud. She laughed on cue and steeled her face into solicitous and interested expressions by turn. She took in nothing, however, as if she were separated by a thick wall from any meaning any of the partygoers might wish to convey. Since her marriage, she had learned popularity required only one be a talented actress capable of mimicry. Apparently, she was that.

Yet, every time she glanced Gabriel's way, and she sought him with an alarming regularity, a strange pull of longing seeped through her anger like syrup through a sieve. She couldn't help but notice he had lost weight, so his cheekbones stood out like sharpened blades. The shape of him was hauntingly familiar, but he was as like her old assistant as a hunting lion was to her fat Persian cat.

There was a feral quality to his stance, and he moved

as if he would just as soon stalk from the room or pounce for the kill. Waves of impatience wafted from his skin, although his visage was as composed as an even floor. Had she met him now, for the first time, she might even have been frightened.

For certain, she would have been wary. Never, not ever, would she have allowed this man to drag her around her bedroom without screaming down the house. Never would she have met him in secret, visited his home unchaperoned, or seduced him in her own bedroom. He was not the same person at all as the one who had acted as her patient, supportive assistant.

Her heart, however, didn't seem to recognize the difference or the danger. When dinner was announced, she realized she was in serious trouble. Following the custom of the day, husbands and wives were separated so that Justin had to find his place at the other end of the long table and the opposite side from her. That was no hardship. However, when she looked across the width of the wood, she found herself impaled upon two twin beams of green lightning glaring their displeasure.

Trembling, she shrank back into her chair, but although she clutched her hands in her lap, nothing could hide their shaking.

"Lady Manning," Gabriel acknowledged stiffly, barely inclining his head.

Arabella managed to nod, how she did not know.

He narrowed his eyes as he studied her. "Been tripping over your cat, have you?"

Though his tone was light, the tic in his cheek beat a fast rhythm, and there was something in his demeanor that spoke of banked but smoldering rage.

The heads of those seated near turned her way, so she

stiffened her spine and gritted her teeth.

"Kismet currently resides with my mother," she replied, as evenly as she could manage. "Thank you for your kind inquiry as to his welfare."

"It was not kindness for his welfare that caused me to ask," he replied shortly.

"Mr. Freebody," she exclaimed, turning quickly to the companion seated to her left, so her bruised cheek was hidden from the table, "I hear you have uncovered a map of Dilmun. Do tell me all about it," she begged. "Spare not the least detail."

David Freebody slit his gaze across the table then returned it to her. "Lady Manning, as you must be aware, Lord Brynley has expressed a similar interest. Indeed, I feel quite privileged in announcing we have entered into a partnership, the two of us."

"A partnership?" asked a simpering, too-beautiful young woman seated to Gabriel's left.

"Yes. In fact, we are agreed, are we not, Brynley? He will leave for Baghdad at dawn." Looking up and down the table and apparently noting he had captured the attention of all the assembled guests, Mr. Freebody added, "Join me, friends, if you will, in wishing success and prosperity to Brynley's hunt for the most fabled city in all of ancient lore. May he return with evidence that will advance the cause of Assyriology upon our fine shores."

His toast was immediately taken up around the table. Even Justin raised his glass, though with a considering look that spiked a new level of fear in Arabella's heart. His manner was too calm, and somehow, too determined.

Arabella glanced across at Gabriel and discovered he was studying her, not his cousin. Carefully, along with the rest of the guests, her fingers shaking gracelessly, she raised her glass of the deep and hearty Cote de Rhone to him. Taking the smallest of sips to hide the evidence of her nervousness, she could still barely force her throat to swallow.

"But you can't be leaving tomorrow," said the same annoyingly lovely woman, whose dark hair was a mirror to the baron's own. Her perfectly formed mouth turned down becomingly like a sulking kitten, and all Arabella wanted to do was pour her glass of wine over the vapidly gorgeous head.

"I'm afraid I'm quite anxious to be off," Gabriel murmured.

The woman frowned further, which suddenly made Arabella feel much better about where the contents of her wine glass continued to rest.

"Where is this Dilmun?" Lady Asterly demanded. Seated to Gabriel's right, she sniffed at the name of the foreign city. "Is it in France?"

Amusement sparkled across Gabriel's face, but the moment so quickly passed, Arabella wondered if she had imagined it.

"Dilmun is both a place and a concept," Gabriel replied, peering around the table. "That it exists on a map, or did exist, is clear from many of the ancient references to the place. It is almost certain that Gilgamesh, a once-great warrior king, discovered this kingdom of his ancestors. It is conjectured that within its borders grows the original tree of eternal life, an ancient concept much like the Garden of Eden. Like that Biblical locale, Dilmun is also conceptual, an ideal filled with running brooks, veritable feasts, and all manner of heavenly accoutrements."

"So, you seek eternal life then, cousin?" Justin yelled

down the length and laughed. "I wish you success, although, to my Christian mind, the only eternal life is the one you will find in the hereafter."

Gabriel's smile tightened. "Never fear, Manning. I've taken particular care to create a new will recently, lest I accidentally stumble upon that eternity which you suggest. I am aware of the perils I undertake."

"Any fiend so foolish as to harm you, my friend, will meet my wrath," Peter Bartholomew promised in a deliberate tone, before adding in a lighter voice, "After all, as your partner in many a venture, should you leave me to handle all matters on my own, why, however, will I find enough opportunity for idleness? Any ne'er-do-well who would cause me such trouble should surely be punished." Peter stared at Justin until finally, he turned toward Arabella.

Appreciative laughter rang around the table, as Arabella, startled to have heard the familiar voice, met Peter's gaze. "Mr. Bartholomew," she acknowledged quietly. "I hadn't realized you were in attendance this evening. It is a pleasure to see you again."

Peter raised a hand to his chest. "I am wounded, Lady Arabella. You have thus far overlooked my presence. I'm afraid I see a pattern here. I say, Brynley, do you remark upon how your former pupil singularly forgets my existence at every turn? Why, it is enough to make me question my stature among the fairer sex."

"Why should Lady Manning trouble to recognize any man not her husband?" Justin's frown was menacing.

"Never fear, Mr. Bartholomew, you are handsome as ever," Lady Asterly intoned dryly, swamping Justin's voice, her volume resonating down the table.

Not quite recognizing the old dowager's sarcastic

tone, the younger ladies were quick to assure Peter he was extremely noticeable indeed and quite a pleasant addition to any gathering.

"Pupil?" one of the men asked, raising an eyebrow.

"The term is not completely correct, but I did have the opportunity to aid Lady Manning with her studies of cuneiform," Gabriel responded smoothly.

"As did I," Justin intervened, stepping on the end of his cousin's words. He glared at the baron. "Why Gilcanesh's tale is the glue that binds our marriage, is it not, my dear?" he asked.

"Gilgamesh." She mouthed the correction, careful not to be overheard, but when she peeped across the table she found Gabriel's gaze upon her.

"In any event, Lady Asterly," the baron continued, addressing the dowager, "if there are any tablets left that tell of ancient times, they will most likely be found at the sacred and holy site of Dilmun. That is why I go."

Lady Asterly sniffed in response. "If you will excuse my saying so, Brynley, I don't countenance all this archeological nonsense that has become fashionable of late. Everyone understands the Bible tells us all we need ever know of history, and surely we may rely upon our preachers to inform us, even then, of what little is of interest in that book?"

"Though I must disagree, Lady Asterly, your opinion seems not to be an unpopular one." Gabriel bowed his head.

"I, for one, am hoping you locate gold statues, eh Brynley?" David Freebody interjected loudly. "Perhaps of a lovely goddess or a cache of jewels."

"Jewels," echoed another young lady.

Arabella could hardly keep track of which since they

seemed interchangeable, and all terribly young.

"Speaking of, have you heard about the latest exhibit at Westminster? The queen has decided to put her private collection on display."

As talk turned to other matters and their first course was served, Arabella chanced to peep across the table again, only to find Gabriel engaged in conversation with anyone other than her. It was as if she had ceased to hold any interest for him at all. She couldn't even spot hatred for her apparent betrayal.

As she chased one course of sawdust after another around her plate, Arabella's fatigue and unhappiness grew until she felt like nothing so much as a dark, inert boulder of despair. Finally, Mrs. Smithson rose, a signal to the ladies to leave the gentlemen to their drinks and cigars. Tossing a last glance Gabriel's way as she followed the other women out of the room, Arabella was further depressed to see he was already engaged in picking out a fat cigar from the box a solicitous servant was passing around. He took no notice of her leaving.

Probably because he wasn't disconcerted by her presence. After all, he wasn't the one in love. That would be her, and more fool she. How had she been so contemptuous of the sentiment only a handful of weeks ago when it was consuming her now like an acid bath?

Her hand pressed to her stomach as if warding off the insidious thoughts, but it was not successful. Having seen Gabriel again, she could admit she had still held out some hope he would rescue her, as he had offered to do before her marriage. How he would have arranged to do so, she did not know, beyond what he had already done in buying her *Epic*. Still, she had hoped, somewhere deep inside herself, somewhere she hadn't even wanted to explore, that after his anger had passed, he would find his way toward missing her. Instead, his sense of betrayal had led him to a different place entirely, a place in which her absence was of no account whatsoever.

Perhaps it was best his disinterest had been revealed. She would no longer wait upon him to save her, but instead take action to save herself.

And she would take it. Soon.

She sat by the French doors that led out onto the patio. On the other side of the room, one of the younger, more accomplished women had commenced playing an airy tune upon the small piano. Most of the remaining females had gathered into little groups, the better to discuss the different men at dinner, who had worn what, and what the latest gossip revealed. It was all pointless noise.

"You look pale, Lady Manning. Are you quite all right?"

Arabella startled at the voice next to her ear. She found herself looking into Peter's angelic face. Over his shoulder, the men returned to join the ladies.

Trying her best, she smiled. "Mr. Bartholomew."

"I thought we had established you might call me by my given name, although I suppose we are not quite in private," he murmured.

She craned her neck to see around him. Gabriel entered the doorway. Despite her resolution, she drank him in hungrily. When his gaze landed upon her, he only frowned and looked away.

It was all she could do not to cry out as an aching pain stabbed at her again.

"Yes, it's too bad all the otters flung themselves into the cooking pot, but what could we do?"

"Yes, too bad," she agreed, looking down at her clasped hands as she fought back the incipient tears prickling at the corners of her eyes.

"Arabella."

She looked up into Peter's sympathetic gaze.

"I find it difficult to maintain my enormous ego when you so clearly are attentive to someone other than me."

Arabella's cheeks heated, but she couldn't find the words to deny his accusation. She swallowed hard, but a giant lump in her throat prevented her from doing so.

"I wasn't being facile, Arabella. You look quite peaked. I expect marriage is taking its toll."

"Yes, it is."

The words slipped out around the boulder before she could restrain them. They were too honest, given the environment. She tilted her head to look toward the doorway where Gabriel had just been standing. There was no one there.

Peter dropped down into the chair beside hers. "There's no need to look for him any longer. He's just left. Said something about more packing, but the truth is, now that he's got his map of Dilmun, he needn't suffer the party further. Nor you," he added blithely, but his voice was deliberate for all of its lightness.

Arabella closed her eyes. When she opened them again, he watched her closely, his gaze full of pity.

"You've made him suffer, Arabella. You must know that."

She nodded, shook her head, and then shrugged. "He doesn't look as if he's suffering."

Peter tilted his head. "Looks are deceiving. For instance, you appear to be positively mired in torment. How could that possibly be true, given this was your choice?"

The kindness in Peter's regard robbed Arabella of any false pride she might have donned.

"It wasn't my choice. Gabriel warned me, but I didn't realize…"

"Realize?"

She shook her head. "I didn't intentionally betray him; please know that. Both of you have been so kind, so very kind, and I…"

The burn in her chest, the unshed tears and desperation that had mounted, day by day, stopped her voice again.

When she could manage, she added, "In any event, it seems Gabriel has recovered from whatever brief prick he might have felt from my hurried marriage. How excited he must be to be traveling to Dilmun."

"Ah, the infamous understanding of one scholar for another. It is too bad the both of you can't see further than the page spread under your noses. Tell me, what did you mean when you said you didn't intentionally betray him? What do you believe there was to betray?"

Everything.

"Nothing. Of course, nothing," she replied quickly, stung. She popped out of her seat, only to have Peter rise as well.

"Now is not the time for lies," he said softly, suddenly very serious.

She wouldn't have credited he could wear such a severe expression. He shot a glance toward the far end of the room where Justin stood talking to their host.

"Tell me why you married. Indulge me."

Arabella glanced toward her husband as well. He glared at her. She skipped her gaze around the room.

People had begun to turn toward them, their expressions questioning as they noticed her lengthy and intimate conversation with a man only barely acceptable, especially as she was only recently wed.

"Justin is watching."

"Everyone is watching. Tell me."

The last thing Arabella wanted to do was talk about her marriage, but with people beginning to stare, the one thing she had to do if she wished to avoid a scandal was to derail Peter.

"I don't know, is that what you wish to hear? One moment, I was leaving the Stapleton ball with Justin and his father, and the next I woke up, and Gabriel…he was looking at me, and Justin…"

Arabella's throat closed. She cleared it and glanced to the side, away from Peter's piercing blue eyes.

It was an unbelievable story.

"You were drugged?"

Arabella shrugged. "I believe so, not that it matters now." Quickly, she looked back at him. "Now, if you will excuse me?"

She began to move toward her husband, who had happily been stopped by Lord Rutledge, but Peter grabbed her elbow.

"Has the marriage been consummated? Tell me the truth," he hissed in her ear.

She paused but then shook her head. "No. No, he has left me alone, until he can be certain I do not…am not…"

She had no more words.

Peter dropped her arm, and Arabella crossed the room, not only to appease Justin's volatile temper or to avoid the scandalized looks the other women wore, but also to escape the sympathy Peter's expression held.

He didn't need to tell her she was trapped or that her own inexcusable stupidity was the cause.

There was no one to save her except herself, but save herself she would.

Soon.

Chapter 32

There were only two places the baron could reasonably be found after an evening spent ignoring the woman who had broken his heart. Peter wiggled two metal picks against the locked doors of the museum. He was either polishing Shu's saddle to a mirror finish, or he was holed away in the Assyriology section of this venerable institution. As Shu was currently in Ireland being put to stud, it had been easy to decide where to travel.

An ardent benefactor, board member, and a researcher of some value, Gabriel had the keys. Peter wasn't as lucky, but he was very good at entering locked dwellings. He slipped inside on silent feet, his way in the dark lit by the reflective glow of light from the end of the row of offices. When he reached the partially opened door, he skated through it without making a sound.

"I knew you'd come looking for me. Can't ever mind your own business, can you?" Gabriel swiveled his chair, so it faced the door.

"Damnation, how did you even hear me?" Peter dropped into the seat across the rather small expanse of wooden desk. Evidently, the board wasn't actually supposed to work from these tiny spaces.

"I expected you to meddle."

"You would do the same for me."

Gabriel reached into his pocket. He took a rolled

document, fastened with red wax, and slid it across the wood top toward him. The symbol pressed into the wax was familiar.

When he cocked an eyebrow in question, Gabriel said, "My will. After the dinner, I stopped by my solicitor's office to retrieve a copy. He wasn't pleased to be roused from his bed."

"Ah." Peter pocketed the document inside his jacket. "He has the original?"

"He does. I told him if either you or Reggie requests it, he is to hand it over without issue."

"There is something else."

"No. There is nothing else." Gabriel fiddled with a letter opener. He must have been perusing a pile of mail, but Peter doubted the contents had truly been processed. His friend wore the distracted look he often held when studying cuneiform. Now, something else obsessed him.

"Normally, I would warn you that pressing me upon this particular subject is unwise, especially given you lied to me about her presence tonight," Gabriel muttered. "The bonds of brotherhood can only stretch so far before they break, you know, though you seem not to care."

"Though I am indeed surprised the letter opener you are fondling has not yet found its way into my heart, my reasons for keeping quiet about Arabella's presence were sound." Peter paused, feeling his way. "This trip you intend will take the better part of a year, perhaps two."

"Perhaps more," Gabriel acknowledged easily. "I haven't yet decided."

Peter could see no way to raise the subject except baldly. "Then you should know, by the time you return, Arabella will be in the ground, and any babe of yours she might be carrying will be similarly interred."

His all-but-brother flinched. "Justin would not risk killing his child. Arabella and I were together only one night, the very same night she wed and bedded my cousin. If she is pregnant now, the chances are it is his seed." He wrinkled his nose. "Disgusting, wrenching thought."

"I asked her if the marriage had been consummated."

Gabriel visibly started. His stare was diamond-sharp. "You what?"

"She denied it, which makes excellent sense from Justin's perspective if he knew she had been with you. I suspect he is aware. He would not risk his title passing to your issue."

"How is that possible?" Gabriel demanded, leaning forward. "I saw them in bed together. Do you think I can ever erase that image from my mind, her, almost naked, and that cretinous villain's leg thrown over her body, his fingers toying with her? It is burned here," he growled, thumping his forehead, before shuddering.

Then, he stilled, as if re-evaluating the scene he had witnessed, perhaps for the first time seeing it from a perspective uncolored by the agony of betrayal. Finally, reluctantly it seemed, he nodded.

"Oh." His fierce expression melted like pudding in the sun.

"Exactly. Justin and your uncle must have drugged her, as she has no memory of the ceremony. However," he added quickly, when Gabriel's expression suddenly lightened, "I am equally certain they are truly, legally wed, or Justin would never have presented her to Society as his wife."

It wasn't easy watching the hope evaporate from Gabriel's face, knowing his next words would be even more painful. The stubborn, prevaricating scholar needed to be jolted into action, but that didn't mean the process was pleasant.

"Arabella was extraordinarily pale tonight. She ate nothing. If she is pregnant now, Justin will kill them both. You know this is true."

"You watched her."

"Of course."

Gabriel's palm slapped down upon the desk. "Why bring this to me now? What do you expect me to do, even if it is all exactly as you say?"

"Let us not waste more time with dispute," Peter retorted. "You may choose to do nothing. You may choose to run to the desert and ignore whatever happens upon these shores. However, you know as well as I do that it strains credibility to believe Arabella decided to marry Justin under such conditions. Under any conditions. I firmly believe none of this was her doing, poor lass." He took a deep breath. "If you do nothing, then I tell you now, I will do whatever I can to help her."

"You are soft in the head," Gabriel growled, but his bark had no bite.

Peter left him to think for a few moments.

Finally, he asked, "Drugged?"

"Ask yourself whether it is in her nature to have chosen a man of little learning, a man of questionable character whom she did not favor, when she could have chosen no one at all, or even, Lord help her, you?"

Suddenly, Gabriel groaned as he sank his head into his hands. "What have I done?" he whispered, sounding tortured. "What have I left her to endure through my blindness, my stupidity?"

Peter understood. Arabella was a gentle soul. It was

easy to want to protect her, especially from the worm she had married.

"The better question is, what will you do now?"

"I will steal Arabella and take her to the desert, far from anyone's reach, just as a brighter man would have done weeks ago."

"Even though she is legally Justin's?"

Gabriel's eyes gleamed, and the candlelight wavering within his pupils made him seem dangerous. "Wives can be made into widows, and if Justin kidnapped and drugged her then I shall have little hesitancy in performing such a service."

"You mean to kill Justin then? In cold blood?" Peter asked conversationally.

"Want to come and find out?"

"Wouldn't miss the opportunity for the world."

****

Justin had been strangely silent all evening. Arabella had expected him to rail about Gabriel's presence at the dinner party or even Peter's, but instead, he had contented himself by humming a strange tune she couldn't place. The constant refrain gave her goosebumps. The ride, which should have been short, was beginning to seem interminable. She shuddered, but it had nothing to do with the night chill.

Actually, it was taking far longer than it ought to return to Kildare's London home, where they all resided. The curtains over the windows had been drawn, but the city streets were never completely dark, and light should have peeped in around the fabric.

Attempting to keep her voice steady, Arabella asked, "Are we expected elsewhere tonight? I had hoped to sleep away this headache."

Even to her ears, her speech sounded overloud in the quiet confines. Justin acted as if he hadn't heard her question for all that.

"Justin?" she demanded again, trying not to let fear warble the edges of her words. "Justin, where are we going?"

When he still failed to acknowledge her, the incessant hum his only response, she raised her arm, intending to pound on the roof to signal the driver to stop. Justin caught her wrist.

"You are always so difficult," he complained. "Now, look what you've done. You've dragged me from my pleasant reverie and to no good end as John Coachman has orders to take us to Ripemoor. Nothing you say or do will supersede my orders."

"Let go of me, Justin. You are hurting my wrist."

Smiling, he did as requested, and she rubbed at her aching bones.

"What is Ripemoor?" she finally asked.

She could not read his expression. Darkness surrounded her, although outside, she knew a large moon shone.

"I've decided a short honeymoon with my bride is in order. We will be spending some time together."

"What does that mean? What are you planning? Justin, answer me!"

But he remained unresponsive, and finally, after further entreaties failed, she lapsed into silence as well. A chill caught hold of her neck. She rubbed at it quickly, trying to restore warmth, though the rest of her body flushed with heat.

It was a long ride. Arabella had just begun to doze when the carriage stilled. In a moment she was awake, some feeling of foreboding reaching out on the condensing fog to wrap her within its icy tentacles.

"Good. You're up. Watch your step, my dear." Justin helped her from the carriage and to the front steps.

With a nod of his head, he dismissed the driver. Arabella had to restrain herself from calling out to John Coachman to stay, help her, take her far away. Instead, she followed her husband's lead as he unlocked the door and led her into the Stygian-draped foyer. He lit a taper, but it did little to relieve the black.

"Watch the stairs."

"Where are the servants?" she asked as she measured the tread of the steps.

"There aren't any. Now do be quiet, Arabella. You disturb my thoughts."

When they reached a doorway on the upper landing, he paused. Searching above the lintel, he withdrew a key. It turned in the lock with a grating click. The door creaked open to reveal a room bathed in further darkness. With her new night vision, however, Arabella could make out the dim outlines of a bed, dresser, and armoire. She hesitated at the doorway, even though the pressure on her arm indicated she should travel within.

"Do you mean to-to bed me?"

"I meant what I've said. I won't risk a bastard for an heir, although I do plan to use other parts of your body for my comfort. Now, I'm going to leave you for a little while. I suggest you get some rest."

"What are you going to do?"

"I'm not quite certain. Something will come to me. Don't worry, my dear," he added, patting her bruised cheek. "If you're good, I promise to make our time together as painless as possible."

When he had gone, the key grating again in the lock, she leaned against the door and nearly wept.

She had left her escape too late.

Chapter 33

Gabriel was desperately afraid they wouldn't arrive in time. Precious moments had been spent searching his uncle's London townhouse. He and Peter had learned that the newlyweds had not returned from the party.

Armed with pistols and knives, they were ready. As ready as they could be. The problem lay not in their being wrong about Justin's destination, but in their right. At Ripemoor, his cousin had full authority. There was no one to gainsay him, no one to stop him from hurting Arabella in any manner he wished.

Flying hell for leather they might be, but the speed was still too slow. Every second ticked like knife thrusts through his heart. Gabriel leaned forward as if to make the horses run faster.

"Do you really plan on killing the bastard?" Peter asked, petting the barrel of the gun he held.

"Would you care?"

"Not for the act, no, but I would mind quite a bit when the noose tightened about your neck afterward. Put me off women for a good few months, I should think."

"Then I'd best not be caught."

Peter drummed his fingers on the weapon. "Might I suggest a stealthy escape to Baghdad and the procurement of an annulment instead of murder?"

"I was considering divorce."

"Unfeasible. Even if you could obtain one, such legal

278

action would place Arabella, you, and any children you should beget far beyond the pale of Society. No reputable home would have any of you. You know that."

"So you do recommend murder then?"

Peter clicked his tongue against his teeth.

After what seemed like forever, the carriage finally turned sharply onto a private drive. The pain in Gabriel's chest dissolved.

He would make up for not saving Arabella weeks ago. He should have pulled his revolver and taken her away that first moment he had come upon her in her marriage bed. Instead, his foolish pride had left her at the mercy of merciless men. If she ever forgave him, it would be a miracle, but he could try. This was his chance.

Peter shifted in his seat. "I must say, this newfound recklessness is refreshing."

It was. Gabriel's insides thrummed with resolve. For once, he didn't need or want to balance action against outcome. He didn't need or want to find the best way forward. His only goal was to save Arabella, and in that single-minded pursuit, any action was justified.

"I'll tell you what; I'll put an equitable proposition to my cousin, asking him to release Arabella to my care. When he rushes me, I will have all the legal and moral excuse I need to rid the earth of his stench."

"Except for the minor point that breaking and entering likely voids any self-defense rationale you are contemplating."

"*Tch*. Technicalities."

After knocking on the carriage roof as the house came into view, the two men descended.

With instructions to the driver to remain until he returned, Gabriel checked his pocket-sized pistol and knife, then nodded at Peter. "Stay behind me, but be ready."

"He will be expecting you, I think, but not me."

"That's because he doesn't understand the value of friendship, having never had a friend himself," Gabriel replied.

Peter clapped him on the shoulder, a silent agreement.

Noiselessly, they crept along the edge of the wood, then circled the house to the back. After testing the locks on a series of windows and doors, they came upon the opening to the atrium, where once a grand indoor garden had grown. The portal had more give than the other entrances, so Peter pulled his picks from his jacket pocket and set to work. In a matter of moments, the door swung wide with barely a whisper of sound.

The moon lay on the other side of the house, but what illumination there was revealed rows of empty containers of soil. A smell of mildew and rot permeated, a decayed, dead odor. Gabriel's nose wrinkled.

The house had, indeed, been closed up a long time. No great care had been taken to ensure it remained in working condition should it be reopened again. Clearly, his uncle and cousin had not foreseen a need to plan for future penury. How assured they had been of keeping the title.

He narrowly missed walking into a stack of buckets. "Careful."

"Feel free to take the lead if you think your vision is better."

In response, Peter's hand gripped his shoulder again. Gabriel exhaled, then nodded when he felt calmer.

That Arabella was here, in this place of rot and death,

was unbearable. What kind of callous monster would consider taking a gently bred woman into such a location during the dark of night? Though he had been filled with hot rage earlier, what settled into his bones now was ice. The thought of truly killing his cousin gained traction with each step across the dirt-strewn floors.

Having reached the end of the atrium, Gabriel slipped through another door. Once in the main part of the house, he stopped to take his bearings. He had only visited this place once in his youth, but he seemed to remember the general layout. Library to the left. Bedrooms to the top of the winding stairs he would find by turning right.

The grave-like stillness was breached by a small clink. It echoed from the left. He waited, but hearing nothing further, he decided to try the bedrooms first. Arabella was his first priority.

If she were in the library having a drink with her husband, he would have heard more than the almost inaudible sound of glass meeting table. Peter touched his arm, cocked his head, and then slipped around him to the left. Gabriel watched until he disappeared into the darkness.

Taking a steadying breath, he advanced down the long hallway and up the stairs. He leaned heavily upon the balls of his feet and kept to the outer rim of the steps so as to avoid their creaking under his weight. When he arrived on the upper level, he stopped to listen. A faint rustle, and then a curse, floated to his ears.

Relief washed over him, weakening his legs. If Arabella could blister the air with her call to Humbaba, the demon who guarded the sacred forest, then she was still in fine form. He knocked softly and whispered her name.

"Gabriel?"

"Shh," he replied, pressing his lips to the keyhole. "Quietly. I presume you don't have a key?"

"No, but Justin took one down from above the lintel. Perhaps he replaced it there?"

He looked where she had indicated, and his fingers found a long piece of metal. "Good lass." He pressed the key in and turned, wincing at the sound. "If that doesn't wake the dead, I don't know what will." He pushed open the door.

Arabella stood on the other side, her hands folded at her waist. The glow of a single candle flickered over her form. She had lost her gloves, and her hair was a mass of tangles escaping from pins. Everything about her screamed her fear, from the rigid way she held herself to the tightness about her lips and eyes. The fact she had managed to push a heavy armoire halfway to the door spoke volumes.

"Are you all right?" he asked softly, holding out his hands as if he would gentle a skittish mare. He stepped into the room. "Has he hurt you?"

"Yes. No. I tried to barricade the door. I might have managed if he drank at the pace of a snail. I only required another hour or two."

"You are a pillar of unanticipated strength. I'll remember when we're married. We'll be traveling so much, it will be a relief to let someone else heft the trunks."

"M-married?"

"Well, I believe you did agree, though I suppose it was so long ago now you've forgotten." He crossed the space and pulled her into his arms, luxuriating in the warm, soft, delicate frame that housed such inner fortitude. He pressed his lips to the crown of her head and stayed there, just drinking her in until she softened against him. Then, deliberately, he pulled away, just enough to look into her eyes. "I have failed you. I am so, so sorry."

"I thought you hated me," she mumbled, burying her face against his chest. "Am I dreaming?"

"I could never hate you. I think I merely hated myself for not figuring out how I felt and what I wanted earlier before it was too late. I have acted like the world's biggest fool, and I would not blame you for consigning me to the devil for what I've allowed to happen." He pressed a kiss to the top of her bounteous curls again and inhaled the gardenia scent that would forever remind him of her.

She seemed not to know what to say and when she cocked her head up, tiny tears had formed in the corners of her eyes. He reached up with his thumbs to wipe them away, and she smiled.

"Will you trust me for a little while, Arabella?" he asked softly. "We will discuss everything, and I will answer all the questions I see brimming upon your lips, but just now I think it wiser to focus upon escape. If I can ferret you away without Justin knowing, I think it would be wise to do so."

"Then we should leave immediately. I assume he is in the library, wherever it is. His habit is to take a drink after we return from our nightly entertainment."

Gabriel pushed away the queasy feeling that pitted his stomach at her words. "Our entertainment." It spoke of a relationship, even if it was an unwilling one. He pivoted, but she caught his arm.

"Wait." Arabella searched his face in the dimly lit room. Finally, she nodded shortly, as if reassured by whatever she read there between the flickering shadows. "I need you to know, despite how it looked when you saw us, Justin, he never…"

"Never touched you," he finished for her. "He saw the blood upon the sheets after we made love and did not want to risk a bastard. Yes. Peter told me the unspeakable vermin hasn't attempted to make your marriage legal. I take it that is still the case."

It wasn't a question. He needed it to be true, or he would never be able to live with his own guilt. Arabella bobbed her chin.

Slowly, so as not to startle her, Gabriel pressed his lips lightly against her own. Pulling back, he stroked her soft cheek.

"There is no punishment great enough for my inattention or my folly," he whispered. "I intend to live a long life making up for every pain the wretch has caused you." Clearing his throat of the strange tightness binding it, he added, "Come. Let's get out of here."

Without hesitation, she placed her hand in his and they exited the room. Gabriel took care to turn the key behind them and to replace it upon the lintel, hoping to cost his cousin precious moments in pursuit. He led Arabella down the hall toward the servants' staircase, straining to see the way in the dark. No sooner had they tiptoed their way to the bottom than he stilled. His instincts shouted there was something wrong, but he saw nothing in the gloom.

He leaned down to whisper in Arabella's ear, "I'm going to get you out of the house by means of the kitchen, but if we should be spotted, I want you to run toward any exit, out into the woods, and then down the line of the drive to the carriage. My driver waits there with a pistol, and though he might not leave without me, he can protect you until I can make my way there." He sensed she was about to argue, and he placed a finger against her lips. "Trust me," he demanded.

Silently, she placed a kiss against his finger.

They had just turned toward the bowels of the house when a shadow loomed in front of them. Before Gabriel could do more than press Arabella behind him, something heavy connected with his forehead.

As the world spun out of focus, she screamed, and the sound followed him into the deeper stillness, torturing him for his ineptitude.

Chapter 34

"Please be all right. Please be all right," Arabella whispered, her pleas dragging him from out of the black like a rope line.

A chill, wet cloth pressed against his brow. Its iciness eased a small part of the rhythmic drumming within his skull. He concentrated upon prying open his eyes, desperate to ascertain Arabella was uninjured, but no sooner had he managed a crack than a ray of blinding sunlight pierced his brain like a serving fork.

"Gabriel," she exclaimed. "You're alive!"

"Shh." He licked his cracked lips. "Water."

"I'm sorry, but there's nothing to drink. The towel holds only raindrops from earlier, the little I managed to wipe off the window. It stormed a couple of hours ago."

He would have nodded, if it was possible to keep his head upon his shoulders while doing so. "Where's Peter?" he whispered instead.

He tried to rise, but she pushed him down upon the soft mattress that gave off a smell of fungus and damp.

"Lie still now. That was a great blow Justin struck. I feared…" Her voice trailed off. "Never mind. The point is, you are alive. We all are," she said, answering his unspoken question before he could ask it, "at least for the time being."

Gabriel tried to open his eyes again, just the tiniest peep, and was rewarded as the earth slowed its ceaseless turning. He focused upon the tattered and ripped hangings that had once been pulled back against the bedposts but now hung at odd angles. Perhaps the smell of mildew and dust rose from these scraps of decaying fabrics and not just the dirty sheets beneath him.

"Where is Peter?" he asked again.

Arabella shrugged, although her expression remained concerned. "I don't really know. Justin made him carry you here, and then the two of them left. At gunpoint. I imagine he's locked in one of the other rooms."

"Good," Gabriel muttered, relaxing.

"Yes?" Arabella bit at her lip. "Only, well, it might also mean Justin has shot him."

"Humph. I'd like to see that."

She switched hands against his brow. "You don't seem to have a fever."

"I meant only Peter is slippery. Never fear." He pressed her cool fingers to his skin, beneath which a thousand fiery anvils banged. Then, he reached for her other hand, and raised it to his lips. "My angel," he whispered against her skin. "Tell me what happened. I seem to recall a blow from above."

"Justin jumped out of a statuette hole over the doorway, although how he accessed it in the first place, I have no idea. Perhaps he spent time in a circus. Using a replica of Zeus, he hit you over your head. I screamed, Peter came running, but by the time he arrived, Justin had a gun pressed against my temple. Peter swore a blue streak and threatened all sorts of bodily injury, but he gave up his weapon to save me."

"Good man." He smiled. "At least I was blasted by a major god."

Her hand stilled upon his forehead.

"Peter would have appreciated that retort," he told her seriously.

"You must keep hold of your wits, Gabriel. I think Justin means to kill us all."

Her words didn't surprise him. He closed his eyes and kissed the palm of her hand. "I am reminded of the passage where Gilgamesh used an axe to cut down a cedar tree. Humbaba raged against the destruction of what he considered to be his property."

"Like Justin. He imagines I am his property."

"He is wrong. You are no one's property, though I hope you will make me yours. Soon."

His eyes popped open again just in time to see her lips spreading in a delighted smile. Her joy filled him with an odd floating feeling, and for a moment he savored the sensation. Even the pain in his head disappeared.

"You are correct. Justin won't quibble at murder any longer if he ever would have. We must be off." Gabriel rose again, gently pushing away her helpful hands that tried to still his efforts.

When the room stopped spinning, he lifted his chin carefully. Better and better. His head still ached fiercely, and he could feel the large bruise forming on his right temple, but at least he could stand and move without collapsing.

Slowly, almost staggering to the door, he stooped to examine the lock. It was old, a concoction of springs that would require something of heavy weight to trip them. Carefully, he leaned his head against the wood and tried to still the pounding within his skull. Perhaps he might throw a bedside table, or…?

"Here."

Arabella leaned into his back and reached around his

waist. She held two long Chinese sticks that she had taken from her coiffure.

"I decided to be prepared. Justin thinks he notices dress, but never once has he examined my hairstyle." She clicked her tongue. "Sir Austen, who bore a certain regard for my mother, gifted me with these years ago when I was first expected to make my debut. He told me women in the East find these types of accoutrements quite useful for protection."

Taking the sharply pointed objects, Gabriel was surprised to find they were painted metal and not wood. "The benefits of a broad education. You are a goddess."

"I would have stabbed him had he touched me."

"No court would blame you."

He turned back toward the lock, and in a few moments, the catch sprung free.

"Come," he said, holding out his hand to her.

It was a short but harrowing trip to the kitchen and through that door into the garden beyond.

"We're not safe yet," he murmured in her ear. "We shall skirt the house by taking the forest to the drive. I hope to find my coach still waiting. If not, we'll hike to the village, where I can procure another weapon and transportation."

"And Peter?" she asked. "Shouldn't we try to rescue him, too?"

"There is no need. A lock has never yet been invented he cannot pick. Now, stay low. Your skirts are an easy target."

They crept along the edge of the wood, and though Arabella limped as stones and sticks bit through the fine kid of her evening slippers, they didn't pause until a thorn branch skewered her upper arm. Disengaging the pricker,

Gabriel leaned over to press a kiss beneath the wounded flesh. She swayed into him, and he hugged her quickly before releasing her.

"Later, my love," he whispered, taking a moment to stroke back the wild curls that tumbled across her forehead. "Come. We're almost there. I hear a horse. Possibly a good sign."

But when they rounded the curve, Justin stood in front of Gabriel's carriage; his gun squared upon Arabella from a distance that couldn't miss. Behind him, the driver lay tied and sprawled upon the earth, unconscious. The earl stood next to his son. He shook his head as if disgusted.

"I told you, Father. I will have to kill them, you see? They're slippery," Justin said, confirming Gabriel's worst fears about his cousin's intentions.

"And I told you to watch out for Darkie, didn't I?" the earl complained.

"I watched. I waited," Justin snapped.

He drew closer. His eyes glowed as if lit from within, fever-bright even in the low light of the early morning copse of trees. His tongue snaked out to wet his full lips. His skin bore a disquieting, reptilian sheen. The hairs along Gabriel's arms rose with foreboding.

"Anyway, it is all to the good. Finally, I will be able to rid myself of the thorn that has made me bleed, over and over, since I was a child." His hand shook, the revolver moving as if attached to a well-crank.

"Be calm, boy," the earl ordered, sidling up beside his son. He touched his wavering arm, then lifted his pistol. "You are right, however. A hunting accident will be explanation enough for Darkie's corpse. Your wife, on the other hand..." His voice trailed to a purr as his pig-like gaze raked Arabella. "She has her uses, temporarily, and we've a deserted house in which to play before we send her to her maker. Drowning afterward, do you think? There's a pond out back, and the bloat will hide the bruising and cuts."

"If you touch her, I will kill you. That is a solemn vow." Gabriel tried to inch closer to Arabella as he spoke, the better to shield her with his own larger frame.

"Don't move another finger-length, Darkie, or I'll aim for a part of her that will hurt her dearly and kill her slowly." Justin giggled. "Oh, how I have waited for this day! I've wanted you dead since I was a child, and Father had you brought to the estate." His manic good humor suddenly departed as quickly as it had appeared. "Just because you're his half-brother's whelp, he took you in. Then, you and that half-wit friend of yours proceeded to make my life miserable, always mocking me, setting a bad example for the villagers who shunned me as if I smelled." His pistol rotated slightly toward Gabriel. "Did you think I'd forgotten?"

"I think you've reversed which one of us caused the other misery."

"Actually, I took Darkie in because of the stipend," the earl said, his smile fat with malice. "The money more than made up for any slight inconvenience you suffered, Justin."

"The stipend?"

Gabriel waited for a moment of distraction in which he could move away from Arabella and draw their fire. Their weapons remained too steady.

"The stipend left by your parents in trust for your care, Darkie. Your father, arguably the most profligate gambler and womanizer ever born, was unaccountably aware of his own proclivities. From the day of your birth, he took care to bank funds monthly in a trust. It was to be used for your benefit should he die before you reached your majority. When your parents passed to the next world, I, as your closest relative, became your guardian. And the trustee." He simpered.

"You snake," Gabriel hissed.

The earl seemed unconcerned by the insult. "The money came in handy. Ironically, we've used the last of it to battle you in court for the titles. Too bad. I've quite a few bills in need of paying, but your demise should provide a remedy to that unfortunate circumstance."

"Why didn't I know about this trust?" Gabriel demanded, rankled despite the danger in which they found themselves. "And why, if it was left for my care, did I receive so little of it?"

"You didn't starve. You had a lovely place to live on the grounds with that drunkard you love so well, and you had an education, of sorts, even if you did most of your learning on your own. You've no reason to complain."

"I would beg to differ, Uncle." He paused as a terrible thought occurred to him. "Did you kill my parents?"

Arabella squeezed his fingers. The little gesture steadied him.

"*Tch*. What a vivid imagination. After my *illegitimate* half-brother ruined and killed his archenemy, the Earl of Winslow," Kildare said, shooting a glance toward Arabella, who gasped, "the very man who was responsible for his ruin, by the way, he and his wife died in an unfortunate boating accident. Well, not unfortunate for me, of course." He paused before adding, too lightly, "The Thames never has been easy during the thaws of late winter, especially when candied plugs melt too far from shore."

"Murderer!"

The earl began to laugh, big belly sounds of mirth as if his part in his half-brother's death was the funniest joke he had heard in years. Perhaps he was only amused Gabriel's and Arabella's fathers had been enemies and each responsible for the other's ruin.

"Steady," Arabella murmured. She squeezed his hand again.

Gabriel swallowed his rage and let it burn in his belly. "You are the bravest female I have ever known."

She was, too. He might have jumped right into the guns if she hadn't been there, anything to smash that fat, florid face into paste.

Justin made a retching noise. "Please. The dull thing never even realized she held the key to your fortunes, Darkie. Brave? Arabella's an imbecile."

Before Gabriel could object to the insult, Arabella startled. "The ring! The day after we wed, Justin's first act was to fetch a seal ring my father gave me when I was quite young. He told me your father had lost it to mine in a card game." Then, she pressed his fingers again. "I swear I didn't know it was important to you."

"That's because you have the imagination of a stoat, darling. Yes, the ring was everything," Justin purred and then giggled again. "It originally belonged to our grandfather, Darkie. I used it to forge the symbol upon the will, the one responsible for your ultimate loss," he gloated. "And it was always right under your nose."

As the final pieces of the puzzle fell into place, Gabriel tensed, his instinct demanding he rush the double-dealing cad.

"Careful, Darkie. I wouldn't move if I were you. I already have half a mind to let my father have Arabella while you watch. You are aware of his perversions, yes? His predilection for knives?"

A low, high-pitched moan, like the whine of a dog waiting to be allowed dinner, issued from the earl's throat.

Ice trickled down Gabriel's spine.

"Whatever our fathers were or weren't," Arabella snapped, clearly not as alarmed by the threat as Gabriel believed she should be, "compared with the two of you, they were saints. You're nothing but vile, kidnapping blackguards, and I'll be glad to see the last of you." Despite the guns, she drew nearer to him, ignoring the immediate outcry by the earl and his son. "Whatever your father did, Gabriel, you must know you are no more responsible for his actions than I am for my father's. We are not such barbarians we hold the innocent to blame for the actions of the guilty, are we?" She lifted the hand he did not hold and touched his chest over the place where his heart beat wildly. "I know what it feels like to have a scapegrace for a father," she whispered. "It is a thing that unites us, not cuts us apart."

"You are the most wonderful woman I have ever met," he fervently assured her. He meant every word.

"Enough," the earl ordered, practically spitting. "My boots are leaking water, and I long for my breakfast. Justin, let us get to the killing now so we might enjoy our leisure…and the afterward." His tongue snaked out to tickle the corner of his upper lip as he stared hard at Arabella's bodice.

"Agreed." Justin gestured roughly with the pistol. "Turn around now, the two of you. Arabella in front.

March down that path. There." He pointed with his chin.

Thinking to resist in the momentary confusion of action, Gabriel angled his foot, hoping to jump into Justin and knock him into his father, thereby forcing their weapons in the opposite direction from Arabella. Instead, a deafening explosion rocked the clearing. A blast of heat rushed a finger's width from his skull, ruffling his hair. Arabella screamed.

"Don't toy with me, Darkie."

The earl threw down his expended weapon upon the sodden earth and pulled another from his inside pocket, denying Gabriel any hoped-for advantage. Carefully, seeing the clear intent in his uncle's gaze, he lifted his hands in surrender.

"Do as Justin says," Gabriel said loudly to Arabella, but as they turned, he leaned in to add, "When I say 'epic,' throw yourself to the ground and roll to the right."

She nodded, and relief rushed through him. It felt like more of a victory than it probably should when he also managed to brush a kiss over her golden head before stepping back.

"You are aware, Justin, are you not, that I have friends who will avenge my untimely passing? You should rethink your plans for cold-blooded murder," he called over his shoulder.

His cousin was but a step behind him. There was added danger in his proximity, of course, but it also meant he might be toppled and thrown off his mark.

"It isn't murder if it is a matter of expediency," Justin snapped. "Even the Bible forgives such things."

It didn't.

The path they walked bent just ahead. In a moment, Arabella would arrive at a hairpin turn, blocked from

Justin's gun by the narrow trunk of a tree.

"Prelates would disagree with your theology, cousin," he called, rotating his head and seeing his chance. "But then, this really is an *epic* struggle."

He turned and kicked up and out. A dangling branch foiled his aim, and his foot made contact with Justin's wrist instead of the pistol itself. As Justin's finger tightened upon the trigger, the gun went off, more deafening at proximity than the earl's had been. With no time to trace the path of the bullet, as the earth tilted and the world became a massive, high-pitched whine, Gabriel continued in his attack. Each second of surprise might make the difference between Arabella's life or death.

He followed his kick with a well-placed punch. Cartilage broke under his fist. Satisfaction filled him. Justin's symmetrical face would never again be so handsome. His delight was short-lived as his cousin quickly retaliated by delivering up his own fist to Gabriel's stomach, knocking the air from his lungs.

Gasping, Gabriel lunged forward, capturing Justin around the middle. Under the force of his charge, the viscount's legs gave way. He prepared himself to use his cousin's body to break their fall to the earth, but then another loud crack of gunfire issued, and the impact with the ground was more cushioned than it should have been.

Rolling off Justin quickly, Gabriel pretzeled into a fighting stance despite his noise-induced imbalance, all his focus upon the body that lay perfectly still at his feet. He raked Justin's splayed form. A splotch of red unfurled like a rosebud upon the center of his chest. Vacant Champagne eyes, always before filled with a vague disdain and contempt, gazed emptily at the sky.

Reflexively, Gabriel glanced down at his chest.

Justin's blood stained his shirt where his black jacket hung open, shredded.

"My boy! My boy!" the earl wailed, struggling to rise from under his son's body. When the earl had managed the feat, he knelt beside his child, pressing his hands to the gaping wound in Justin's chest. "Oh, my God! Oh, my God, look what you've made me do, Darkie! I've killed him! I've killed my boy!"

With a timing that seemed too orchestrated to be chance, Peter stepped from behind a tree. He shook his head in disgust before turning to examine Gabriel. "You all right?" he shouted, pointing at the tear in Gabriel's jacket.

"It's Justin's blood."

"When you pushed your cousin into Kildare's gun, his hand must have jarred. What a mess."

Gabriel pivoted, expecting to see Arabella, but the space was a wash of lonely trees. He took a step forward just as nausea and dizziness speared through him. Though it felt like moving through molten sand, he stumbled on as an odd heaviness began dragging him downward. Another step, and the stinging in his torso flamed.

A glint of white, gold, and pink, almost covered from sight by a hillock of decaying leaves and green sprouts, caught his attention. Forcing his legs to advance, he staggered toward it, his feet unusually clumsy over the litter of foliage and roots.

He shouted, or thought he did, but Arabella did not move. As he flung himself to the ground beside her, he reached out to cup her cheek, willing those beautiful amethyst eyes to open.

A terrible bright stain of red painted the side of her gentle head crimson.

The world flipped again as the silk of her golden hair slipped through his numb fingers. The damp earth, loamy and dark, reached up to drag him down beside her. He closed his eyes and sighed.

Arabella was his epic love.

How stupid of him not to have realized it while there was still time.

Chapter 35

"He will recover? You are certain of it?"

Arabella sat upon the edge of her bed, where an insensate Gabriel lay deep in unmoving sleep. The bullet that had killed Justin had also torn a hole through the baron's upper abdomen, glanced off a rib, and exited through his side. Though narrowly missing his heart, the projectile had still done its damage.

"He will, but Arabella, you may not. That branch knocked you senseless. You must rest yourself," Peter said as he paced her bedroom-turned-sickroom like a tiger in a cage. "You're so pale you could be mistaken for a corpse. What will Gabriel think when he awakens to find you've perished into one of the perambulating dead?"

Despite her fatigue and worry, Arabella's lips twitched.

"Reggie is in your kitchen fixing you a tray. I want you to promise to eat every bite of whatever he concocts, before or after you sleep is of no concern. You wouldn't want to disappoint that poor old man, would you, especially with all he's been through?"

Peter's voice was as hypnotic as a snake-oil salesman's pitch at a county fair. Arabella knew she wouldn't buy into his hawking, no matter how much she needed to follow his advice, not so long as Gabriel refused to open his eyes.

It had been five days now, five long days, albeit she

had only been awake herself for the last four of those. When Justin's gun had fired, the bullet had struck a tree branch. The wood had splintered and knocked her senseless to the ground, which was just as well. She had been afraid of Justin, true, but it would have haunted her to have watched him die. What must the earl be feeling, knowing he had killed his only son? She would have felt more pity for the old man if it hadn't been his bullet that had laid Gabriel low as well.

Somehow, after the debacle, Peter and the coachman had managed to get them all into the carriage and then into town where a doctor had seen to Gabriel's wounds directly and sewn him back together. It had been Arabella who had insisted upon Gabriel's transfer to her own home and bed. Superstitious though she was undoubtedly being, she wanted Gabriel to heal in a place where she had recovered from many childhood illnesses. It was also where they had first leaned into each other in what seemed like a different life entirely.

Even with Gabriel's wound cleaned and sewn, the larger problem was still infection. The fever had kept Gabriel insensate. All Arabella had known how to do was to apply cold rags to his forehead, though she had also followed the village wise-woman's advice of adding combed honey and wine to the bandages. The doctor had neither agreed nor disagreed with the crone's advice, but Peter, who had spent some time in the East, thought the remedy sound.

Arabella trusted him implicitly. If anyone was more concerned for Gabriel's wellbeing than her, it was him.

The treatment was working, albeit too slowly. Just this morning, Gabriel's fever had broken for the first time. Now, he seemed to rest normally, if normal was a sleep from which he would not wake.

"Please come back to me," she begged.

"He will, Arabella," Peter said softly, stopping beside her.

He placed his large hand upon her shoulder. During her long watch, he had been an unflinching companion, and she had been made more peaceful by his lighthearted company.

"But you need to eat and rest."

His hair was uncombed, sticking up in patches like an inverted rooster comb. Beneath his eyes lay two large bruises of fatigue. Unshaven, with his glittering blue eyes filled with a seriousness he strove to hide, he finally looked less like an angel and more like a violent highwayman.

"I'll rest when you do," she said gently. "If I look like a corpse, then you look like the devil himself. Not a single woman will drop handkerchiefs in your path if you don't take better care."

"Were you always so mean-spirited?"

She smiled and patted his hand before turning back to watch Gabriel breathe.

"He'll be an earl now, you know, or he will once the court officially deprives his uncle of the title. The queen has weighed in."

"She has?"

That surprised Arabella. How had the queen even heard of the affair?

"After we transferred Gabriel to this chamber, I escorted Robert to Her Majesty directly. He's in prison now, with a list of charges against him that would see him hang, were he a commoner, which he is in reality, but why quibble over legitimacy at this point?" He shrugged.

"As it stands, the queen does not wish for word of this debacle to spread, if for no other reason than because the Thauleys are distantly related to her husband's father."

"I wasn't aware," Arabella murmured.

"Few are. Robert has no claim to the throne, of course, but things could get sticky anyway, especially with the recent rumblings of the various underground groups set to end the monarchy. So, instead of hanging as he should, Robert will be stripped of his titles and quietly transported as a convict to Australia, to make his way there however he can. For Society, it will be as if he has died. In all important respects, he has. The titles and estates are to go to Gabriel as soon as the court agrees his line was the legitimate one. They will do so. There's evidence and testimony to prove the Thauleys' will was forged."

Arabella nodded. It was probably too good an ending for Robert Thauley and far better than the price Justin had paid for his nefarious deeds. She looked back at Gabriel, sleeping deeply but peacefully. She removed the cloth from his head, dipped it in the water again, wrung it out, and placed it back upon his brow.

Without warning, his eyes popped open. Arabella was speared by green, vivid despite his convalescence.

"Oh, thank goodness," she exclaimed as she almost swooned with relief. She caught the side of the bed to keep her steady. "You're alive."

"I told you he was too cantankerous to die," Peter exclaimed. He leaned over Arabella's shoulder to examine his friend, and then sighed deeply. "Good. It's good."

He patted Gabriel on the arm, and retreated toward the door. "I'm taking Arabella's advice and resting, because if women cease throwing handkerchiefs in my path, then they will inevitably stop tripping into my bed. That's unacceptable. Gabriel, we've much to discuss, but I think it can wait a day. If you need me, call. Otherwise, I'm going to wrestle with Morpheus for a bit and let the old reprobate win." He raised his hand in farewell and opened the door.

"Peter."

Peter turned, his hand upon the knob.

"Thank you, my friend," Gabriel said, his voice hoarse. "For my life. For…everything."

Peter's face pulled taut as if he were about to cry, but then he was out the door. Arabella barely noticed the closing door, so intent was she pulling the blankets up while Gabriel tried to shove them down.

"I was so afraid," she whispered, finally acceding.

He held her gaze and moved his thumb up to touch her cheek. His fingers trembled slightly. "Me too. You were lying upon the earth, so terribly still, and I couldn't find my balance to lift you. My ears were filled with a piercing ring, and in the next moment, the world receded."

"The doctor said any hearing loss caused by the discharge of the guns should be temporary."

He blinked his eyes as if it were an effort to keep them open. "What happened after I lost consciousness?"

Arabella told him, as quickly and succinctly as she could, including the news Peter had just shared. "So, it seems the titles will be yours after all, albeit not in a way you could have anticipated."

"My uncle's punishment is Justin's death at his own hands." Gabriel's expression was drawn. "I'm not certain how I feel about that." He paused, blinked his lashes rapidly, then asked, "And you, Arabella? How are you coping? You are a widow now."

She hadn't had time to dwell upon the fact, with Gabriel so ill, but she knew she would have to consider it more fully with time. Too much had happened for her emotions to be easily untangled. There was a relief, yes, but there was sadness, too.

Her confusion must have been written upon her face. Gabriel reached up again, and this time his fingers were steady as he stroked her cheek. "You don't need to be strong anymore. You may weep for him. I would understand."

"Would you?" she asked. She took a deep breath. "I never loved him. I'm not even certain I liked him. It is difficult to imagine we were married."

"Difficult for me to imagine as well."

She pulled the covers up again for something to do. This time, he let her. "I've been wondering what I might have done differently, had I not been so afraid. Had I not been positively steeped in misery at your absence."

"I'm so sorry," he whispered. "I was wrong."

She bent her chin and kissed his palm. "I should have listened to you. I should never have left the ball in their company. You have nothing to be sorry for because the entire situation was my fault."

"No."

"I've also been thinking of what Justin might have been had he had a better father. He possessed some interesting qualities. I'd like to think, if he had been raised by my mother, for example, he would have grown into someone honorable and kind. Decent." She frowned. "I am relieved he is gone from my life. I won't miss him, but…" She shrugged, helpless to describe the mix of feelings within her.

"My cousin was ever a thorn that bled me, but he was also my blood. I think I understand." He patted the space beside him with his free hand. "Will you lie next to me? I want to hold you and assure myself the dastardly tree branch did no permanent damage."

With an alacrity she knew was unbecoming, she jumped over him and burrowed into his side, her lips pressing to the fabric of the nightshirt covering his flesh.

"You cannot know how I have longed to hold you near like this," he purred. "You will marry me, Arabella, now you're free again?"

"Silly man," she whispered, her heart racing.

He didn't notice her evasion. Already his eyes were drooping, and in moments he slipped back into slumber. Arabella managed to hold her eyes open a few minutes longer, but then she too drifted off into a healing sleep, the feel of his pulse calming her as she floated down.

He was alive.

Somehow, all would be well now because of it.

Chapter 36

Lady Winslow sat in the ballroom, gazing at the portrait of the man she had long loved and lost, even before he had left behind the earthly plane.

Despite his profligate ways, John Winslow had not been a terrible person. He had often been understanding of her moods, interested in her thoughts, and carelessly kind, but he had never loved her, not as he should have done and not as she had so often willed him to have done. His heart had always rested with another, a secret she had kept from everyone, though she could not keep it from herself. To his credit, he had told her about his love before they wed, and in fairness, she had therefore been warned. But what woman wants to believe she can't win the adoration of the man who made her soul dance?

She shook her head and turned away. It was all gone now anyway.

The creak of the door startled her. Peter Bartholomew stood bracketed in the doorway.

"I am hardly likely to attack you, Lady Winslow. Please do not complicate matters further by having one of your convenient fits."

Glenda's spine stiffened. Affronted, she asked, "Who are you to tell me what to do in my own house?"

He inclined his head as he entered the room, his pale golden-white curls catching and refracting light. "My apologies. Such was not my intention."

"You look like a highwayman," she snapped, not only because he did but also because his beauty was breaking her heart all over again.

She had never met this man in Society, but when he had arrived with Arabella, carrying Brynley over his wide shoulders like a sack of well-dressed potatoes, she had known exactly who he must be. It was no surprise he ran with the person whose goal was to ruin the Winslows, but only a wonder life could interweave the knots of the cloth so seamlessly.

Peter gestured toward the other straight-backed chair, one of a pair Annette had not yet recovered though Arabella's sortie had been a lifetime ago. The spindly furniture looked adrift in the cavernous room otherwise devoid of appointments. "We haven't spoken much, but there are some questions I would like to put to you, Lady Winslow. May I?"

Hesitating, but seeing no help for it, she grumbled, "If you must. What do you want, Mr. Bartholomew? Has the baron given up the ghost?"

He took a seat, then pressed his palms to his legs. "Happily, no. He is finally awake. Thank you for your obvious concern."

"His death would not concern me."

He hesitated. "Yes, so it seems." He appeared confused. "In any event, I came to speak with you on a matter of some urgency. You are removing to the continent shortly, I understand?"

"I have already delayed my departure once."

"And you plan for Arabella to join you."

"*Lady Manning* is to accompany me, of course, especially now as she is widowed and otherwise alone in the world. What is it to you?" She stared at him,

307

challenging him.

Peter held her gaze steadily. "Quite a lot. Surely, you must see she and Gabriel are meant for each other? He is to be given his uncle's titles, so if your objection to him is merely one of standing, that matter is about to be rectified."

As she stared at the young gentleman, Glenda couldn't help but search his features, hoping to find that what she knew was not true. Instead, all she saw was a younger version of the man in the portrait. How had Arabella not guessed when the two men shared even the same lightness of humor, the same sparkle in their differently colored eyes? But then, children never truly saw their parents, did they?

Something in her expression must have alerted Peter, a certain softening maybe. When she glanced over his shoulder toward the painting again, he hesitated and then pivoted. When he drew in a long, audible breath, she knew he had seen it too: the same eye shape, the same cheekbones, the same long and elegant nose, the same sensuous lips, but it was the chin that was most alike. It was a strong plane cleaved by a seductive hollow, a rapscallion's bulwark. Though the haughty lord in the portrait was slightly older, he was most definitely imprinted upon the rogue seated adjacent to her now.

"Yes. From the moment I first saw you, when you carried the baron upstairs, I knew it. You are an uncanny miniature, such that I cannot see your mother at all."

Lady Winslow waited.

She had to wait many, many minutes while he processed the information.

"The timing is correct; the age and even your name led me to the inescapable truth," she added gently.

"Funny we've not crossed paths before, but London is a large city, and your standing within it is, well…"

Finally, he turned back to her, his eyes glittering. "I have wondered my entire life about my father's identity. Gabriel and Reggie always insisted he must have been a nobleman, but I doubted it because why would my mother keep such a secret from me? She hated the nobility." He laughed ruefully. "I suppose that rabid dislike makes a strange sort of sense, now that I know. Is it true?"

"John Winslow was a noble, all right, at least in title, and although I wish I were uncertain, there is no doubt. I knew of your mother, you see." She leaned over and touched Peter's arm. "And John, God help me, he loved your mother, Peter. May I call you Peter?" When he bobbed his dimpled chin, she sighed and sat back. "He would be so pleased to learn he had fathered a son. And you would have loved him unconditionally, I think. He would have doted upon you just as he did Arabella. Despite his unfortunate predilections for cards, ponies, and women, he was something of an expert in holding unflagging adoration deep within his heart. Unfortunately, I was not one of the lucky few to be grasped so tightly."

Glenda inhaled a long, deep breath, her lungs, for once, remaining open. Her chest still ached, torn between the righteous indignation she imagined she should be feeling, entertaining her husband's bastard in her ballroom, and the actual sympathy she felt for the young man. He had been born of a great love she had ever resented. She should hate him. Instead, she was comforted by his presence. It was a little like having John back again.

Peter stared at the portrait. "Tell me about him."

Glenda thought a moment. "He was terribly shallow,

and much given to excess, but much given to kindness and laughter too. His tongue was quick, his brain quicker. I found it difficult to follow his thoughts most days. Often, I could swear he deliberately courted danger. What I remember most, however, is how life seemed so terribly trivial in his presence, nothing but a game or a dance. But when he absented himself, the world grew heavy. So heavy."

She rose from her chair and traversed toward the open window. Beyond, the air was sunny and warm, the kind of day that made a person want to rest in England forever. Birds twittered, the grass gleamed, and the scent of roses was so strong it permeated the entire room.

She turned back. "John never escaped his one true love," she continued softly. "Mathilde Bartholomew. They had been forbidden to wed, of course, given she was a gardener's daughter. I have always thought it ironic that my unhappy marriage was the result of Society trying to arrange a perfect union while refusing to join two intertwined hearts. The rules made none of us happy, though I am deeply grateful to them all the same. Arabella," she added by way of explanation.

"My mother…" Peter swallowed. "She would never name him, but when I was little, she would run her fingers through my curls, and little tears would escape the corners of her eyes. I have just realized it must not have been because my presence made her sad, but rather that my image did."

"It is the same with Arabella. I would look at her after John died, and I would see so much of him it would tear a little hole, right in my chest, here." She laid her hand flat over her heart. "In the end, however, she became a person in her own right. The similarities became easier to accept, given how much I loved her. And she, me."

Peter stood. "Then do not make the same mistake. Give Gabriel your blessings. Allow Arabella to follow her heart, which will lead her directly to him. I have never met two so meant to be one."

Glenda shrank back from the sting of his hit. "You don't know anything at all."

"Then tell me."

She couldn't. They were friends, her husband's bastard and the baron. He would never believe her or see the man from a woman's point of view.

"No. Not now."

"If you leave in mere days, then when?"

She turned to look outside. It was closing in on her. Everything was coming to a head.

"We will talk before I go," she finally said. She managed to smile at him. "I give you my word."

She thought he would pursue their conversation. Instead, with a little jut of that rapscallion's chin, he left. Glenda gazed at her husband's portrait across the room and then turned back to look out into the little garden.

Just now, she preferred the view of the roses.

Chapter 37

Arabella stretched and then stopped, her movements unnaturally constrained. Panic filled her, but it washed away quickly as the faint scent of vanilla and fir teased her nose, and she remembered.

"Good morning," Gabriel whispered, his fingers stroking the hair from her face. He leaned over and placed a kiss upon her forehead.

She arched up to meet his lips when a peremptory knock startled her backward. Peter entered, carrying a tray. Behind him, Lady Winslow trailed with a teapot. Her mother was so surprised to find Arabella in bed with the baron, she cried out and dropped the vessel. Tea puddled across the floor as the porcelain broke into three large pieces.

"Let me get that." Peter gently brushed her mother back and picked up the shards. "Lady Winslow, we'll need some rags?"

Instead of rushing off to get them, her mother stared at her and wailed, "Oh, Arabella, can't you stay away from that man? Don't you realize the scandal, and...oh!" Quickly, she disappeared out the door, but Arabella was fairly certain she wasn't planning to fetch cleaning supplies.

Peter looked after her, then back toward them. "I think she's holding up rather magnificently under the circumstances, don't you?"

Arabella didn't. As she tried to scramble over Gabriel, his arm shot out, preventing her.

"Stay," he murmured. "Peter was just leaving."

"Peter is leaving." He leaned against the wall next to the door. "Peter, however, expects to engage in some important conversations with his lordship in not more than a half-hour's time. And, might he suggest the lock be employed when the bed is occupied by two?" He pushed off and strode out the door without another word.

The pool of tea remained. Kismet stretched himself to a standing position and jumped from the bench to investigate. Arabella threw back the sheets.

"Where do you think you're going," Gabriel murmured, grabbing her around the waist and pulling her back into him.

"I thought to gather some rags from the linen closet, then wash my teeth, and perhaps attend to other necessities. If you must know," she retorted, pushing at him.

Gabriel sighed dramatically but released her. He flopped back upon his pillow. Draping his arms beneath his head, wincing at the pull across his chest, he tracked her as she picked her way across the room. Altogether, she wasn't certain if his stare disconcerted her more than it pleased.

He was alive. He was in her chamber. She had prayed for his recovery, and every part of her being was overjoyed he appeared to be well, but just now his presence was also perturbing. He was so masculine, so large and magnetic, and she felt too weak and tired in comparison. Arabella shook her head, unable to come to terms with her emotions.

Anxious to escape for a few moments and order her

thoughts, she gathered a small towel, hairbrush, and some pins and fled toward the door.

"You will marry me, won't you? Now that there is no impediment?" he demanded, stalling her.

And there it was, the question she was trying to avoid.

Slowly, reluctantly, Arabella rotated, although she could not make herself meet the piercing, knowing expression in his eyes.

"It is very kind of you to ask."

"Yes, isn't it?"

"Now I'm a widow, and you have the *Epic*, well, we aren't pressed to act precipitously, are we?" She swallowed hard, searching for better words.

"We are pressed. I am pressed," Gabriel retorted, slowly sitting up. He winced again from the effort and strain upon his muscles.

Arabella opened her mouth, then closed it again. Finally, she slipped from the room. She gathered the rags, returned briefly to throw them upon the spill, and left again before the glaring, disconcerted male could challenge her with his logic.

The bathroom was ancient, but it was equipped with cold running water, if not hot. There was a water-closet, and a cabinet with tooth powder, cream for her skin, and a sliver of fine-milled gardenia soap. She placed the items she carried upon the small table and turned on the taps in the tub.

Arabella gazed into it as she ran the water to a level that would allow her a quick rinse. The basin was small, too small for Gabriel's bulk. She hadn't been thinking, when she had installed him in her home, of just how difficult it would be to fit a virile male into their female-oriented world.

Life had become so complicated during the past weeks. She had been kidnapped, and through violence, become a widow, nearly joining her departed husband in the hereafter when he had sought to kill her. Having hoped she might be pregnant, she was strangely hurt by the loss when she discovered she had never been. More than that, she had fallen in love, hopelessly, irrevocably, so-that-she-now-understood-her-mother in love.

And the man she loved still professed to want to marry her. So, why was she so unsettled?

Because much had happened, but the essentials hadn't changed, had they? She was in love with Gabriel, but he was not in love with her, and if he was not, her mother's warning still applied. Oh, it would take a longer-suffering mind than hers to believe he did not care for her at all. Of course, he must. After all, he had endangered his own life to save hers, an act indicative of feelings beyond mere guilt for having bedded her. Physically, they shared an attraction. More importantly, they shared a solid friendship, one that meant the world to her.

Their solidarity would be the hardest part of the relationship to lose.

No, they were unarguably perfect for each other in every way, except he had never said he loved her, which could only mean, given all they had been through together, he did not. He was too upright to profess an emotion he did not feel, and she applauded him for that innate honesty. Still, honor did not change the basic equation. Unless and until Gabriel loved her, she had no choice but to keep her distance. To marry him otherwise would be to kill herself by painful degrees.

The sting of the cold water was not as knife-sharp as

the agony in her heart. Arabella could only hope time and distance would lessen the pain.

Unfortunately, she feared there was a lifetime ahead of her to find out.

Chapter 38

The tiny garden was bright, the normal English rain and smog for once hidden behind fluffy clouds and blue sky, a Constable painting made wild by the unkempt beds and trails through which weeds pushed toward the sun. Arabella hadn't been able to resist walking those paths.

It wasn't a large property. Half the original plot had been sold in her great-grandfather's day, before the entail. Still, what was left was perfect. Overgrown, the wildflowers sprang from the lawn, creating swathes of bright hues like spilled watercolors. Having chosen to use their funds upon sustenance rather than the proper upkeep of the garden, both she and Lady Winslow had been surprised to find the wild nature ensuing between the walls suited them better than manicured shrubbery and flower beds would have done.

"There you are. I've been looking for you." Gabriel had to duck under a wayward rose bush that arched over the near-hidden flagstone.

"I thought to try to memorize it," she said, tearing her gaze from him.

He seemed much improved, in any event.

As if to confirm her thoughts, he said, "I will take my leave later this afternoon. There is much to oversee, and Peter has impressed upon me the need to attend to our business concerns since my plans have changed. I'm afraid he is out of patience with my neglect. I should meet with him soon if I can find him. He seems to have disappeared."

"I'm certain he simply needs time to process some startling news. I've spoken to my mother, and it is the most marvelous thing." Quickly, she told him everything she had learned of Peter's parentage.

If Gabriel was shocked, he hid it well.

"You knew?"

He shook his head. "No, but when I met you, I remember thinking how easy it was to joke with you. It felt too natural. Then I noticed your physical similarities. Both of you resemble your father. I waited for Peter to remark how alike you were, but he never seemed to want to know. I'm glad he finally discovered the truth."

"Me too. I have a brother." Arabella smiled.

It was wonderful news, even though she knew she was expected to resent having an illegitimate half-sibling. It would have been difficult to be unhappy, however, given that Peter was Peter, and even Lady Winslow seemed less-than-secretly pleased.

"Yes. And I will have an adoptive brother for a brother-in-law," Gabriel said in a pointed tone.

She thought he would reach out to her, but he didn't. It was as if he knew what she would say. It only took the saying it, which was harder than it should be.

Finally, finding her voice, she whispered, "I'm not going to marry you, Gabriel. I'm sorry."

"You are."

She shook her head. "I am removing to the continent with my mother."

"Why?"

Arabella gazed at him, helpless to explain. Anything she said would only lead him to profess sentiments he did not feel. She would not be able to live with that lie between them.

"This is not over," he said gravely. Then, astonishing her, he simply walked away, back to the house, maybe back to his own home, she didn't know.

She watched him recede, wondering why it hurt so to keep herself from pain.

****

From the garden, Gabriel searched determinedly through every room until he caught Lady Winslow packing some boxes in the library.

"Even murdering weasels deserve their social due," Lady Winslow said rigidly after he complained about Arabella's decisions and stated his case. "Arabella has at least a year of mourning ahead of her."

"I am doubtful that mourning is the only consideration, but if so, I am happy to come retrieve her in six months' time. Convention be damned. We can marry in France unless there is another reason of which I am unaware?"

"You are as insufferable as your father," Lady Winslow snapped, dropping a book roughly upon the table. Her gaze burned into his. "It was all about what he wanted, what he believed was true, but he was wrong. My husband gambled, yes, but he never cheated. He won that fortune from your father fairly. There was no cause to ruin John. To ruin us."

"I agree."

Lady Winslow started.

"I agree," Gabriel repeated. "My father was in error in taking his anger out on your family, whether his assumptions were true or false. I have never held with punishing the innocent, especially for unproven

319

allegations."

Lady Winslow blinked at him. "Do you mean that?"

"I do. Completely."

"But then…"

For the first time since he had met her, she didn't shrink from him. He held out his hand, and slowly, as if he were trying to tame a rabbit to take a carrot, he waited until she tentatively placed her fingers within his.

"Come, sit, so we might discuss important matters."

Leading her to the couch, he waited until she composed herself. He took a deep breath, appreciating the fine weather. The fires were banked; all the windows stood open to let in the sun and warm breezes.

"I believe we labor under a misapprehension. May I?" He gestured to a chair, and she inclined her head. Taking his seat, he continued, "I am not my father, Lady Winslow. I do not wish to contribute to your ills. I never have."

"Then why have you dogged Arabella's heels?"

Gabriel couldn't imagine how she wouldn't know. "Because Arabella is wonderful," he replied patiently. "Because she is perfect. Because she shares my passion for Assyriology. Because she ignites something within me." He shrugged. "Just because I need her next to me in order to be happy."

Lady Winslow was silent for a few moments. Gabriel let her think.

"You paid her for her copy of the *Epic*. If not to ruin us, then the book must be what you wanted, yes?"

"No. The purchase was merely an unanticipated bonus." The little fudge of truth was necessary. Otherwise, she might feel honor-bound to return his funds. "It is true I made Arabella's acquaintance while

320

trying to uncover my cousin's schemes. I did not know about the ring, you see, not until recently. Justin's interest in your daughter made no sense to me, because she is not the type he would normally find pleasing. That is a compliment to Arabella, I assure you," he added when she appeared set to object. "In any event, although my initial reasons for courting Arabella may not have been enviable and pure, I harbor quite different motivations now."

"That you are only happy when you are with her?" Lady Winslow repeated in a disbelieving tone.

"Yes." Gabriel rose and sauntered to the window, looking out to where Arabella sat on the old rusty iron garden chair.

Her face was lifted to the sun, and he suspected she would be sporting some freckles across her nose when she returned indoors. He smiled.

Lady Winslow, who had risen as well, joined him. "I could almost think you loved her."

He startled and faced her. "Of course, I love her. Isn't that what I've been saying?"

"Not precisely, no." Her shoulders relaxed. A ghost of a smile played upon her lips. "If I could be certain your feelings were true and you would endeavor to make her happy, I would grant my permission."

"Then you must believe me."

She tilted her head as if considering. "Here, come sit on the window seat. Your wounds must pain you still."

Gabriel accepted her invitation, grateful she had already lowered herself as well. Standing, sitting, or even breathing for long periods of time was difficult. His wounds still piqued him, but he was alive, and he was determined.

"The truth is, my confidence in my opposition of you

ceased to have any real teeth the moment you rescued my daughter. When I think of what that fiend had planned…" She shivered. "He fooled us s-so completely."

Gabriel noticed the rasp underlying her words.

"Please, do not distress yourself, Lady Winslow. We are well past the worry, and even the gossip, unfueled, will have died long before you return to these shores."

Taking a deeper breath through her nose, she seemed to calm. "You are right, of course. All is well that ends well."

Gabriel waited, wondering what other sentiments he needed to find to convince Arabella's mother of his sincerity. Words were so fragile, so easily incomplete. How could he explain that by being with Arabella, he felt more alive, that color was brighter and deeper, the sound was clearer, air was easier to breathe? He raised his hand as if to beseech her, but she cut him off before he could find more ill-fitting expressions.

"I understand," she said simply. "Perhaps I have been altogether wrong. I was so in love with my husband, you see. Many women are not, and that lack, I believe, generally favors a happier marriage. No, do not interrupt," she added, raising a hand as if to forestall argument. "You are not a woman. One day, perhaps, a wife will have an equal say in marriage. She will be a true partner and not a necessary accessory. One day, perhaps, a woman will be able to leave a man who hurts her, or at least make demands of him with the expectation he will try and fulfill them. That day has not yet arrived."

"Do you believe I would physically mistreat Arabella?" he demanded, shocked.

Lady Winslow snorted gently. "I might pity the man who tried."

"Justin tried." It still swamped him with guilt and impotent rage.

"Exactly, and if he hadn't died, I would have helped her bury him." She shook her head. "Terrible jest aside, the cruelty of which I speak is indifference. In the face of a woman's love, that hurt is far deeper than bruised skin."

"Did your husband malign you?"

"Never. He was always courtesy itself, and when not involved in his own selfish pleasures, he was kindness too. But every kindness he did me was more of a blow than even his evil deeds. When he smiled, or laughed, or held me in his arms, I nearly cried of the heartbreak, knowing he would rather be with another. I almost welcomed the losses, the infidelities, the arguments, because then I could gather the pieces and hold myself together with the glue of anger and righteousness. When he was loving, I had no defense." She paused. "Can you understand?"

He rather thought he could, though he had never contemplated such a plight before. What if Arabella had loved another but married him? The very notion folded his heart until his chest ached.

He took the woman's hand in his. He looked into her pale blue eyes that he now recognized were rimmed with pain. "I swear to you, on my honor, on my name, I will never give your daughter cause to question her place in my life. She is, and she will always be, everything to me."

Glenda Winslow searched his eyes, his shoulders, his chin. Then, she moved her other hand to cover Gabriel's own. "Go to Arabella, my lord. Tell her you have my blessing. Tell her what you have told me. Tell her not to be afraid."

"I love her," he added again in reassurance.

"Then be quick," she retorted, "and do not let her argue. Once she begins, you will lose."

"Yes, I'm finding that to be true. One more thing?"

She lifted her brows.

"You knew about our morning study sessions, didn't you?"

Slowly, she inclined her head.

"Several times, I sensed a presence, and I wondered. You did nothing to stop them, even though you feared me, feared my motives. Why?"

Lady Winslow sighed. "Ah, well, I thought, at the time, it would be the better course to watch you closely. I stayed outside the library door every morning, you know, to make certain you took no advantage."

"I didn't. Not then, anyway." For a moment, guilt pinged his conscience.

"It is a wash, now, or will be. Go."

He didn't waste any further time. He found Arabella in the garden, perched upon the same chair.

"Such deep thoughts," he murmured, breaking the heavy silence.

She jerked her head up, and he thought he saw a glimmer of tears before she turned away. The deep black of her high-necked gown paled her complexion even further than normal.

"Gabriel. I thought you had gone."

"Only to speak with your mother." He knelt before her on the damp earth and reached for her hands. "I have secured her blessing."

Arabella's head whipped around. Her eyes widened. They sparkled, violet jewels glossy and wet from crying.

He wiped a moist trail from her cheek with his thumb. "I understand your surprise. Cornering her required the bravery of Gilgamesh, believe me. In the end, though, all it took to convince her was my assurance I loved you. Loved you with all my heart and being. I do."

"You do?"

"Yes, and I have been remiss in not saying the words earlier. It is not that I didn't feel the emotion, Arabella. I think it was only I didn't realize what it was I felt. It took almost losing you to recognize how life without you was impossible. You are everything to me. I promise, if you have me, I will devote every day of the rest of my life to making you happy. My life is yours."

Her smile was so bright, it hurt to look at it. He leaned forward, and she rushed to meet his lips with her own as he dragged her up and into his arms.

It was the ending any Sumerian hero would have envied had he possessed the intelligence to look for love rather than eternal life.

The consideration passed through him, but then there was only Arabella, his Arabella, in his arms, under his lips, in this moment, with the scent of roses heady on the air.

It was better than any epic ending, and it was his.

Epilogue

Five years later

"Leila, get down from there. You naughty girl. What have we told you about climbing the ziggurat?"

"Do not climb it unless an adult is with me," the little girl answered as if reciting a memorized passage.

Black curls framed an ivory face and fearless purple eyes. She stood at least six feet above Arabella's head, and though her children were far more capable than she of climbing over the ruins, having grown up doing precisely that, she still worried.

"Well, come down now for luncheon, please. Your father and Uncle Peter have just come in from the desert, and they have wrangled something you will certainly find interesting."

"A baby camel?" Leila squealed, already tumbling pell-mell down the rough edges like a little monkey. She came to rest, unharmed, at Arabella's feet.

"Kindly wash your hands and face, and then we shall see. If your brother is awake, he might also wish to view the little surprise."

"He is only two years old, Mother. He requires his rest," the little girl said. "He will also try to take my camel, and then we shall fight, so it is altogether better he stays in bed."

Still, she ran off to wake him, shouting his name,

which only made Arabella laugh.

Since coming to the desert, they had discovered a life unimagined by those consigned to the rigidity of Victoria's country. Away from the imperial jingoism that marked the British upper class, they were simply free to exist as they would. Gone were her corsets and tight clothing. Instead, they all wore sweeping cotton robes that caught the rare breeze and deflected the heat. Sometimes, just to provoke a response from her handsome husband, she forgot to wear anything under her robe at all.

Though Gabriel had grown quite bronzed by his time in the sun, his excavations had not yet proven fruitful. Dilmun remained a myth. Their nights together were much more real.

A pair of arms wrapped around her waist from behind, startling her, but she knew his touch in an instant.

"Does this crumbling ziggurat capture all your attention, my love?" he asked softly, nuzzling her ear.

His touch still sent lightning bolts of pleasure down her spine. She said a little prayer of thanks every time she felt them.

"Actually, I was wondering how you will react to the news we shall soon be chasing after a third little monkey?"

He swirled her around; joy etched upon his face.

"Are you certain? How are you feeling?"

She laughed. "Never better. Besides, now your uncle is dead, you are officially the Earl of Kildare in every sense. We shall require a minimum of three boys to carry on all the titles properly."

"And I want at least ten girls to replicate your absolute perfection." He swung her around before swooping in for a long and utterly knee-bending kiss.

She laughed when she was able to draw breath again.

"Ten girls? I will love my nieces, of course." Peter strolled toward them. "But I feel obliged to remind you, my sister is not merely a reproductory tool, and childbearing is a risky proposition. I suggest you find separate tents in which to sleep at once."

Peter, she knew, was only partially joking. He had grown fiercely protective of Arabella since learning she was his half-sister. Even better, he had unexpectedly found a mother figure in Lady Winslow, who saw her beloved husband's face every time she looked at his. She had declared Peter was as good as adopted, and he hadn't seemed to mind at all. He called her "mother," and she called him "son."

After six months in Nice, Lady Winslow had decided that she found the desert air better conducive to her condition. Once her grandchildren had appeared, her extended visit had become permanent. Dressed in a white caftan robe, she sat inside the tent entrance just now. An elderly Kismet stretched over the desk. She penned a letter around his paws to her friend, Annette de Veer, attempting to convince her once again to come out for a visit.

Lady de Veer had taken, of late, to asking for weather reports, an encouraging sign. The woman had never quite recovered her spark after Robert Thauley had spoken those terrible words to her. Since her husband had recently passed on, there was no reason why she shouldn't find a life among people who were more her family than any she had ever known elsewhere.

The desert was good for that. The high winds, the rough weather, the endless sun, all sloughed away the restraints that kept people apart from each other. It was a better life than any Arabella could ever have hoped to know, and even if all of the people she loved moved on, back to England, off to other parts of the globe, should they ever choose their own adventures, she would still have Gabriel, the light of her life, beside her.

Their door would always be open because somehow they had found the best of days, and their hearts were complete enough to share.

Theirs was more than an epic love.

It was a right love. It was an easy love, and she knew with every day the best was yet to come.

A word about the author…

Judy is a sort-of-retired litigation attorney, a current homemaker with a propensity to ignore any and all domestic chores, and the mother of an outrageously comedic teenage boy and a fur-baby named Chocolate-the-Dog, so named because he thinks he's a cat.

Judy has been writing since she first learned to read, and has stories constantly going through her head. With a passionate interest in archaeology, most especially alternative archeology, she still hopes to one day uncover the true history of the world.

As a graduate of Mount Holyoke College with a degree in Art History, when she ventures away from books, it is to find the nearest art museum or purveyor of High Tea.

She has lived in four states and in France, and currently makes her home in North Carolina, which she loves, except for the bugs, snakes, and humidity.

Visit her at www.judylynnichkhanian.com for excerpts and information, tall tales and small ones.

If you loved this book, please leave a review online. Your support is greatly appreciated.

Thank you for purchasing
this publication of The Wild Rose Press, Inc.

For questions or more information
contact us at
info@thewildrosepress.com.

The Wild Rose Press, Inc.